Book Four of a Series

The List

By K J Scott

K J Scott

This book was written for Carmen, Candice and Megan, Thomas, Monique, Chloe, Callie, Charley, Blake, Case and Fonz.

K J Scott

LIKE TARA MAGEE ON FACEBOOK

Taramagee@Taramageebookseries

THE AUTHOR, K J SCOTT, WOULD LOVE TO HEAR FROM YOU!

Contact info:

Instagram@author_kjscott

https://twitter.com/author_kjscott

https://www.facebook.com/profile.php?id=100004414414351

http://www.littlebeckypress.com

Acknowledgment

I would like to thank my readers for choosing this series.

I would also like to thank my son Thomas for his support and encouragement through the writing process. He was the first person to read the complete series.

WARNING

READ BOOK **1, 2, & 3** BEFORE ATTEMPTING TO READ BOOK **4**.

READING BOOKS OUT OF ORDER MAY CAUSE YOUR BRAIN TO MALFUNCTION WHICH MAY LEAD TO RANDOMLY WALKING BACKWARDS AND PROBLEMS TYING YOUR SHOES.

CHAPTER 1

On the Train

We found our assigned seats. Mine was next to the window. I sat down and watched out as the train left the station. The two men who followed us ran towards the train. They stopped as it moved farther away from the station.

"Look Rachel." I pointed at them as the train moved slowly down the track.

"We're lucky they didn't have time to get a ticket," Rachel said as she leaned over and looked out the window right before they were out of sight.

"I'm glad we made it out of this place."

"Me too. We were lucky. That was way too close for me, Tara."

"I know, me too, but let's not think about it now. We made it on the train safely. So, that means it's a good day. Do you have the train schedule Jess gave you?"

"Yeah, it's in the backpack, let me get it for you." Rachel unzipped the front pocket of the backpack and dug around until she pulled out the schedule. "Here it is." She opened it to the page with the seven-sixty-three Surfliner schedule and handed it to me.

"Oh no, the train will be stopping at the San Diego Old Town Station at six-twelve a.m. that's in five minutes," I gulped. "Those two men could drive to the next station and board the train there, if they wanted. Rachel, what are we going to do?"

"Let's hope they get stuck in traffic or they get a flat tire. I don't want to die today," Rachel shouted.

1

"You don't want to die today? Oh boy, you are funny," a voice said from the seat in front of us.

I looked at Rachel and we both shook our heads. We didn't know what to think. A stranger eavesdropped on our conversation and thought we were joking.

"Now… why would you girls think dying today would be any worse than dying tomorrow or dying another day of the week? Besides, you don't get to decide when it's your time to go," the stranger laughed. The top of a head popped up from the seat in front of us and a set of big blue eyes looked at us. "Hey, you guys are twins."

"Who are you anyways?" I asked.

"Who do you want me to be?" he laughed.

"Are you serious?" Rachel rolled her eyes.

"If that's what you want me to be," he laughed.

"Yes, we want you to be serious… who are you?"

"I'm the one and only Houston. Not to be confused with the place in Texas of course." He stuck his hand between the seats and held it out for a handshake. "How are you ladies?"

Rachel and I looked at his hand, looked at each other, and laughed.

"Ouch, that hurt," he said as he stretched his fingers out for a second and then dropped his hand as if it were sad no one would shake it. Then he pulled it from between the seats.

Rachel and I laughed.

"So, you think I'm amusing do you?" He batted his eyes at us over the seat.

"You are funny," Rachel and I said at the same time.

2

A voice came over the loudspeaker announcing the next stop.

"And you girls have that twin thing going on. That's amazing." His eyes moved back and forth between Rachel and me. "So, how long have you been freaking people out doing that twin thing?" he asked.

"Doing what?" I asked.

"The twin thing? You know, saying the same thing at the same time, you know, stuff like that."

"I guess since we could talk," Rachel said. She looked at me and we laughed.

"Well, of course. That was a stupid question I guess," he rolled his eyes. "So, what are your names?"

"I'm Tara," I smiled

"I'm Rachel."

I felt the train slowing down Rachel and I looked out the window as it pulled up to the station and stopped.

Rachel and I looked at each other with fear in our eyes hoping we didn't see the two guys who were at the first station.

"Boy, you girls look scared. What's up with that?" he asked.

Rachel and I kept our eyes peeled out the window. The train started to move again, and we both breathed a sigh of relief.

"Wow ladies, what has you so scared?"

I grabbed the schedule and looked for the next stop.

"Solana Beach at six-forty-three a.m. That's a half hour from here. What do you think Rachel?" I asked.

"I have no idea. Maybe they will. I don't know," Rachel said, trying to be vague just in case Houston was listening to our conversation.

"So, what's up with you girls?" Houston popped his whole head up and we had a better look at him as he looked back and forth at us.

Houston was a handsome boy who I guessed to be around eighteen or nineteen years old.

"Oh, nothing," Rachel smiled.

"Well, if it's nothing why is your face turning red?"

I looked at Rachel and Houston was right. Her face was turning red right before our eyes. I thought I'd keep my mouth shut, or I'd look the same as her.

"I have allergies. My face gets red when I'm close to something I'm allergic to. I must be allergic to you if my face is turning red." Rachel stared him in the eyes and didn't blink.

If I didn't know she was lying I would have believed her myself, she looked so honest.

"Well, if you're allergic to me then why isn't she turning red too?" Houston pointed out the obvious.

"Just because we're twins doesn't mean we share everything," Rachel smiled.

"Well, I hope you're not allergic to me," Houston laughed. "So where are you girls headed?"

Rachel and I looked at each other. She nodded her head for me to tell him.

"We're heading to Seattle for a visit," I said. "Where are you heading?"

"Why, the *Happiest place on earth* of course," he smiled. "My girlfriend and her family are picking me

4

up from the train station. We're going to be there for three days."

"Really? You're going to Disneyland?" I said.

"I want to go to Disneyland," Rachel and I said at the same time.

"There you go with that twin thing," Houston laughed. "Have you been to Disneyland before?"

Rachel and I shook our heads no.

"What, you've never been to Disneyland? Don't tell me you're here on the train headed straight for the *Happiest place on earth* and you're not going? Ah, girls you have to go to Disneyland. What would life be like if you never went there? Well let me tell you. Life without Disneyland is pretty meaningless," he nodded his head. "Yep, just a bunch of people walking through life with no purpose, living a meaningless life," he shook his head. "Pretty sad I'd say." He turned around and sat in his seat.

I looked at Rachel and we burst out laughing.

The conductor came by and asked to see our seat markers. Rachel and I handed them to him. He put the markers over our seats by the seat numbers.

"This is where they go girls. That way we know these seats are taken so we don't assign them to someone else," the conductor said.

"Oh I see," Rachel said as she looked over her head.

I looked at the schedule, counted the number of times the train would stop between here and the place we were getting off in Los Angeles. There were eight more stops before we'd arrive at the station. That meant eight more chances they could catch up to the train and grab us. My stomach turned. There were six stops to Disneyland. I figured it was two fewer chances plus a whole bunch more fun.

"Rachel, I want to go to Disneyland," I whispered.

"I was thinking the same thing," Rachel smiled.

"I heard that," Houston laughed. His eyes peered over the seat at us. "So, you should call your parents and tell them you'll stay one night at Disneyland and head north on the same train tomorrow. Just have them wire you extra money. You can't pass it up."

"Now, that's a good idea Houston," Rachel said.

"Yeah, that's a good idea," I went along with Rachel. We weren't going to tell him our parents didn't know where we were, or the truth we actually had no parents. "Hey, Houston how do we get our tickets changed?"

"You talk to the conductor and he can take care of you." He turned around and sat in his seat.

Rachel looked up the aisle, "Hey Tara, lets catch up to the conductor and ask him."

"Okay." I followed Rachel up the aisle to the conductor.

"Sir... we'd like to change our tickets and get off the train at Disneyland. We want to catch the train tomorrow to finish our trip. Can you help us?" Rachel asked.

"Why sure girls, just call reservations and let them know you want to change your ticket."

"We don't have a phone," I said.

"What, you don't have a phone? Well, give me a minute and I'll call for you," he smiled. He talked to the passenger who was sitting in the seat next to where he was standing and asked him for his seat marker. Then he went on to the next person who

6

hadn't put their seat marker up themselves. He went all the way to the end of the train car doing an empty seat count, then he turned around and came back to where we were standing.

"Okay girls, let's see your tickets, I need the numbers off them."

"Okay, I'll be right back." I walked down the aisle and grabbed the backpack took the e-tickets out of the zippered compartment and headed towards the conductor.

"Are you getting it taken care of?" Houston yelled.

"Yes, I think so," I yelled back at him as I headed towards the conductor.

The conductor held one hand out waiting for our tickets and his other hand on the phone talking to customer service. He took the tickets and looked at them.

"Yes, the reservation number is 9CA072 and 9CA073. Okay... Okay, I'll let them know. Thank you. Okay sounds good. It was good talking to you also... bye." He hung up the phone. "Okay, girls you are all set. You can hop off the train in Anaheim and go to Disneyland. Then be at the station at eight o'clock to catch the train leaving tomorrow morning. Now you realize you won't get into Seattle until the day after tomorrow right?"

"Okay, that's fine with us we're not in a big hurry anyway," I said.

"Yeah, we're not in a hurry anyways," Rachel repeated.

"Well good, now you can go to Disneyland and enjoy yourselves," he smiled.

"I'm really excited." I smiled and headed back to our seats with Rachel behind me.

"Yippy! Me too," Rachel laughed.

"Did you get it taken care of?" Houston asked.

"Yes we did," Rachel laughed.

"You girls are going to Disneyland," Houston laughed. "We can probably give you a ride if you want." He looked over the seat.

"How far is Disneyland from the train station?" I asked.

"Oh... not far just around a mile I think. It would take you a half hour to walk there maybe a little more. But, I'm sure we can give you a ride. You're going to want to save your feet for walking around Disneyland. There's a lot to see for one day. You really need two or three days to see everything. I've been lots of times and I still haven't seen everything. You're going to have a great time."

"If you could give us a ride we would greatly appreciate it. Do you think it would be okay with your girlfriend's family?" Rachel asked.

"Let me call my girlfriend and ask." Houston turned around and sat in his seat.

"Hey girl, how's it going?" I heard him say. He was silent. I could hear the muffled sound of his girlfriend's voice. "That sounds great Eva. Hey, quick question. Do you think your mom would mind if we gave a couple of kids a ride to Disneyland?" He was quiet for a minute. "Okay, I'll let them know. Talk to you soon. Yep...Yep... See you at eight-o-eight. Love you too. Bye." He hung up the phone. "Okay girls, you have a ride. We're going to the hotel and you can walk straight across the street from there and go right into Disneyland," he yelled over the seat.

"Oh, we forgot about that. We are going to need to find a place to stay for the night. Do you think they have any rooms at the hotel where you're staying?" I asked.

"I'm sure there are plenty of rooms to stay in. It's midweek in October kids are in school now. Hey, why aren't the two of you in school anyway?"

"We're home schooled," I said.

"Oh that's nice."

"What about you... why aren't you in school?" Rachel asked.

"I graduated this year. I start college winter quarter in January."

"What are you going to college to study?" I asked.

"I haven't decided yet. I'm still trying to figure it out. I'm going to do my prerequisites first and then I'll make my decision."

"Prerequisites? What's that?" Rachel asked.

"Oh, just required classes everyone has to take."

"Oh... I didn't know that." Rachel said.

"Yeah, well... there's a ton of them. So, I'm going to get them done first. Then I'll decide what I'm going to do for the rest of my life. Maybe I'll be a brain surgeon," Houston laughed.

"Hey Tara, can you look at the schedule and tell me what time we'll be getting into Disneyland?" Rachel asked.

"We'll be arriving in Anaheim at eight-o-eight."

"I just said that. Didn't you hear me?" Houston laughed.

"No I didn't."

"I heard you Houston," I said.

Houston peeked his head over the seat. "So, I'll tell you how it's going to go down. My girlfriend and her family will pick us up at the train station. She'll take us to the hotel and you can hang out with us for an hour until the park opens. Then we'll head across the street into Disneyland and you can buy your tickets. Make sure you get a hopper pass so you can go into both parks."

"Both parks?" Rachel questioned.

"Yeah, there's Disneyland and California Adventure."

"So, how much money are the tickets, do you know?"

"I think it's about a hundred and fifty bucks for a hopper pass."

I looked at Rachel and we both gasped.

"Really? That's a huge amount of money for us to spend right now. What's the price for one park?

"It's about a hundred."

I looked at Rachel. I could tell she was thinking the same thing. We each had five hundred dollars, and it had to last us. We had no idea where we were going or how much money it would cost us to live. I wanted to go to Disneyland in the worse way, but I wasn't sure if we should spend the money. Jess told us he would wire us money, but we knew if we contacted him again someone would find out where we were. The men who were following us now knew Jess was involved and would probably be watching every move he makes.

"Tara, I know we don't have a lot of money, but I was thinking... we should go anyway. Tomorrow is your birthday, let's celebrate it today. Let's worry about money another day," Rachel whispered in my ear. She didn't want Houston to hear her talking about my birthday.

"Okay, let's celebrate our birthdays today," I said aloud.

"So... when's your birthday?" Houston peeked over the seat again.

"Tomorrow's our birthday, so we are going to celebrate it today," I smiled.

"How old are you going to be?"

"We're going to be fifteen," Rachel laughed.

"I remember when I was fifteen. It really sucked. "My birthday's in August. All my friends were turning sixteen and getting their driver's license before me. I was one of the last people in my class to get my license. Well I'm glad that year is over," he laughed.

"We're only going to go to one park today Houston. Which place should we go?" I asked.

"I think you should go to Disneyland it has a ton of great rides. California Adventure is great too, but I think for first timers you should go to Disneyland. California Adventure is like going to a big carnival. Disneyland is more unique. Oh, I'm getting so excited." Houston did a drumroll on the seat with his hands. "I love Disneyland!" He sat down in his seat. "Well girls, I'm going to close my eyes for a while. I'm resting up for a big day. You girls try and keep it quiet back there," he laughed.

Rachel and I rolled our eyes and shook our heads.

"I think we should rest up too," Rachel whispered to me.

I nodded.

I closed my eyes, listened to the sounds on the train, and drifted off to sleep.

The next thing I knew. I felt someone patting me gently on the head. I opened my eyes and Houston

11

had one-hand on my head and one-hand on Rachel's. He was patting us both. I reached up, grabbed his hand and took it off my head. I looked at Rachel who was doing the same.

"Ah, you're awake. The train's going to be in Anaheim in nine minutes. We're just leaving Santa Ana now."

"I must be a little tired. I didn't hear any announcements," Rachel said.

"Me either."

"You were both snoring pretty good," Houston laughed.

"Really?" I asked.

"No, just joking. They haven't announced it yet," he laughed. "Hey, we need to be by the doors when they open. The train just stops for a minute."

Just as Houston finished talking the announcement came on for the Anaheim stop.

"Are you girls excited or what?" Houston stood up stretched his legs and walked down the aisle towards the door. He seemed very tall to me.

"Well, we're not as excited as you are. Of course, we've never been to Disneyland, so we don't know what all the excitements about," Rachel said.

"I guess we'll know when we get there," I said.

Rachel grabbed the backpack and followed Houston. I was right behind her.

We stood by the doors and waited.

"Once you go, you'll never be the same," Houston smiled. "You are guaranteed to be a happier person for the rest of your life," he laughed.

"Well, then that's a good thing," Rachel and I said at the same time.

"There you go," Houston nodded and smiled. "That's an amazing trick."

The train stopped, and we followed Houston to a blue van parked in the parking lot.

"Eva this is Tara and Rachel," Houston said when the girl who was driving the van rolled down her window.

"Twins?" she smiled. "Hi, nice to meet you. Are you two ready for Disneyland?" she asked.

"Yeah," we both said.

"Okay, hop in the back," she said.

Houston opened the sliding van door and jumped inside. Rachel followed him and sat in the backseat. I jumped in, closed the door behind me and sat on the seat next to a little boy about six years old.

"Hi, I'm Tara... who are you?" I asked.

"I'm Griffin. I'm six," he held up five fingers and smiled. "Are you going to Disneyland?"

"Yep, we're going to Disneyland," I laughed.

"I like Disneyland," he smiled. "I like the birds."

"The birds?" I asked.

"Yeah, they sing songs," he nodded his head. "Tiki, tiki, tiki, tiki," he sang.

"Nice," I laughed.

"You want to go see them?" he asked.

"Sure," I smiled.

"Hi, I'm Clare. I'm Eva's mom," the woman in the front passenger seat smiled and waved.

"Hi, I'm Tara," I said.

"I'm Rachel," Rachel waved from the backseat.

"Thanks for giving us a ride," I said.

"Yeah thanks," Rachel said.

Someone sitting behind me tapped me on the shoulder, I turned around to see who it was. A little girl about ten years old waved at me.

"Hi," I smiled.

"I'm Parker," she smiled.

"Nice to meet you Parker," I said.

"Okay girls, we'll be going to the hotel for a little while then we'll head over to Disneyland about ten to nine," Clare said.

"Where do we get our tickets?" Rachel asked.

"You can get your tickets once we're at the park. Are you getting hopper passes?"

"No, not this time," Rachel said.

"That's okay it doesn't matter, you will enjoy which ever park you go to," she smiled. "Is this your first time at Disneyland?" Clare asked.

"Yes," I said.

"Oh, how exciting! We're all veterans here. You are going to love it," she smiled. "Where do you girls live?"

"Richmond Connecticut," I said.

"Well, you girls are a long way from home. How long are you planning to stay in town?"

"We're just staying the night and heading to Seattle tomorrow," I said.

"Visiting relatives?"

I nodded my head and smiled hoping I wouldn't turn red.

"That's always fun," she said. "Eva, make a right here."

We pulled into the parking lot of a hotel.

"Mom do you have the ticket?" Eva asked as she pulled up to a gate and put her hand out.

Clare handed her a ticket, which she put in the machine, then handed it back to Clare. She waited for the gate to rise, drove in and found a parking spot.

"Oh, I have the room key somewhere," Clare said.

We climbed out of the van and waited while Clare searched her purse for the key.

"I found it. Here's the key," she pulled it from her purse and waved it in the air. "If you kids have anything you want to leave or put in the room do it now so we don't have to make another trip," she said.

"I think we're going to the front desk and get a room," I said.

"Okay, girls it was nice meeting you. Boy, you two, are identical aren't you?" Clare smiled as she took a closer look at us. "You know, you girls are welcome to hang out with us if you want."

"Yeah, you girls can hang out with us if you want. We know our way around the parks," Eva said.

"Okay, that would be great. We'll come over to your room as soon as we check in. What's your room number?" Rachel asked.

"Room two-twenty-nine," Clare said.

"See you girls later," Houston said. He had Griffin on his shoulders and was holding Parker by the hand. Griffin was wearing Houston's backpack and was holding on to his forehead to keep from falling backwards from the weight.

"See you later," Griffin said.

"Yeah, see you later," Parker waved.

15

Rachel and I waved as we headed towards the hotel lobby.

"Do you have the ID Jess gave us?" I asked.

"Yeah, I put them in the side pocket." Rachel searched through the side pocket of the backpack while we walked to the lobby of the hotel.

"Here they are," she pulled out two drivers' licenses and handed one to me.

"I'm Rita Cook," I laughed. "What's yours say?"

"I'm Martha Cook and by the birth date on here I'm twenty-three," Rachel laughed.

"Oh yeah, our birthday is June seventh, how about that," I smiled.

"Do you think we can pass for twenty-three?" Rachel asked.

"Yeah, we look young for our age," I laughed.

The desk clerk was staring at us as we walked up to the counter.

"Can I help you ladies with something?" he asked.

"Yes, we would like a room for the night please," I said.

"Will that be cash, check or credit card?"

"Cash," Rachel said as she unzipped the pouch on the backpack.

"Your name please," the clerk asked as he typed into the computer.

"Rachel, I mean, huh, Martha Cook," she turned red.

I stepped in front of Rachel and asked him how much the room was.

"It's one-hundred-seventy-four thirty-three with tax," he said.

I gasped. "Rachel that's a lot of money for a hotel room isn't it?" I whispered.

"Yeah, a lot more than we usually pay."

I took the money from the backpack, counted one-hundred-eighty dollars and handed it to the clerk.

He took the money typed on his computer, handed me change and printed a receipt.

"Sign here," he turned the receipt around and handed me a pen. "Also can I get your vehicle make, model, and license plate number please?"

"We don't have one," I said as I looked at the receipt. "Martha it's in your name, you need to sign this." I handed the pen to Rachel. I watched as she signed her name as Martha Cook on the bottom of the receipt. She handed it to the clerk, smiled and didn't say a word.

"No vehicle, okay. Here are two room keys." He handed us the key cards and showed us a map. "You're in room three-twenty-nine. You go out the door and take a left. The elevator's here and your room's right here on the third floor. The pool is open till ten p.m. and check-out time is eleven a.m. Okay, you are all set. Do you have any questions?"

"No, I think we're good, thank you," I said.

I grabbed the map off the counter and headed out the door. Rachel followed me.

"I almost choked at the price of the hotel room Tara. That's a lot of money for one night."

"I know. We aren't going to have very much money left after today. We're going to need jobs when we get to Seattle or we're going to be living on the streets."

"Well, we can look at it this way. At least we get to do one fun thing before we end up homeless or dead," Rachel shook her head.

"That's right. We can take Disneyland off our bucket list after today," I smiled.

"Bucket list? You have a bucket list?"

"I didn't, but I'm going to start one today," I laughed. "Because you never know when we're going to kick the bucket."

"Yeah, we should make a bucket list. That would be fun," Rachel laughed.

"Stairs or elevator Rachel?"

"Let's take the stairs." Rachel pointed to the stairs right in front of us.

We walked up the stairs to the walkway and found our room. Rachel put the key card in the door and opened it. I followed her in the room. There was one king bed in a very nice room.

I put the backpack on the bed and took the rest of the money from the zipper pouch.

"Rachel, it's going to cost us a couple hundred dollars to get into Disneyland for the day. We're going to be down to a little under six hundred dollars. And we're going to need to eat."

"Hey, I'm a little hungry now."

"Me too, should we find someplace to eat around here before we go into the park?"

"Yeah."

We took our fake ID and three hundred dollars and headed out the door.

We went to the lobby and asked if they knew where any fast-food restaurants were. There happened to be one right next door. We went over, ate a breakfast sandwich, and headed to the hotel.

As we were walking through the parking lot, we saw Houston, Eva, Clare, Griffin, and Parker coming down the stairs.

"Hey look." Rachel pointed and waved. "Hi."

"Oh, there you are. We were hoping we would run into you. We weren't sure if you were coming by our room or not. Did you get checked in?" Eva asked.

"Yeah, we're on the third floor."

"Are you two ready to go to Disneyland?" Houston asked.

Rachel and I nodded our heads.

"Me too, me too," Griffin and Parker screamed.

"Okay, Let's do it," Clare yelled.

We followed them through the parking lot to the crosswalk. We were the only ones standing there so Houston reached his foot up to the signal button and pressed it with his shoe.

"I am multitalented," he laughed.

By the time the walk sign flashed, there was a crowd of people waiting to cross the street with us.

As we crossed the street, I noticed the Disneyland sign on the other side.

"Look Rachel," I pointed.

"We're here." Griffin and Parker ran under the arch.

Clare pulled out her camera.

"Okay, all of you stand under the arch and I'll take your picture," she said.

"I'll take your picture if you want me to," a woman said to Clare.

"Thanks, that would be great," Clare handed the camera to the woman and found a place to stand

19

between Parker and Griffin. Everyone smiled while the woman took several pictures.

"Thank you," we said.

"Can you take our picture?" the woman asked as she handed the camera back to Clare.

"Sure," Clare took the woman's cell phone from her.

"Just point and press the screen," the woman said.

Clare took a bunch of pictures and handed the phone back to the woman.

"Thank you," she smiled.

We walked through the parking lot to a green tent. There were people standing in line waiting to have their bags and backpacks checked. The lines were moving quickly.

"Do you girls have your backpack?" Clare asked.

"No, we left it at the hotel," Rachel said.

"Okay, you two can go right there and get your tickets," Clare pointed to the ticket booths. "Just wait for us there, it will only take us a couple of minutes to check our bags."

Rachel and I walked through the line and headed to the ticket booth.

"Two tickets please," Rachel said as I handed her the money.

"Your names please," the clerk asked.

"Rachel, I mean Martha Cook and Rita Cook," Rachel stuttered.

"That will be one-hundred-ninety-two dollars please."

Rachel handed the clerk two hundred dollars. The clerk handed her two tickets and some change.

"Have a magical day," the clerk said.

"Thank you, we will," Rachel said as she handed me a ticket. I looked at the ticket, noticed the picture of Minnie Mouse and the name on the front. I handed it to Rachel.

"This has your name on it Martha," I laughed.

"Oh, I didn't see they had our names on them Rita," she handed me the ticket she had and laughed.

We stood in front of the ticket booth looking to see where Houston, Eva, Clare and the kids were. They were standing in the middle of the open area waiting. Rachel and I waved at them as we walked towards them.

"Oh, there you are," Eva shouted when she spotted us.

"Are we ready? Do we have our tickets?" Clare asked.

"Yes, we are all ready," Griffin screamed with excitement.

"Then let's head for the gate," Clare took off in the direction of the Disneyland gates. "It's three minutes to nine now."

"Are you girls excited?" Houston asked.

"We're getting there," I said.

"I'm excited," Parker screamed.

"Me too," Griffin screamed.

"What ride do you want to go on first?" Eva asked.

"I think we should go on the Indiana Jones ride first, then the Pirates of the Caribbean. What do you think?" Houston asked.

"Yeah, Griffin should be tall enough, this year, to go on Indiana Jones with us," Parker said.

"Yep, I grew since last time," Griffin smiled. "I want to go on that ride first."

"Okay, Indiana Jones it is," Clare smiled.

We stood in line just as they started scanning tickets. There were groups of people already in front of us. It surprised me since the park was just opening. The line moved quickly.

I was getting excited as I waited my turn. When I reached the front of the line, the woman scanned my ticket and I walked into Disneyland Park.

CHAPTER 2

Pre-Birthday Celebration

There in front of me was a large flower arrangement of Mickey Mouse's face in the middle of the lawn. On the hill behind it sat an old time brick building with a sign that said Disneyland in great big letters. There were several windows across the building and a big old clock. One side had a steeple roof with a weather vane up high. At the top of the weather vane sat a silhouette of Tinker Bell.

"Wow," I said.

"Wow," Rachel said.

"That's the train station up there," Houston said. "Come on, follow me. We're going to Adventure land."

We followed Houston and the others through the main entrance to a beautiful little town with happy music playing. The music sounded like something out of an old-time movie. I kept looking for a barbershop quartet to start singing along with the music.

"This is Main Street. You can buy souvenirs here. We'll come back here later tonight on our way out of the park. That way if you want to buy anything to take home you won't have to carry it around with you all day," Eva said.

"So... we're finally in the happiest place on earth. I can see why they call it that. I'm feeling happy already," I smiled.

"Yeah, me too. Look how the people dress, their clothes fit this old-style town. It's like going back in time. And it's so clean," Rachel said.

23

"The people who work here are called cast members. I love how they're dressed too. Just wait till you see a princess walking around," Eva smiled.

"I know, I could live here," Parker said.

"Me too," Griffin said as he squeezed in between Rachel and me and grabbed ahold of our hands.

I looked down at him and he was smiling at me.

"You two, can sit with me on the Indiana Jones ride okay."

"Okay," Rachel and I said.

We watched as a horse and buggy went by us on the street.

"This is great," I said.

"Tara, look over there. See the double-decker bus," Rachel pointed.

"Wow," I said.

We followed the crowd down the street. I could see a beautiful castle at the end of the street right in front of me.

"Rachel, look at the castle isn't it beautiful," I sighed.

"Oh, Wow! Now that's a castle."

"That's the entrance to Fantasy land," Eva said.

"We'll go there later," Clare said.

We followed them to a place with an arch that read Adventure land. There were wooden buildings that looked like huts with grass roofs.

"I want to go there," Griffin let go of my hand and pointed to a building.

"Enchanted Tiki Room what's that?" I asked.

"That's where the birds sing," Griffin smiled. "Momma can we go there?" he asked.

"Yeah, we'll go there but I thought you wanted to ride the Indiana Jones ride?" she asked.

"I do," he said.

"Okay, we'll do the Tiki room in a little while."

"Yeah, yeah, yeah!" Griffin did a little dance as he walked. Then he grabbed ahold of my hand again.

Everyone laughed.

"There's the Jungle Cruise ride. We'll go on that later," Parker said as we walked by it.

We walked under a sign that read *"Indiana Jones Adventure. Temple of the Forbidden Eye."*

"Here's the entrance. I hope you enjoy your first ride girls. Come here Buddy let's see if you're tall enough," Houston said as he waved for Griffin to stand by the height sign.

Griffin stood next to it and he was an inch taller than the sign.

"Good job Buddy. You grew a lot since the last time we were here," Houston said as we walked down the path.

The path looked like a long winding trail through the jungle where there were pillars with snake carvings and snakes everywhere.

Next, we walked through an Egyptian pyramid. We looked at the hieroglyphics on the walls and floor.

"We still have a ways to go. I think we're going to be some of the first ones on this ride this morning," Houston said.

We walked into a room with an old black and white movie playing on the screen.

"What's that?" I asked.

"Oh, they play that for everyone. It tells you about the ride and safety," Clare said.

We made our way through the pyramid. It looked like Indiana Jones and his crew, were looking for treasure as we walked down and around to the place where the jeeps were. There weren't very many people in front of us in line.

"You girls are sitting with me right?" Griffin asked again.

"Yep, we'll sit with you," Rachel smiled.

"Let's let Griffin and the girls get in front of us so they can be in the front seat, since it's their first time," Clare said.

"Thanks," Rachel and I said.

"Yeah, thanks Momma," Griffin said.

"You betcha Sweetums," Clare said as she moved aside and motioned us to move in front of her.

"How many people do you have in your party?" the cast member asked.

"Seven," Clare said.

"Rows one and two," she said.

We waited our turn and soon it was time to ride. Rachel, Griffin, Parker and I sat in the front seat. Houston, Eva and Clare were sitting behind us.

"You guys are going to love this," Houston yelled.

The Jeep took off down the track moving slowly into the dark. An Egyptian gold mask with snakes on each side was the first thing I saw then we were twisting and turning around corners. Big bugs were crawling everywhere. Snakes were slithering in front of us. Flames shot out of nowhere. Stuff was on fire everywhere I looked. There were huge cobwebs above us. We were laughing and having a great time. I heard the sound of air darts flying through the air at us. Then I saw Indiana Jones hanging onto a rope dangling from the ceiling. I saw a giant ball right in front of us. It scared me for a second as the jeep went in a dark tunnel to avoid the huge ball coming straight for us.

When the ride came from the tunnel and the jeep stopped, I wished the ride would continue.

"Let's do that again," Griffin yelled.

"Okay, who wants to ride one more time?" Clare asked.

"I do, I do," everyone said.

"Okay, let's get in line again."

We headed out and around to the path again. We headed from the building to the end of the continuously moving line. More people were in line this time, but it didn't take us long to make our way to the front.

We jumped in the jeep and enjoyed the thrill of the ride for a second time. When the jeep came to a stop, Griffin wanted to go again.

"We have more rides to go on Griffin. We can come back to this one later okay Bud," Houston said.

"Okay, then let's go to the Tiki room," Griffin said.

"Let's go to the Pirates of the Caribbean first before the line gets too long and then we'll do the Tiki room," Clare said.

"Okay," Griffin moaned.

"Griffin you like the pirate ride. It's one of your favorites," Eva said.

"Yeah, Griffin don't you remember? That's the one with the big ships in the water," Parker said.

"Oh yeah. I remember now," he smiled and grabbed Rachel's and my hand.

"Okay, let's go there," Houston walked in the direction of the ride.

"Look there's Tarzan's tree house," Griffin pointed to a tall tree with steps leading up and around a big tree.

"That's a big tree house," Rachel said.

"Do you want to go up there Griffin?" Houston asked.

"Yeah," Griffin smiled.

"Okay, let's go up and look around," Houston took Griffins hand and headed to the tree house steps.

We followed them up the steps of the tree house to the top where we crossed a rope-and-plank walking bridge. We walked across the bridge and looked at the book that welcomed us into Tarzan and Jane's home in the trees. We continued up steps to a hut with a ferocious looking cheetah inside. The growling sound of the cheetah made Griffin stop for a second.

"That's scary. It sounds real," he said as he shook his head and went by it.

We crossed another wooden bridge and went down the steps to a grass roofed hut where Kala the ape raised Tarzan when he was a baby. We went down more steps to look in the window at Jane while she sat in a chair sketching a picture of Tarzan as he posed for her in their home. We went farther down the steps to the bottom where I saw many barrels, wooden boxes and metal buckets. There were also metal drums and other musical pots and pans in Tarzan and Jane's jungle area. The monkey sounds and the sounds of the jungle made the adventure in Tarzan's tree house a lot of fun.

"Did you like it?" Houston asked Griffin.

"Yeah, but the big cat sound scared me," he nodded.

"It didn't scare you last year," Parker laughed.

"I don't remember the big cat being there last year," Griffin said.

"It's always been there," Clare laughed.

We walked around the corner to the Pirates of the Caribbean ride.

"This is a fun ride, girls. You will like this," Eva said.

We walked under the walkway and through a chained area.

"Why do they have all these chained areas?" I asked.

"When it gets real busy the lines of people weave through these chained areas. You'll see later this afternoon when it gets busy," Houston said.

"I can tell you as many times as I've been to Disneyland, no matter how busy it gets, Disneyland keeps people moving through the lines. You're never standing in one spot for more than a few seconds. I would say Disneyland is an expert on moving people," Clare said.

"Really?" Rachel questioned.

"Yeah, and if they keep you in one spot for longer than a few seconds they always have something entertaining for you to see. You're never just staring at the back of someone's head or at a brick wall. I can tell you, in all the times I've been

29

here I've never seen anyone unhappy or yelling except maybe a cranky baby. I can tell you this is truly the happiest place I've ever been on earth," Clare smiled.

"Just the music alone makes me happy," Parker smiled.

"If I could live here I would," Griffin smiled.

Everyone laughed.

We walked through the chained area and up a ramp with a beautiful metal railing.

"So, all the ropes at the last ride weren't just part of the scenery?" Rachel asked.

"Nope, it's designed to keep people moving while they're enjoying their surroundings," Clare said.

"They do a great job," Rachel laughed.

We went inside a dimly lit building where there were people in boats sitting in the water.

We walked up a ramp where lanterns hung from the ceiling.

"How many people in your group today?" the cast member asked.

"Seven," Houston said.

"Rows one through three," the cast member said.

Clare and Parker took the first row, Houston and Eva were in the second row. Rachel, Griffin and I were in the third row.

As the boat moved through the water in the dark, I heard the sound of crickets, frogs, birds and a cougar. I saw an old shack and a small boat. I noticed an empty restaurant on the other side of the water and figured they must not serve breakfast there.

The boat went by an old man rocking in a rocking chair on the porch of a small cabin. Then we were in complete darkness. Then I saw a pirate's flag with a talking skull and heard screaming in the distance.

As we came closer to the flag and skull, the skull said *"dead men tell no tales"* and we plummeted into the water at a fast speed. I screamed as the water splashed everywhere.

Everyone laughed.

Then the pirates sang *"Yo ho ho ho a pirate's life for me"* and we plummeted again. We were in a dark cavern underground, with water falling from holes in rocks around us.

There were bones, treasures and the sound of the voice saying *"dead men tell no tales"* as we moved through the water. There were pirate skeletons everywhere I looked. A skeleton sat in bed reading while a ghost played a piano. Another skeleton sat on a pile of gold, silver and jewels guarding his treasure. Then there was a mist spraying and Davy Jones the squid-faced pirate was saying *"Dead men tell no tales"* as we went through the mist.

"There's the big boats," Griffin pointed and whispered.

We went by the boats as they shot cannonballs at each other. Then we went through and amazing city of pirates. I saw pirates everywhere.

"Look there's Jack Sparrow peeking out of the barrel," Rachel whispered and pointed.

I saw many things happening as the boat traveled through the underground city near the water. As we went upward, we saw Jack Sparrow sitting in a rocking chair singing *"a pirates life for me."*

"They sure made him look real," I whispered.

"Yeah, just like in the movie huh," Griffin said.

"Yep, just like in the movie," Rachel said.

When the boat reached the top of the lift, I saw we were at the beginning of the ride where we started. The boat eased around the corner and stopped. We hopped out the boat and headed out the building.

"That was great. Can we do it again?" I asked.

"We can but let's hit a few other rides before it gets busy," Clare said.

"Yeah, let's go on Splash Mountain before the lines get too long," Eva said.

"I want to go to the Tiki room," Griffin whined.

"Look Griffin. We'll go to the Tiki room after we go on Splash Mountain okay Bud. I promise you," Houston said.

"Okay," Griffin pouted. "What's Splash Mountain?"

"You couldn't go on it the last time we were here. You were too short," Parker laughed. "You are going to love this ride Griffin. It's way better than the Tiki room."

"No, it isn't. I like the Tiki room," Griffin laughed. "It's my favorite."

We came out of the Pirates of the Caribbean ride onto a French street.

"What is this?" I asked. "It looks like we're in France."

"New Orleans French Quarters," Clare said. "Isn't it nice?"

"Yeah, I've seen a few paintings of streets in France. This street looks just like it popped out of a painting. It's amazing," I said.

"Let's go this way," Houston pointed to the left.

We walked along the street and came to an open area. I saw a huge mansion across the street from a lake.

"What's that?" Rachel asked.

"Oh, that's the Haunted Mansion," Eva said.

"Oh yeah, can we go in there?" Griffin asked.

"I thought you wanted to go to the Tiki room after Splash Mountain?" Clare asked.

"Huh, can we go there first and the Tiki room after that?" Griffin asked.

"Sure kiddo. I think that will work," Clare smiled.

We followed Houston into Critter Country and over to the Splash Mountain barn. We weaved through the building, went by a fireplace, and up a few steps with a wall of stones next to it. Then we went through a wooden tunnel and into a cave like place where we waited for our log.

"How many in your party?" the cast member asked.

"Seven," Eva said.

"We can only put six of you in a log. Who wants to ride in the next log?" the cast member asked.

"I will," Houston volunteered

"Okay, the rest of you, rows one through five. Put the little guy up front please," the cast member said.

"Mom, can I sit in front with Griffin?" Eva asked.

"Why don't you sit behind Griffin and Parker? I'll sit in back. Maybe the drop won't feel so bad from the back," Clare laughed as she hopped in the rear of the log.

I hopped in the seat in front of her and Rachel sat in front of me.

"The drop?" Rachel asked.

"Oh yeah, when you go down the big waterfall you will feel the drop and don't forget to keep your eyes open. They take your picture on the way down as you're screaming," Houston laughed as he waved. "Bye ladies, see you on the other side if you make it," he smiled.

"Bye," Eva smiled and waved.

Everyone laughed.

We moved slowly through the water, went around a corner, and up a track.

"For your safety just stay seated and keep your hands, arms, feet, and legs inside the log and be sure to watch your kids," a cartoon voice repeated.

I wondered how many people were dumb enough to stick their hands, arms, feet, and legs outside the log. I laughed. I knew Rachel was thinking the same thing as I heard her laugh too.

When we reached the top, the log turned another corner where there were thorns and a beautiful waterfall as we headed into a small building with another track taking the log up another level. We went by a hooting owl. The music was playing an upbeat tune. There were animals everywhere I looked as we glided through the water towards Brer Fox Den. It was a nice comfortable ride as we went down our first waterfall. There were singing frogs, alligators and birds in the make-believe forest. And a smiling bear strung up by a fox, hanging by his feet in a tree. There were bunnies, foxes, more bears, and crocodiles. All of them singing. Then the log took us down a level into a darker room where there were bee's buzzing around lit up bee's nests. There were mushrooms lit up and animals singing as we weaved through the darkness. A voice sang "*You must beware the fox is there.*" The log went up a ramp and stopped below two buzzards. It sounded like the buzzards said... "*We'll show you the laughing place.*" But I wasn't sure. The log continued upward I could see a bunny tied up with rope as the shadow of a hungry fox showed his teeth. When we reached the top it was a straight shot downward into the water. I felt my stomach cringe as we plummeted. Everyone screamed as we sped down the steep hill. We hit the bottom with a big splash. As the log made its way back meandering around corners I heard a deep voice say "*dead men tell no tales.*" Then the music played, "*Zip-a-dee-doo-dah, zip-a-dee-ay.*" I saw chickens, pigs and other animals singing and dancing on a riverboat. As we meandered through the water taking in the sights, I thought this is amazing. The log came out the tunnel and stopped. The cast member said thank you watch your step as I stepped out of the log.

"That was fun," I laughed.

We walked through a passageway and came to a place where I saw six photo screens on the wall.

"Hey, there we are," Eva laughed.

"Everyone has their eyes closed except for you Griffin," Parker pointed at the picture.

"I think my stomach is still back on the ride," Clare said.

"Mine too," Rachel and I said.

"Let's wait here for Houston," Eva said. And just as she finished her sentence Houston was standing behind her.

"Are you waiting for me?" he laughed as he put his arms around Eva's waist and lifted her off the ground.

"You scared me for a second," Eva laughed.

"Look Houston," Griffin pointed at the screen with the picture of Houston in it.

"Oh yeah, I had my arms up," he laughed.

Everyone looked at Houston's picture. His arms were in the air and he had a great big grin on his face.

"At least your eyes are open. Everyone except Griffin has their eyes shut in our picture," Parker said.

"Let's go to the Haunted Mansion," Griffin danced around from foot to foot.

"Okay, let's go," Clare said.

We followed Clare and Griffin as they walked out the building and down the street.

"Well, girls what do you think of Disneyland so far?" Clare asked.

"I think it's the happiest place on earth," Rachel smiled.

"I think so too," I smiled.

We walked through the gate into the courtyard of the Haunted Mansion.

There were headstones of pets with funny things written on them. Like *"Rosie was a poor little pig, but she bought the farm."* We walked up the steps and into a big room with a chandelier hanging above us. There was creepy organ music playing and a voice of a man who said.

"When hinges creek in doorless chambers, and strange and frightening sounds echo through the halls. Whenever, candle lights flicker where the air is

deathly still. That is the time when ghosts are present, practicing their terror with ghoulish delight!"

A door opened, and we walked into another room where the voice continued speaking.

"Welcome, foolish mortals, to the Haunted Mansion! I am your host, your ghost host. Kindly step all the way in please and make room for everyone. There's no turning back now. Our tour begins here in this gallery where you see paintings of some of our guests as they appeared in their corruptible, mortal state. Your cadaverous pallor betrays an aura of foreboding, almost as though you sense a disquieting metamorphosis. Is this haunted room actually stretching? Or is it your imagination, hmm? And consider this dismaying observation: This chamber has no windows and no doors, which offers you this chilling challenge: to find a way out! Of course, there's always my way."

The room went dark, and I heard a clap of thunder. Lightning lit up the room. I looked up to see a skeleton hanging from the ceiling. Then the voice spoke.

"Oh, I didn't mean to frighten you prematurely; the real chills come later. Now, as they say, look alive, and we'll continue our little tour. And let's all stay together, please."

The door opened and we walked into another room down a creepy hallway where there were weird paintings that changed as the lights flickered, and statues of heads.

"There are several prominent ghosts who have retired here from creepy old crypts from all over the world. Actually, we have nine-hundred-ninety-nine happy haunts here, but there's room for a thousand. Any volunteers? If you insist on lagging behind, you may not need to volunteer. The carriage that will carry you into the moldering sanctum of the spirit

37

world will accommodate you and one or two loved ones. Kindly watch your step as you board, please. We spirits, haunt our best in gloomy darkness, so remember, no flash pictures, please... And now, a carriage approaches to carry you into the boundless realm of the supernatural. Take your loved ones' by the hand, please, and kindly watch your step. Oh yes, and no flash pictures, please! We spirits, are frightfully sensitive to bright lights."

I followed Rachel into the black coffin looking car and sat in the seat.

"Do not pull down on the safety bar, please; I will lower it for you. And heed this warning: the spirits will materialize only if you remain quietly seated at all times."

As the carriage made its way down the ramp I saw ghosts dancing in the ballroom right around the corner. I watched in amazement. There were howling dogs, screaming people, and a floating glass ball with a talking head in it. I saw singing stone sculptures at the gravesite, I couldn't figure out how they made them look so real.

We came out of the darkness and I heard a voice say.

"Ah, there you are, and just in time! There's a little matter I forgot to mention. Beware of hitchhiking ghosts! They have selected you to fill our quota, and they'll haunt you until you return! Now I will raise the safety bar, and a ghost will follow you home!"

As we went by a mirror, I noticed a ghost image sitting in the seat between Rachel and me.

We reached the end of the ride, stepped from the coffin, and walked up the ramp. I laughed when I saw the little dead bride who said.

"Hurry back! Hurry back! Be sure to bring your death certificate if you decide to join us. Make final arrangements now! We've been dying to have you!"

I thought of the dream I had with someone holding a knife to my throat while I was in a wedding dress. It gave me a chill for a minute. I looked at Rachel. By the look on her face, she was remembering the same dream. I decided I wasn't going to think about it and just enjoy being in Disneyland.

"That was fun," I said as we came out of the building.

"Yeah, they sure have a lot of fun rides here don't they. I can't figure out how they made those stone sculptured heads talk," Rachel said.

"I know, I was thinking the same thing," I laughed.

"Okay, we're going to the Enchanted Tiki Room next," I heard Griffin say as he came out of the building.

"Okay, Enchanted Tiki room it is," Clare said.

We followed everyone to the Enchanted Tiki Room, and sat outside in the seating area waiting for our turn to watch the show. The seating area had trees and totem poles that talked.

The drums beat and a horn blew. The doors opened to the Tiki room and a cast member stepped outside and greeted us with an "Aloha come in side."

We went inside the grass-roofed hut and took a seat. Within a couple of minutes the show started. There were parrots telling jokes and singing. I saw an enchanted water fountain with multicolored water shooting up into the air. White birds descended from the ceiling singing songs from the Mary Poppins' movie. I tapped my foot and danced in the seat to the music. There were baskets of singing flowers that sang songs from Hawaii. The totem poles Tikis on the walls joined in singing and their eyes moved. There were other Tikis playing drums. It was a great show I enjoyed the whole thing.

When the show ended, I followed the crowd out the building.

"Tiki, Tiki," Griffin sang.

"Tiki, Tiki," all of us sang back to him.

"Makes you want to dance, doesn't it?" Clare laughed.

"Yeah," Houston grabbed Griffin's hand and danced around as we walked through the crowd of people.

"Where do you want to go next?" Eva asked.

"Let's go to the island. That's always fun," Parker said.

"Island?" Rachel and I said at the same time.

"Yeah, there's an island that has all sorts of neat caves and other stuff on it," Parker said.

"Okay, let's head over to the raft," Eva said.

We followed Eva and Parker as they made their way through Frontierland. We walked around the waterfront to a dock where I saw a wooden raft full of people making its way across the water towards us.

The cast member pulled the raft up to the dock and let the people off, and then she asked us to board the raft.

As soon as the people were aboard, we drifted slowly across the water to the island. We pulled up to the island and the cast member told us to watch our step as we came off the raft.

"Look, there's were Mickey performs his Fantasmic show," Houston pointed to an old wooden stage.

"What's that?" I asked.

"Oh, it's this amazing show with water and lights. We'll watch it this evening when the sun goes down," Clare said.

"Look there's a cave," Griffin shouted as he took off running towards the entrance of a cave.

"Slow down Griffin. You need to wait for us," Clare scolded.

Griffin kept running and stopped when he came to the entrance of the cave.

"Hurry," he motioned to us.

"What's your hurry little dude?" Houston asked.

"I want to go in the cave," Griffin whined.

"Wait for us," Clare demanded.

There was a sign at the cave entrance that read "*Injun Joe's Cave there are thousands of caves in America. Many of them unexplored-even today... here is a labyrinth of secret tunnels... colorful strata and curious fossils... hiding place for buried treasure... stalagmites form fantastic shapes... and eerie sounds sometimes echo through the silent rooms.*"

"Hey, this is Injun Joe's cave," Houston said.

"Come on let's go in," Griffin smiled. "Who's Injun Joe?"

"I don't know but this is his cave," Clare laughed.

As we walked through the cave, you could hear the sound of the wind blowing strongly. It made me laugh since there was no wind blowing outside the cave. I heard the sound of thunder and someone screaming.

We saw a sign on the wall Houston read it aloud.

"Chamber of the bottomless pit... Legend has it that the ghost of Injun Joe haunted the bottomless pit and is doomed to wander forever through its subterranean passages, if you listen, you can hear his mournful wails. However, there are some who can only hear the singing of the wind."

As he read the sign, we could hear the wind blowing stronger and more screaming.

"That Injun Joe is pretty scary sounding," Parker laughed.

"Yeah, will you hold my hand?" Griffin asked Eva.

Eva grabbed ahold of Griffins hand. "Are you scared?" she asked.

"A little," Griffin had the look of fear in his eyes as he heard the screams of Injun Joe. "Where is he?"

"He's in the bottomless pit," Houston laughed. "Be careful you don't want to fall in or you'll be in the bottomless pit with him."

We walked through the cave as it twisted and turned. The howling wind and the screaming sounds continued as we made our way through the small passageways in the rock. Soon we came out the other side of the cave and walked down a path leading to a pontoon bridge. It moved under our feet as we crossed. There were waterfalls and wooden sky bridges to cross as we made our way around the island.

"Hey, let's go in the tree house," Griffin pointed up the trail.

We followed him up the ladder into the tree house.

"This isn't as tall as Tarzan's tree house," Parker said as she looked out the window. "This tree house has a great view of the water."

We climbed out of the tree house, walked a little further down the trail, and came to an old mill with a big wooden waterwheel. We walked down the path a little further ending up at the big rustic wooden building and the stage.

"This is where Mickey will stand tonight," Parker stood in the center of the stage and waved her arms in the air.

"That's what Mickey does," Griffin said to Parker as he ran and stood next to her and waved his arms in the air too.

Rachel and I laughed.

"You two must really like the show," I said.

"Yeah, it's great. Just wait till you see it," Parker said.

"Yeah, it's a great one all right," Eva said.

"Hey, here comes the raft are we ready to head to the other side?" Clare asked.

"Where are we heading to next?" Rachel asked.

"I don't know gang. Where do you want to go next?" Clare asked.

"Let's take the train to Toontown," Eva said.

"Yeah, let's do that," Griffin said.

"Does everyone want to go to Toontown?" Clare asked.

"Yeah," everyone said.

Once we were on the other side, we walked to New Orleans Square and waited for the train to arrive.

"Are any of you getting hungry?" Clare asked.

I looked at Rachel and she looked at me. I knew she was as hungry as I was.

"I am," we both said at the same time.

"There you go with that twin thing," Houston laughed.

"You girls do that a lot don't you?" Eva laughed. I went to school with twin boys they were always doing that stuff. They'd finish each other sentences too. Do you two do that?"

"Sometimes," Rachel and I said at the same time.

"There you go," Clare smiled. "Okay let's get something to eat before we go to Toontown. There's a little restaurant here in the French quarter where they serve clam chowder in a bread bowl. Are we hungry for Chowder?"

Everyone said yes at the same time.

"See that's not just a twin thing," Rachel laughed.

Everyone laughed.

"Follow me," Clare said as she headed over to the restaurant.

After we ate, we headed back to the train station, and waited for the train.

"What's making that clicking sound?" Rachel asked.

"That's the little building right over there, someone's sending out a telegraph," Parker pointed.

The train pulled to the station and we watched the passengers climb from the train.

"All aboard," a cast member shouted.

Everyone climbed on board the little open-air train and took a seat on the wooden benches. The seats faced the French quarters, which made for a good view of the park.

As the train headed from the station, we went into a tunnel.

A voice came over the speaker, it said, "*Welcome aboard the Disneyland railroad, to insure a safe ride remember to keep your hands, arms, feet inside the train and watch your kids.*"

At first it was dark inside the tunnel then I could see light and hear the singing. The sound of music came from the splash mountain ride below the train. I heard "*zip-a-dee-doo-dah, zip-a-dee-ay my, oh, my, what a wonderful day plenty of sunshine headin' my way, zip-a-dee-doo-dah, zip-a-dee-ay.*" I could see parts of the ride through windows placed in the cave walls. At one point I could see the birds dancing and the big wheel riverboat. As we came from the tunnel we went by a restaurant then a forest full of deer. I could see the island we were on earlier across the water. We went by an Indian on a horse and what looked like an old town. There were barrels, old milk containers, benches and other things. Then the announcer came over the loudspeaker and said. "*Okay our next stop is Toontown.*" We went into another dark tunnel and came out next to a stage then we were at the Toontown station.

"I love Toontown," Griffin said.

"Me too," Parker said as we jumped off the train.

The music was playing *"Who's afraid of the big bad wolf."* As we walked through the town, I noticed all the buildings were cartoon like in shape.

"Let's go on Gadget's go coaster," Griffin said.

"Okay," Clare said.

We followed Clare to the entrance of the ride. The line moved fast and we took our seats on the roller coaster in a matter of minutes.

"Are you girls having fun?" Houston shouted from the last car.

"Yes," I said.

"Yes," Rachel said.

The roller coaster went up the track slowly. Once we came to the top, it flew down the track at top speed. I screamed as we went around a corner. I felt my stomach go in and it made me laugh as it twisted and turned one way and then the other. Rachel was laughing too. The roller coaster slowed down, right before it entered the building. We were still laughing when we hopped from the car and headed out the building.

"That was fun," I laughed.

"Yeah it was," Rachel laughed.

"Let's go ride the Rodger Rabbit Car Toon Spin," Eva said.

Everyone followed Eva as she made her way through the people to the entrance of the ride.

"You girls are going to like this one," Eva said.

"I like them all so far," Rachel laughed.

"I do too," I nodded.

"Me too," Parker and Griffin said at the same time.

"Hey, you two have that twin thing going on too," Houston laughed.

"No we don't. We're not twins," Griffin glared at Houston.

"Okay Buddy, I know you and Parker are not twins. I was just kidding," Houston laughed.

"Can I ride with you Rachel?" Parker asked me.

"I'm Tara, yes you can," I said.

"I want to ride with the other twin," Griffin grabbed ahold of Rachel's hand.

"Why sure you can Griffin," Rachel said.

"Eva, why don't you ride with your mom and I'll take the cab behind you," Houston said.

"Okay," Eva said.

When it was our turn Parker and I hopped into the cute little cab. Rachel and Griffin took the cab behind us followed by Eva and Clare. I saw Houston had a cab to himself right behind them.

The light turned green, a hand popped up and pointed the way. Our car went slowly down the track. It turned and drove into a dark room. Roger Rabbit was in his car like ours spinning in circles. He said, *"Want to spin come on in,"* he laughed. Then I heard a voice say, *"Holy smokes Roger we've been...aah."* There were weasels pouring dip from containers. A weasel stood near the rear of a car where a pair of women's legs were sticking out the open trunk. Next we were driving through a cartoon house and then into what looked like a cartoon alley at night. We drove into the Powerhouse where I heard. *"Danger, danger"* the music playing was creepy. The lights went out and it was completely dark until we came to a weasel, who was electrocuting Roger Rabbit. I heard birds tweeting and saw stars spinning. Then we were driving down a hole and I could hear a woman screaming. I saw stairs on all sides as we went through the middle. I saw the rabbit and he said something, but I couldn't make out what it was. We drove through a place with Jack-in-the-boxes and carnival music playing then we were in the dark again. I could hear noises but I wasn't sure what sound it was. I heard a woman say this is going to hurt you a lot more than it's going to hurt me. She had a mallet in her hand. The ride was wild with twists and turns. There were cartoon characters everywhere and weasels wanting to dip the rabbit.

Parker and I laughed as the cab turned around and we saw Rachel and Griffin laughing.

"That was fun," Parker laughed.

"It sure was," I laughed as I stepped out of the taxicab.

We waited near the exit for our group to finish the ride.

"I want to go see Mickey Mouse," Eva said.

"Yeah, Me too," Griffin said.

"Okay, let's go get our picture taken with him," Clare said. "Girls, do you want to get your picture taken with Mickey Mouse?" she asked.

"Yeah, that would be great," I nodded.

"Seeing Mickey would be the perfect birthday present."

"Is it your birthday girls?" Clare asked.

"No, our birthday is tomorrow, but coming to Disneyland today is like an early birthday present."

"Well, happy early birthday girls," she said.

"That's right you told me on the train and I forgot all about it," Houston said.

"Happy early birthday girls," Eva said.

"Happy birthday," Griffin laughed.

"Happy birthday," Parker said.

"Thanks everyone," Rachel said.

"Yeah, thanks everyone this is my best almost birthday ever," I said. "Rachel and I will never forget it as long as we live. You guys are so great to let us hang out with you and show us all the sights in Disneyland. We'd be lost and wondering around the park trying to figure out stuff if it weren't for you showing us where to go."

"Well, it's been our pleasure girls," Clare said. "Now, let's go see Mickey Mouse," she headed into Mickey Mouse's house with all of us right behind her.

Mickey's house was big and yellow with green trim. We walked into the cartoon like house and there was a staircase leading to the second floor. His closet was stuffed full and had stuff sticking out the door.

"Look," I pointed and laughed.

"Yeah, it looks like your closet at home Griffin," Parker laughed.

We walked through his living room area and looked at his things on his desk. I saw Mickey's list of things to do today and read it to everyone.

"1. Wake up at five a.m.

2. Mousersize,

3. Play with Pluto

4. Eat a balanced breakfast

5. Water lawn

6. Call Minnie

7. Be in movie barn by six-thirty a.m.

8. Open barn to greet guests," I said.

"Boy, he keeps a tight schedule," Clare laughed.

"I'm sure he's in the movie barn by now," Parker laughed.

"Poor Mickey never gets a moments rest with all of us guests walking through his house every day," Eva laughed.

We walk through the house and saw pictures of Mickey all over the place. There was a player piano playing music and a small black and white TV playing old cartoons. Mickey had pictures of him and Minnie on the fireplace mantel. In the laundry room there was a washing machine with a window to see Mickey's white gloves washing in it.

"He uses Freeze detergent for really cold water, Toonox bleach, Toonite, and Toowny laundry detergent," Rachel laughed.

"Cartoons are funny characters, aren't they?" Houston laughed.

"You are so funny Houston," Eva laughed.

We walked out Mickey's back door and went through a lattice hallway into Mickey's backyard. There were birds singing. Pluto's doghouse and his dog dish were out there. There was a big bone in his dish.

We watched as the carrots popped up in his garden and then disappeared again. When the last carrot was gone, a mole popped his head up and laughed.

"Mickey has a mole in his garden again," Clare laughed.

"Mom, the mole has been eating Mickey's carrots for years," Parker laughed.

We walked into Mickey's Movie Barn. He kept his movie props and chicken coop in the same area.

"Look kids, there are pictures from Mickey's first cartoon," Clare pointed to the pictures on the wall.

We walked down the hall and saw Mickey's costumes hanging on a pole above us along with many other props from cartoons. I noticed paint cans stacked near an art canvas with trees painted on it. A sign said *"Duck at work."*

I saw a sign in the shape of an arrow that read. *"To screening room and meet Mickey."*

We walked down the hall and went around the corner. There was a big movie screen playing movies of Mickey. I saw old film canisters stacked on shelves and piles stacked high in the hallway.

We reached the room where Mickey was taking pictures, and we watched as the groups ahead of us gathered around him for a picture. As soon as they finished the cast member motioned us to stand by Mickey. Rachel and I waited.

"Okay, let's get in the picture," Clare said as she motioned to Rachel and me.

"Us too?" I asked. We figured Clare wanted a family picture of her and her kids and we weren't planning to be in the picture. We came to see Mickey.

"Yes, of course you too," Clare said

"We're not part of your family," Rachel said.

"You are now," Clare smiled.

I felt all warm and fuzzy.

"Rachel you stand on one side and I'll stand on the other," I said.

"Okay," Rachel said.

Everyone stood next to Mickey and smiled for the camera.

"Hi Mickey," Griffin laughed.

Mickey shook Griffin's hand.

"Bye Mickey. Thanks," we said as we headed out of the movie barn.

"Don't let me forget to stop and pick up our pictures on the way out later," Clare said.

"I'll remind you mom," Eva said.

We walked through Minnie's, and Goofy's houses, then through Donald Duck's boat, and over to Chip and Dale's tree house.

"Let's go ride some more rides," Houston said. "How about we head over to the Matterhorn bobsled ride?"

"Am I tall enough to ride the ride?" Griffin asked.

"Well, you were tall enough for the Indiana Jones ride so you should be tall enough for the Matterhorn," Clare said.

CHAPTER 3

Time Flies When You're Having Fun

We walked out of Toontown and headed for the Matterhorn ride.

"Hey there's the *It's a Small World* ride. Let's go on it since we're here," Parker said.

"No, I don't want to go on that ride right now," Houston shook his head and rolled his eyes. "Every time I go on that ride the song is stuck in my head for days. Let's wait and save that ride for last," he said.

"No, let's go on it right now," Eva laughed as she grabbed Houston by the hand and dragged him towards the ride.

"No!" He laughed as he dragged his feet.

Parker put her hands on his back and pushed him towards the ride.

"Come on, you know you want to. It's a small world after all. It's a small world after all," Parker sang.

Griffin grabbed Rachel's and my hand as we walked along the path.

"It's a small world after all," Griffin sang.

It's a small world song played as we waited for our turn to get on a boat.

"I can't believe you're dragging me on this. You know this song is going to be stuck in my head the rest of the day," Houston shook his head. "And it's a really long ride."

"Ah, you love it," Eva laughed.

We boarded the little boat and headed into the building as the music played. As the boat traveled through the water, I saw dolls from around the world. They were dressed in outfits from their native countries. They were all moving, dancing, and singing it's a small world song, in the language of the country the dolls represented. The buildings look like buildings from the country the dolls represented. The music continued the whole way through the ride. I felt like I was taking a tour of the globe. All the different unique costumes the dolls wore amazed me.

"It's a small world after all, it's a small world after all," I sang.

I could hear Rachel, Griffin and Parker singing too. Eva, Houston, and Clare were sitting in front of us. Eva and Clare were singing while Houston was shaking his head and smiling. Eva laughed at him.

When the ride finished, we hopped from the boat, and went up the ramp.

"It's a small world after all," Houston sang.

We laughed.

"Okay, now to the Matterhorn," Eva said.

We stood in line at the Matterhorn and waited our turn. I watched the waterfall coming down from the ride.

"We go in that big mountain?" I asked.

"Yep, the sleds go right through the middle," Eva said as we approached the front of the line.

I was in the first bobsled. It went down the track and slowly climbed a dark tunnel. I could hear people screaming in another bobsled. I saw eyes in the darkness and heard something growl at me when we reached the top of the mountain. We glided around the corners with ease. The bobsled whipped down the cliff. It zigzagged through the mountain in no time. I laughed when I saw an abominable snowman who growled as we went by it. I could hear Griffin laughing or crying behind me. I wasn't sure which.

We coasted around the corner and hit the water. Everyone screamed as the water splashed around us.

We came to a stop behind another bobsled and waited our turn to exit our sled.

"That was fun," I laughed.

"It's a small world after all," Houston sang as he climbed out of the last bobsled.

"Houston, *It's a small world* is stuck in my head too," Rachel laughed.

"I think it's stuck in all of our heads," Clare laughed. "How about we go to Autopia next?"

"I want to drive. I want to drive," Griffin jumped up and down and laughed with excitement.

"You can drive the car Griffin," Clare said as she headed towards the ride.

"Okay," he laughed and skipped along the path.

When we came to the ride we walked by 3-D images of cars out camping. They appeared to be alive, like in the Cars movie. There were 3-D images of cars at a gas station too. They were talking.

We walked down the long path to the cars.

"Can I ride with one of you girls?" Parker asked.

"Sure," I said. "Which of us would you like to ride with Rachel or me?"

"How about you Tara," she smiled.

"Only if you drive," I laughed.

"Okay," she smiled.

I watched as Rachel took off down the road in the car in front of us before Parker and I sat in our seats.

"Hey, let's catch up to her," Parker laughed.

"You're the driver. Let's go then." I put the seat belt on and we took off after Rachel.

"Go! Go!" I screamed.

"She's not too far ahead of us, I'll catch her." Parker pushed her foot down on the pedal.

We could see Rachel in front of us, but we weren't catching up to her.

"Darn car, I can't get it to go any faster than this," Parker laughed.

"Well, maybe Rachel will take her foot off the gas and slow down a little."

Every time we thought we were going to catch up to her she would speed away from us again.

"Come on Parker get this thing rolling," I laughed.

I looked behind me and saw Eva and Houston on our tail.

"Speed up Parker. Eva and Houston are right behind us."

"They are?"

"Yeah, they're gaining on us."

"Oh no," she screamed, laughed, and pushed the pedal down as far as it would go.

We went round the corner and their car was out of sight.

"I think we lost them," I laughed.

"Look, there's Rachel right in front of us," Parker pointed.

"Yeah, and there's Eva and Houston right behind us."

"I'm going to catch her," Parker screamed.

Just as she said that, I saw we were back where we started. We caught up to Rachel as she pulled the car up behind another car and waited.

"Well, we caught her thanks to this traffic jam," Parker laughed.

"Yeah, Eva and Houston caught us too." I waved at them as they stopped behind me. "Hey where's your mom and Griffin?"

"I don't know. I don't see them."

I looked around and spotted them in another lane a few cars back.

"I see them right over there," I pointed.

"Mom," Parker yelled and waved.

Clare waved back while Griffin stuck his tongue out at Parker then smiled.

"That was fun Parker. You're a great driver."

"Thanks Tara."

We pulled up to the number three sign and climbed out of the car. We walked out of the gate and saw Rachel waiting. We stood and waited for everyone.

"Okay, it's getting late. Let's ride one more ride and then head to the Fantasmic Show," Clare said. "Which ride do you want to ride on kids?"

"How about Space Mountain?" Griffin said.

"Yeah, let's do Space Mountain," Eva said.

"Does everyone want to do Space Mountain?" Clare asked.

"Sounds good to me," Rachel smiled.

"Me too," I said.

"Yep," Houston said. "It's a small world after all," he sang.

We laughed.

"See I told you it would be stuck in my head the rest of the day," he laughed.

We walked into the Space Mountain ride and looked over the railing at the space cars below us. It was like we walked into the future.

The line moved quickly, and we made it to the front in a few minutes.

"You girls sit in the front since this is your first time," Clare said.

We switched positions with Eva and Houston and took the front seat.

We headed through a tube, which looked like part of a space ship. It was dark and I saw small lights everywhere. Then we moved into a glass tunnel and I could see the stars in the sky. We headed through the tunnel to the solar system. At least I thought it was. Then I realized it was the eye of an evil space creature and we were heading straight for him. The space creature waved its arms and lightening lit up the glass tube. The evil creature flew away, and we were in darkness as we zoomed to the wide-open space. I could see stars again. I felt like we were floating in space. Then we started going faster and faster as we whipped around the galaxy. I screamed as a monster's face came towards me. It felt like we were spinning out of control in the darkness. I saw the monsters hand come out of the stars and reach towards us. Then I saw his upper body as it reached towards us. I screamed again. Then we came to a meteor shower. A few minutes later it was gone and we flew back to the mother ship where we started.

I followed Rachel off the ride.

"Now, that was a wild ride," I said.

"Yeah, I'll say it was," Rachel said.

"You girls sure can scream," Houston laughed.

"I think I screamed like you did the first time I went on it too," Eva laughed.

"I think I'm a little sick from that ride," I said.

"What... are you going to throw-up?" Griffin asked.

"No, just a little dizzy that's all."

"Me too Tara," Rachel said.

"That ride tends to do that to people," Clare laughed.

"Mom, I'm feeling a little dizzy too," Parker said.

"Maybe all you girls just need something to eat. It's been hours since we had anything to eat," Houston said.

"Houston you must be hungry," Eva said.

"Uh... Yeah, I would have thought one of you guys would have been saying you were hungry too by now," he laughed.

"I'm hungry," Griffin laughed.

"That's my bud. Us guys have to stick together," Houston smiled.

"Okay, let's grab something to eat and head over to the Fantasmic show," Clare said.

We followed her to Main Street to the Carnation Café.

"How many in your party?" the cast member asked.

"We have seven," Clare said.

"Follow me."

59

We followed the cast member to our table.

"Your server will be with you shortly," she said as she handed us each a menu.

"Tara, Rachel, order anything you like off the menu. Since it's your birthday tomorrow I'm treating," Clare said.

"That's nice Clare, but you don't have to do that we have our own money," I said.

"I know, but your birthday is tomorrow and you're celebrating it today. I want to buy you dinner. I insist," she said.

"Thank you Clare," Rachel smiled.

"Yes, Thank you very much," I said.

"Eat whatever you want,"

"Can I eat whatever I want too?" Griffin asked.

"Don't you always?" Clare laughed.

"I guess I do," Griffin laughed.

"Look, there's fried pickles and dipping sauce," I laughed.

"Ick," Rachel said.

"Oh no, the fried pickles are good," Clare laughed.

"I think I'm going to have the chicken fried chicken," I said.

"Me too," Rachel said.

The cast member took our order and came back with the food in a short time.

"Are you having fun girls?" Houston asked.

"Yes we are Houston," Rachel smiled.

"Isn't this the happiest place on earth and the happiest place you've ever been to in your whole lives?" Houston laughed.

"Yes it is," I smiled. "I can't think of one place I've been that makes me happy like this place does."

"Me either," Parker smiled.

"Me too," Griffin smiled.

"This has been a fabulous day," Clare said.

"Yes it has," Eva said.

"You know girls I'm going to give you our address and phone number just in case you ever pass this way again. You can look us up and maybe we can do this again sometime." Clare pulled a pen and paper out of her purse, and wrote her name, address, and phone number and handed it to Rachel.

"Thanks Clare. I think we would like to meet you in Disneyland again sometime." Rachel folded the paper and put it in her pocket.

"Yeah, it would be fun all right," I said.

"Yeah, if you come this way again you have to stay longer. There are lots of rides you missed because we just can't do it all in one day," Eva said.

"Yeah, and don't forget California Adventure. That's a whole day by itself," Houston said.

"Hey, look!" Parker was pointing at Griffin, who fell asleep with his face in his plate of Mac and Cheese.

"Oh no not again," Clare laughed.

Everyone laughed.

Clare picked Griffin's head up gently, removed his plate out from underneath it, sat it gently on the table, and brushed the macaroni noodles off him with her finger.

"I'll carry him," Houston laughed.

"Thanks Houston, Let's finish our dinner and then we'll head over to watch Fantasmic. Griffin's going to miss it again. I hope one of these days we won't wear him out so much, and maybe he'll stay awake for the show," Clare laughed.

"I don't know about the rest of you, but the last ride kind of wiped me out too," I said.

"Yeah, all the twists, and turns. It wiped me out and scared me too," Rachel laughed.

"It used to scare me too. I've ridden it so many times now it doesn't scare me anymore. It does make me dizzy though," Parker smiled.

"All those twists and turns didn't make the song fall out of my head. It's a small world after all," Houston laughed.

"The song is really stuck in there good, isn't it?" Eva laughed.

Everyone laughed.

"Is everyone just about done eating?" Clare asked.

I looked at my plate. I was almost done.

"Almost," I said.

"Me too," Houston said.

"I'm finished," Rachel said.

"Me too," Eva and Parker said.

"Okay, I'm going to the restroom and get a paper towel to wipe the rest of the food off Griffin's face before you pick him up Houston. Anyone need to use the restroom?" Clare asked.

We nodded our heads.

"If you're done eating head to the restroom. They're right around the corner," Clare pointed.

Everyone headed to the bathroom except me, Griffin, and Houston. We were still eating and Griffin was still sleeping with his head on the table.

"I think this day is the greatest day of my life so far. Thanks for inviting us Houston," I smiled.

"You're welcome Tara? I think," he smiled.

"Yep, you have it right," I laughed.

"I'm glad I could help you girls have a good pre-birthday celebration."

"By the time I go to bed tonight it will be my birthday," I laughed.

So... Tara, who's the oldest you or Rachel?

"I am," I smiled.

"Well, you hold your age well. You don't look one minute older than her," Houston laughed.

As soon as they all came back to the table, I took my turn. When I came back to the table, I took my seat and noticed everyone looking at me.

"What? Do I have toilet paper on my shoe?" I laughed.

"No, we're just waiting on Houston now," Clare laughed. "I cleaned up Griffin's face the best I could. I hope I didn't leave any sticky stuff."

"Here comes Houston now," Eva said.

"Okay, looks like we're ready to go see Fantasmic," Eva smiled.

"Okay, I'm ready to pick the kid up now. I hope he didn't eat too much, he seems to be getting heavier and heavier every time we come here," Houston laughed.

"Well, of course he is Houston. He's a growing boy," Clare laughed.

We followed Clare to the place where the Fantasmic show was going to start.

"Hold on a minute I have tickets in my purse." Clare dug through her purse and pulled out seven fast pass tickets. She showed them to the cast member who was holding a rope.

"You're in the blue section. That's over there," he pointed.

"Thank you," Clare said. "Follow me," she headed in the direction the cast member pointed.

We walked through the crowd of people until we came to a blue sign. Clare showed the tickets to the cast member standing next to the sign, and he unhooked the rope and let us in the area.

Clare weaved through the people sitting on the ground and found a place next to the water for us to sit.

"Let's sit here. We'll have a great view," she said. She sat her purse on the ground next to her. "Houston you can lay Griffin here next to me. Lay his head on my purse."

Houston sat Griffin down gently with his head on Clare's purse. Griffin was sleeping soundly. He didn't move an inch.

"It's a small world after all," Houston sang.

"Okay, you've convinced me. Next time we go on that ride it will be the last ride of the night," Eva laughed.

"It's a small world after all," Parker sang.

Then the lights went down and a woman's voice spoke.

"Welcome to Fantasmic. Tonight our friend and host Mickey Mouse uses his vivid imagination to create magical imagery for all to enjoy. Nothing is more wonderful than the imagination. For in a

moment you can experience a beautiful fantasy or an exciting adventure, but beware nothing is more powerful than the imagination for it can also expand your greatest fears into an overwhelming nightmare. Are the powers of Mickey's incredible imagination strong enough and bright enough to withstand the evil forces that invade Mickey's dream? You are about to find out. For we now invite you to join Mickey and experience Fantasmic. A journey beyond your wildest imagination."

Then the lights dimmed further and big beams of light shot up from the island.

"See, there's the stage we were standing on," Parker whispered. "Mickey's going to be there soon."

Poles of lights shot up from the water. Mickey took center stage dancing to the music. There were streams of colored water flowing into the sky and Mickey had sparks shooting out of his fingertips. As the music played, the streams of water fanned out into a fine mist and a movie started playing in the fine mist with cartoon Mickey on the screen. I saw small fireworks shooting off while the movie of Mickey played. I could see beautiful flowers in the mist.

Big flower petals appeared in the center of the stage. They moved across the stage and formed flowers. Then the flowers on the mist screen sank into the water and a big snake moved across the stage as the flower petals parted to let the snake move around the stage. The music changed to a jungle sound. Monkeys danced on a moving stage as it floated across the water in front of us. More monkeys moved across the water on a floating stage coming from the opposite direction and floated in front of us. The water and stage were very busy.

The floating stages disappeared and the water movie continued with elephants and the music changed to an electric guitar sound. Cartoon elephants danced in the mist to the music.

Then the water turned to colored streams and Pinocchio along with two girl puppets danced on the stage. They disappeared as the water mist screens displayed fish and you could hear someone calling Pinocchio. When you wish upon a star was playing as the cartoon fish danced on the screen. Jiminy Cricket appeared in a water bubble in the mist.

The water was building, and the music was getting fierce. Then you could see cartoon Mickey in the mist, he looked like he was caught in the water and yelling for help. He spun in a circle like he was going down the drain. Then it was dark. You could hear Mickey asking, "What's going on?" Then he said, "Uh oh." It looked like a thunder and lightning storm in the mist. The storm stopped and a large old sailboat came towards us.

I saw Wendy standing on deck as Captain Hook chased Peter Pan through the ropes at the top of the sails. Next Captain Hook's pirates were carrying Wendy across the deck. The boat disappeared and a huge sea serpent followed behind it.

Water shot up into the sky lit up with blue lights. I watched as Beauty and the Beast floated across the water on a raft. They danced together as their song played. Next Ariel and Prince Eric floated across the water on a raft. Ariel sat on a rock flipping her tail around and raising her hands to the music dancing with Prince Eric. Next Snow White and Prince Charming dance to the music "Someday my prince will come," as they glided across the water on the raft in front of us.

The rafts disappeared from view and the wicked queen was on stage. She summonsed the magic mirror. The music was evil sounding. I saw the magic mirror appear in the mist. The mirror told the wicked queen three... *"lovelier maids I see and hear in Mickey's imagination beauty and love will always survive."*

She screamed *"No!"* and a black cauldron appeared on stage. The queen made a magic spell with her powers and turned into a wicked witch. She said she is going to turn Mickey's dream into a nightmare.

She said... *"Magic mirror on the wall all the forces of evil I call."* The magic mirror pops up again, and said... *"You have the power to control his mind."* Then I saw a picture of Ursula the evil octopus she said *"Yes, how exciting let's do it"* and she laughed her evil laugh. Then she sang and said she would like to see Mickey obey her every whim, she turned into an evil devil and ghosts flew everywhere.

Then Mickey was on stage. The water screen showed the evil queen cartoon and then the water disappeared and a huge dragon appeared on the stage.

Mickey ran at first as the fire-breathing dragon sets fire to the water. The fire went out and Mickey stood invincible. He grabbed the sword from the stone. He held it in the air. Mickey said to the dragon... *"You think you are so powerful this is my dream."*

He blasted the dragon with sparks from the sword. I heard the dragon screaming and then saw electricity and sparks then the stage went dark.

The water mist was barely visible. Then I heard beautiful music playing and Tinker Bell flew through the mist. Tink disappeared and lights

67

flicker as a big boat came around the corner with fireworks on it.

Every cartoon character was on the Mark Twain paddle wheel boat and Mickey was at the wheel in his original costume. The characters sang and waved with their streamers on sticks.

I saw Mickey, Chip and Dale, the three pigs, Pluto, Goofy, Jasmine, Prince Aladdin, Mary Poppins, Tiana, Beauty and the Beast, Ariel and Prince Eric, Donald Duck, Woody, Buzz Lightyear, and Jessie.

After the boat disappeared, water shot in the air, and lights brightened on top of the hill. I saw Mickey in a cloud of smoke wearing his sorcerers robe and hat conducting the music.

The fireworks exploded all around him, and beams of lights in blue and gold streamed into the sky above him. I saw smoke and fireworks lighting up the sky.

Then Mickey appeared center stage in his black tux and red pants. He said... *"Some imagination huh,"* and sparks surrounded him. The fireworks went off, the lights went out and the music ended. Everyone clapped and cheered.

"Yah!" I yelled and clapped.

"The show was great!" Rachel yelled.

"I've never seen anything like this before," I said.

"I'm glad you liked it girls," Clare said.

"It's amazing," Eva said. "I could watch that show again. I never get tired of it."

"Me too," Parker said.

"Yeah, it's a great show," Houston said.

"Let's sit here until the crowd thins out. Then we can head over to the Photo Pass store and I'll get the picture we took with Mickey earlier," Clare said.

We sat and waited for the crowd to thin out. As soon as it did, Houston picked up Griffin and put his head on his shoulder. Griffin didn't move.

"Man this kid is out," Houston laughed.

"Okay, follow me," Clare said.

We followed her to Main Street and into the photo pass store.

"Why don't you go look around for some souvenirs? We're going to be leaving the park soon," Clare said to all of us.

"Okay, Let's go across the street there's a store with lot's of things in it," Eva said. "I'm taking Parker with us Mom."

"Okay."

We followed Eva across the street into a store filled with Disney stuff.

"I'm going to go look at the hoodies. Come on Houston," Eva said.

"A hoodie? I could use one of those," Rachel said.

"Me too," I said.

We followed her to the aisle where the hoodies were and I found a hoodie with Minnie Mouse on it I liked. I showed it to Rachel.

"I like that one too," Rachel said.

"Well, of course you do," Houston laughed.

"Eva, pick me out a t-shirt please. It's a little hard for me to look with Griffin snoozing on my shoulder," Houston said.

Eva looked through the rack of t-shirts and found a shirt with Goofy on the front.

"How do you like this one?" she asked as she showed it to Houston.

"You know me well girl," He laughed. "That's perfect for me. Can you grab my wallet from my pocket please?"

"Rachel, these are sixty dollars," I whispered to her.

"Really? That's a hundred and twenty plus tax. I don't think we should spend so much money. Let's put them back," she whispered.

We hung the hoodies back where we found them.

"Let's look for something little," I whispered.

"Okay."

We walked around the store and looked at stuff.

"Hey, how about this little box of mints?" Rachel pointed to a small tin box of cinnamon mints with a picture of Mickey and the gang on the front.

"Good idea. Lightweight, easy to carry around on the train, and we can eat them too," I laughed.

We each grabbed a box of mints, went up to the register and paid for them.

Rachel and I went outside and waited for everyone to finish shopping. We saw Clare crossing the street, and we waved to her.

"Hey girls, did you find a souvenir?"

"Yeah," I pulled the boxes of mints out of the bag and showed them to her. "Small, for the train ride."

"That's a good idea. You'll have fresh breath all the way to Seattle, and back home," she laughed. "Where is everyone?"

"They're still in the store," Rachel said.

"Okay, well I'm going to see what I can find for Griffin. I'll be right back."

Clare went into the store and a few minutes later Eva, Parker, and Houston, carrying Griffin, came out of the door with a couple of bags.

"Hey girls, my mom will be right out," Eva said.

A few minutes later Clare came out of the door with a couple of bags of stuff.

"Okay, are we ready to head back to the hotel?"

"Yeah, I need to put this kid down. He's getting heavier by the minute," Houston said.

"Hey girls, what time does your train leave in the morning? I'm going to give you a ride to the station," Clare said.

"Oh, thank you Clare. Our train leaves at eight-o-seven a.m.," I said.

"We can get up and have breakfast together upstairs in the breakfast room then, I'll drop you off at about ten till eight so you won't miss your train."

"Thanks Clare, what time should we get up?" Rachel asked.

"Six-thirty should give you plenty of time to get ready. We'll meet you in the breakfast room around seven-fifteen."

We headed out of Disneyland and crossed the street to our hotel.

"Goodnight girls," everyone said.

"It's a small world after all," Houston laughed.

Everyone laughed.

71

"Goodnight," Rachel and I said. "See you in the morning."

Rachel and I went to our room and flopped on the bed.

"This was the best day ever," Rachel said.

"I know, I will never forget it as long as I live."

"Me either. Tara, look, it's almost your birthday."

I looked at the clock it was ten minutes to midnight. I reached over and set the alarm for six-thirty.

"Should we stay awake?" Rachel asked.

"No, I'm too tired," I laughed.

I rolled on my side and closed my eyes.

A few minutes later I heard Rachel whisper, "Happy Birthday."

I laughed. "Thank you," I was asleep in seconds.

The alarm went off and Rachel headed for the bathroom.

"It's your birthday today so why don't you go back to sleep while I take my shower. I'll wake you up when I'm done."

"Okay," I rolled over and went back to sleep.

"Tara, it's time to wake up birthday girl," Rachel laughed.

I yawned, stretched, hopped out of bed and headed for the shower.

I jumped out of the shower, dried my hair, brushed my teeth and headed out the bathroom door.

"Happy birthday to you, happy birthday to you, happy birthday dear Tara, happy birthday to you," Rachel sang.

"Thank you," I laughed.

"Well, I thought I would sing it to you before we head down to breakfast, because you know everyone is going to tell us both happy birthday," Rachel laughed.

"Yep, that means we each get two birthdays this year," I laughed.

I looked at the clock it was seven o'clock.

"Let's do a double-check and make sure we have everything in the backpack before we leave," I said.

Rachel and I looked around the room. I found the sack with the boxes of mints.

"Here Rachel, put them in the backpack please."

Rachel grabbed the mints and stuffed them in a side pocket.

"I think we have everything," she said.

"Okay, let's go check out."

We headed out the door and went downstairs to the lobby.

"We're checking out of room three-twenty-nine," Rachel handed the desk clerk the room key.

"Thanks, I hope you enjoyed your stay," the desk clerk said as he printed out the receipt and handed it to Rachel.

"We did," Rachel, and I smiled and headed out the door.

We walked across the parking lot and up the stairs to the breakfast room.

"Room number and name please," the server asked.

"Three-twenty-nine Martha Cook," Rachel said.

I watched and waited for her face to turn red, but it didn't.

We walked away from the counter and I whispered to her.

"How'd you do that without turning red?"

"She just asked for the room number and name. She didn't ask me if I was Martha Cook. I didn't lie. I just gave her the room number and name," she laughed.

We looked around the room and I saw Clare sitting at a table with Griffin. She saw me at the same time and waved me over to the table.

"Hey girls, grab a plate and get something to eat. I'm holding this table for everyone."

"Hi girls," Eva said as she took a seat with a plate full of food.

"Hi," Rachel and I said.

We walked over and grabbed paper plates.

There were eggs, bacon, sausage, biscuits, gravy, fruit, cereal, and anything else we might want for breakfast.

"Let's load up. That way we won't have to buy as much on the train," Rachel said.

We loaded our plates, went to the table, and sat next to Parker whose plate was just as full as mine.

"I see you're loading up," Houston said.

"Yep," I said as I looked at his plate fuller than mine. "I see you're loading up too."

"Yep, we have a long day of fun filled rides at California Adventure. Too bad you girls have to catch a train. Sorry you have to miss out on your birthday," he shook his head.

"Yeah, well we had a great time yesterday. All that fun is already spilling over into today," Rachel smiled.

Clare and Griffin returned to the table and pulled up a chair next to me.

"Happy Birthday girls," Clare said.

"Oh yeah, I forgot, Happy Birthday," Parker said.

"Me too, Happy Birthday," Griffin said.

"Happy Birthday," Eva and Houston said.

"Now remember girls, if you ever come back through and want to go to Disneyland, just give me a call a week ahead of time, and I'll bring the kids, and we'll go with you," Clare said.

"We will. For sure," Rachel said.

"Yes, we will for sure," I said.

We finished our breakfast just in time.

"Look at the time. We need to get you two to the train station. We're running a little late. Let's go," Clare said.

We headed down the stairs, to the parking lot, and looked for the van. Once everyone buckled their seat belts, Eva drove us to the train station and parked. Everyone climbed out of the van to give us hugs good-bye.

"Bye Eva, thanks," I said as I hugged her.

"Bye Tara, you girls are the best," she hugged me back.

"Bye Houston, thanks for inviting us. This was the best time I've ever had," I said as we hugged.

"You're welcome, and you know what they say?"

"I sure do. It's a small world after all," I laughed

"Yep, and you better keep in touch with us," he laughed.

"Parker, you can drive me around Autopia anytime," I hugged her.

"Next time I hope I have a faster car," she squeezed me tight.

"Griffin, sorry you fell asleep before the Fantasmic Show," I bent down and gave him a hug.

"Ah that's okay, I've seen it before and I have it on video at home. I watch it all the time," he laughed.

"Thanks for letting us hang out with your family Clare," I said as I hugged her.

"Any time Tara. It was great fun having you girls with us. You two are like part of the family now. Griffin has something he wants to give you."

Griffin had two gifts, wrapped in Minnie Mouse paper, in his hands. He handed us each one.

"Happy birthday girls. It's from all of us," he smiled.

"Oh wow! Thank you," Rachel and I said at the same time.

"There you go with that twin thing again," Houston laughed.

We hugged everyone one more time.

"Don't open them until you're on the train," Eva said.

"Okay, we won't."

We heard the announcement over the loudspeaker for our train.

"You girls better hurry, the train doesn't wait for anyone," Clare smiled.

"Oh no," Rachel said as she searched the pocket of the backpack for our tickets, pulled them out, and showed them to me.

We both took off running for the train.

"Where are you headed girls?" the conductor asked.

"Seattle," Rachel and I said.

Rachel handed him her e-ticket as I handed him mine.

"Seattle?" the conductor looked at our e-tickets and gave us each a seat check card. He wrote our seat number and SEA in big letters. "You're going to Seattle. Well you're lucky you made it. A minute later and those doors would have shut right in front of you and you would have missed us. We only spend a couple of minutes at every stop. Be listening and we'll let you know when we get close to Los Angeles. The train to Seattle is called the Starlight. Make sure you pay attention to your departure time leaving Los Angeles. Remember... you wait for the train... the train waits for no one."

We climbed aboard the train, found our seats and looked out the window to see Clare, Houston, Eva, Parker, and Griffin watching the train.

Rachel and I waved out the window as the train departed the station.

"Now, yesterday was a day to remember," I said.

CHAPTER 4

No Surprise

"Excuse me, where is the lounge car?" I asked a conductor as she came through the car.

"The lounge car is four cars up," she said.

"Oh, thank you," I smiled. "Hey Rachel, do you want to go to the lounge car with me?"

"Yeah," she said.

I grabbed my present and headed up the aisle. Rachel grabbed her present and the backpack and followed me towards the lounge car. I was having a hard time walking in a straight line as the train bounced on the tracks. As we made our way through the cars people smiled at us and asked if we were twins. We shook our heads yes and continued on our way.

We arrived at the lounge car. Rachel and I sat next to each other in the seats facing the windows. I took my present, set it in my lap, and stared at the Minnie Mouse wrapping paper.

"What do you think it is?" Rachel asked as she stared at the present in her lap too.

I felt the present. "It feels squishy, but it's hard in the middle," I said.

"Tara, you open yours first since it's your birthday."

"Okay," I turned the present over, pulled on the tape, and opened the paper. I was surprised to see the hoodie from the Disneyland store.

"Look it's the hoodie we were looking at," Rachel smiled. "Those guys were watching us."

"They sure were. Weren't they," I laughed. "There's something hard in the middle." I opened the hoodie and saw the picture of us with Mickey Mouse and a card. I opened the card and read it aloud. "Happy birthday Rachel, thanks for being a part of our lives. We wish you a safe journey. Clare, Parker, Griffin, Eva, Houston. They all signed it." I handed the present to Rachel, and she handed the unopened one to me.

"Here you can open this one too it's your birthday. You should always have at least two presents to open," Rachel laughed.

I opened the present and pulled it from the wrapping paper. They bought me the same hoodie, which I wanted and gave me a picture and card too.

"They are so nice," I said as I put on the hoodie.

"Maybe we'll see them again someday," Rachel said, as she put on hers.

"Maybe, one day when we have a normal life again."

"Yesterday was a normal day."

Yesterday was greater than a normal day. Yesterday was a perfectly happy day. Today will be a normal day." Just as I said that, the train stopped.

"Why are we stopping so soon?" Rachel asked.

A woman sitting across the aisle from us heard her.

"Didn't you hear the announcement? We're at Fullerton girls. We're picking up passengers, it will only be a minute," she said.

"No, I didn't hear it. I must have been talking," I said to the woman.

I looked out the window and waited for the train to start moving again.

I looked at the picture of Rachel, Houston, Eva, Parker, Griffin, Clare and me. I thought, what a wonderful blessing to meet them and become part of their family for a day.

Rachel tapped me on the shoulder and I looked over to see what she wanted. She wrapped her arms around me and gave me a hug.

"Ah Tara, it's going to be a great day. Happy birthday," she kissed me on the cheek.

I noticed a man in his twenties sitting a few seats over from us, looking at us with a confused look on his face.

"So, I'm a little confused," he said.

"About what?" I asked.

"You are twins aren't you?"

Rachel and I nodded.

"You have the same birthday don't you?"

"Well, of course we do," I said.

"Then why are you telling her happy birthday? Isn't it your birthday too?" he asked.

"Well, every other year we celebrate my birthday on my birthday and every other year I celebrate the day after. That way... we each get a special day. This year it's my turn to celebrate on my birthday and that's today," I smiled. I knew I was probably very red by now.

"Oh, that makes sense," he said. "I could see how your parents must have wanted you each to have your own special day," he looked at me. "Are you okay? Your face is a little flushed, do you need a glass of water or something?" he asked.

"No, I'm just a little hot, that's all," I said.

"So, how old are you two?" he asked.

"We're fifteen," I smiled.

"I remember when I was fifteen. That's a rough age. Ah, the teenage years... no one ever wants to relive those years," he shook his head and laughed. "Well, it was nice talking to you. I'm going to the dining car for a bite to eat."

"It was nice talking to you too," we said at the same time.

"You have that twin thing going on. That freaks me out." He stood up from his chair shook his head and walked down the aisle towards the dining car.

We need to watch for ears listening to things we say on this train," Rachel whispered.

"I know," I shook my head. "We have to start watching everything we say."

"So Tara, what do you usually do on your birthday?" Rachel whispered.

"I usually have friends over. We have chocolate cake and mint chocolate chip ice cream. We either, go to a movie, go skating, or go swimming at the pool. I can tell you this is a great birthday so far. I never thought I would be spending a birthday riding a train. I mean, just look out the window at the beautiful scenery. The weather is perfect and I can sit and enjoy the view. Plus I get to spend the day with you," I whispered.

"Yeah, I wonder what we'll be doing on my birthday," Rachel whispered.

"Seriously, come to think of it, I don't even know if it's really my birthday today. I mean I hope it is. I feel like it is. If it's not... I'm still going to celebrate on this day, because they told me the eleventh is my birthday. I mean can any one of us be sure the date our parents tell us is our birthday... is really our birthday. We were just little babies. We can't remember that far back."

"Well, I'm not sure if we were born at all," Rachel laughed.

"I know what you're thinking and I was thinking the same thing. Maybe they made us in a factory, and spit us out of a machine, like a Barbie doll. Maybe I should check myself for the manufactures stamp. It's on my body someplace... I know it is," I laughed.

"Check your butt. That's were Barbie's stamp is. If you have one, I know I do too," Rachel laughed.

We laughed.

"Hey Rachel, how far away from the next stop are we anyway?"

"I don't know. But I think we need to be paying more attention. I didn't hear the announcement when we stopped at Fullerton. I want to make sure we hear the announcement for Los Angeles. I don't want to be stuck on the train and end up in the wrong place."

"It really doesn't matter where we end up. It's not like we have any place in particular to go anyways," I laughed.

"You do have a point, don't you Tara," Rachel laughed. "You know Tara, I was thinking about the people who were chasing us yesterday. Maybe they have people on the train who are just watching us to see where we go and what we do. Like that woman sitting over there," Rachel whispered as she tilted her head to the right as if to point at someone.

I looked in the direction she had her head tilted and there sat a woman in her thirties, I guessed, who was staring at the two of us over the top of her laptop. She'd look at her computer for a second and then look at us. She was definitely staring at us.

"Do you think she works for the government and she knows who we are?" I whispered.

"I don't know, maybe, or she just likes to stare. Whatever you do, don't stare back at her."

"Okay, I won't. Maybe she's trying to figure out if we're twins or not."

"Maybe, let's look the other way so she will stop staring at us. She is making me feel very uncomfortable," Rachel sighed.

"Looking the other way isn't going to stop her from staring at us," I shook my head.

"I know, but then I won't notice her staring and it will make me feel a lot better."

We both looked the other way and pretended not to notice her staring.

"Okay, I'm not feeling better. I'm not even looking at her and I can feel the holes she is staring through me," Rachel whispered.

"Me too, I don't like it when people stare. I think I am going to go back to my seat. I can't take this woman staring any longer."

Rachel and I stood up, walked towards the coach car, and the woman who was staring at us closed her laptop, stood up and walked towards us.

"Excuse me," she said.

"Yes?" I answered.

"I noticed the two of you the minute I boarded the train. I couldn't help staring at you. I'm sorry about that but there's something I want to show you. Do you have a minute?"

I was scared and didn't know what to say, but since we were in a train car scattered with people there was nothing the woman could really do to us.

She would be crazy to start things with us in a train full of people.

I looked at Rachel who was shaking her head no.

"I think it will be okay Rachel. She can't do anything to us in front of these witnesses," I whispered.

"Yeah, that's a good point," Rachel nodded.

"Yeah, I guess we have a minute," I said.

"Let's sit down right here. I want to show you something." She pointed to a table. Rachel and I took a seat. She sat down across from us.

"What is it you want to show us?" Rachel asked.

"First, my name is Peggy and I live in Washington. I was down visiting my sister and her family in Texas for a couple of weeks. I'm on my way home now. When I first saw you two, I almost fell over. I'm sorry for staring but you two look so much like my niece, I couldn't take my eyes off you." She opened her laptop, typed something on the keyboard, and stared at the screen waiting.

Rachel and I both looked at each other

"Is your niece Amanda Stevens or Nichole Beck?" Rachel asked.

"No, my niece is Selena Anderson."

"Selena Anderson?" I asked.

"Yeah, here's a picture of her." Peggy turned the computer around to face Rachel and me. On the computer screen was a picture of a girl who looked exactly like the two of us.

For the first time Rachel and I weren't the least bit shocked by the picture of Peggy's niece. It was no surprise to us we saw another girl on the face of the earth who looked exactly like us.

The expression on Peggy's face showed she was surprised. She looked puzzled by our lack of a reaction.

"You girls don't look one bit shocked. I thought for sure you would be shocked by this. What's going on? Don't you think this is strange?"

Rachel and I looked at each other and shook our heads. I could tell she was thinking the same thing I was.

"Should I?" I asked Rachel.

"Yeah," Rachel said.

Rachel and I leaned across the table to get closer to Peggy. I closed the laptop so no one else could see the picture.

"Peggy, we have a favor we need to ask you, and you can't say no," I whispered and nodded my head.

"Please Peggy, you need to listen to us carefully," Rachel whispered.

"Don't tell anyone on this train anything about your niece or the fact we look like her," I said.

"Our tickets are good to Seattle Washington, but we'd like to get off at your stop with you," Rachel said. "We'll go to your house and explain everything to you. Maybe you can help us."

"Whatever you do, don't call your sister and tell her about this or do anything out of the ordinary you weren't already planning to do on this trip," I said. "People are watching and we don't know who we can trust."

Peggy sat quietly looking at Rachel and me. I could tell she was thinking. She didn't say a word for the longest time. I watched as she pulled a piece of paper and pen from her purse and wrote on it.

She handed the paper to me.

"Here's my address and phone number in case we get separated. I want to know everything," she whispered.

"We'll tell you everything we know," I said as I looked at the piece of paper and showed it to Rachel.

"I don't think we should sit together anymore," Rachel said.

Peggy nodded her head, stood up from the table and went back to where she was sitting earlier.

"Rachel, let's sit here for a little while longer. I'm not ready to go to our seats."

"Me either," Rachel nodded. "It's funny how things work out sometimes."

"Yeah, who would've thought?"

"Yeah, who would've thought?"

"So, that makes five of us," I whispered. "Oh, I mean six."

"Six? Where did you come up with six?"

"Well, there's you and me, Amanda and Nichole, Selena and Isabella."

"Isabella... who's Isabella?"

"Kate's niece...I think she's like us. What do you think? Do you think it's possible?"

"Oh yeah, I forgot about her. Yeah, I think anything's possible. I know Amanda said there were only a few of us, but I don't think she knows any more than what Malory has told her."

"Well, I know she doesn't even know Kate. So, she doesn't know about Isabella either."

"I wonder how many girls like us are out there, Tara."

"I don't know but I'm interested in finding out. So, if you add the new girl that makes six of us so far. Which, I think is four girls too many."

"I'm really glad you didn't say five Tara."

"No Rachel, I would never say five."

"I wonder when Selena's birthday is."

"I don't know what month, but I can bet you the day is probably the eleventh, and I know I would win that bet," I laughed.

"Yeah, that's a bet I wouldn't take because you're probably right."

I looked at the piece of paper with Peggy's address on it. "She lives in Ruston Washington. Where's that?"

"Who knows? We'll have to watch her when we get into Washington State and make sure we get off the train when she does."

"What time do we get to Washington State anyhow?"

"I don't know. We haven't made it to Los Angeles yet," Rachel said.

An announcement came over the speaker.

"We'll be arriving in Los Angeles in five minutes. That's Los Angeles in five minutes. For those passengers who are getting off the train in Los Angeles, please gather your belongings. For those people continuing on to other destinations Los Angeles is a rest stop you can get off the train to stretch your legs. We'll be in Los Angeles for approximately twenty-minutes and then we'll continue on to Glendale. If you decide to stretch your legs please be aware the train will be leaving the station on time.

Listen for the boarding call for the Pacific Surfline. Thank you," the conductor announced.

"Let's get going." I grabbed my stuff and headed to the door.

Rachel was right behind me. Peggy was right behind her.

Rachel and I looked at Peggy. Peggy looked at Rachel and me, but we didn't acknowledge we had met or spoke to each other. We stood in line waiting for the train to reach the station.

As soon as it stopped, the doors opened. The line of people in front of us moved slowly out the door. Rachel and I hopped off the train and looked for the Starlight train to Seattle. Rachel pulled out the schedule and looked to see what time it left the station.

"It says we leave at ten after ten."

I looked for a clock and saw one hanging on the wall.

"It's eight-fifty right now."

"Let's find a place to sit," Rachel said.

"How about inside?" I pointed and headed in the direction of the train station.

Rachel followed me through the door and into the station. There were rows of comfortable chairs. Rachel and I found two next to each other and took a seat.

"We're going to be sitting at the station awhile." I looked at the picture of us with Mickey. "I'm glad we met Houston on the train. If we hadn't we would have never went to Disneyland."

"I know, we would have never met any of them if it weren't for Houston. I bet they are having a great time in California Adventure," Rachel said.

"We'll go there someday."

"Yeah, someday."

We sat in the comfortable chairs and watched the people as they went by us on their way to their trains. Some walked slowly, some walked fast, and some were running at top speed. I saw people of all ages, types, and sizes.

"Rachel, I wonder where all these people are going. Wouldn't it be fun to be a world traveler and just go from place to place without any worries or cares just seeing the sights?"

"I feel like I'm already doing that," Rachel laughed.

"Yeah, but we have worries," I laughed.

"Yeah, we do," Rachel smiled. "Hey, did you notice where Peggy went?"

"No." I glanced around the station. "I don't see her anywhere?"

"Well we have her address just in case we lose her," Rachel said.

"Yeah, but we don't know what part of Washington Ruston is in. Maybe we should find a map somewhere so we know where we need to get off the train. Let's find someone to ask where we can get a map."

I looked around the big room. The seat I was sitting in was so comfortable I didn't want to move.

"Hey, look there's an information booth," Rachel pointed. "Do you want to go see if you can get a map?"

"Not really, I'm nice and comfy," I smiled.

"Me too, that's why I asked you if you wanted to go," Rachel laughed.

"We are lazy aren't we," I laughed.

"No, I'm lazy... You're old. I understand if you can't get out of the chair because you're so old," Rachel laughed.

"Rachel, didn't your parents ever teach you to respect your elders?" I smiled as I put my hand out for Rachel to help me to my feet.

"The chairs are comfy," she laughed as she stood up, took my hand, and helped me out of the chair.

We walked to the booth and the man sitting behind the counter asked if we needed his assistance.

"We need information please," Rachel smiled.

"That's why they pay me the big bucks," the man laughed. "What do you need to know?"

"We're heading to Ruston Washington but we've never been there before. Do you have a map?" Rachel asked.

"Yes I do. If you're going to Ruston, it's a part of Tacoma. So, you need to hop off the train in Tacoma."

He pulled out a map and showed us where Tacoma was, then pointed to Ruston.

"So, you see Ruston is right here. Let's see... by the looks of the schedule you will be arriving in Tacoma tomorrow night at seven-o-three."

"Seven-o-three tomorrow night. Okay, thank you," I said.

"You girls have a safe trip."

"Thanks," Rachel and I said.

We went and sat in the comfortable chairs we sat in before and went back to watching people.

The time flew by fast since we saw so many interesting people walking through the station.

We heard the announcement to board the Coast Starlight to Seattle.

"Hey, that's us," I said.

We headed down the hall to our train.

"Twins? Don't try to confuse me girls I'm confused enough as it is," the conductor joked as he looked at our tickets.

"We'll try not to," we said at the same time.

"Ah, you have that twin thing going on," he laughed. "Looks like you were supposed to be on the train yesterday," he said.

"Yeah, but we had the tickets changed to today," I said.

"Oh, yeah I have you here," he looked at his portable device. "Martha and Rita Cook. Which one is which?" he asked.

"I'm Rita," I raised my hand.

"Are you sure? You look just like Martha," he laughed as he wrote SEA and the number sixteen on the seat check and handed it to me.

We climbed aboard the train, went up the stairs, and found our seats.

"This is a long trip Tara." Rachel leaned over and looked out the window as the people boarded the train. She stared out the window a few minutes then she whispered. "Hey look at the man in the gray suit looking in the window. It looks like he's looking at us."

"Is he looking at us?" I whispered.

"I don't know for sure, but it looks like he is. I'm getting an uneasy feeling about this. He's wearing the same type suit those guys were wearing yesterday," Rachel whispered.

"He's not one of the men who followed us yesterday is he?"

"I don't know for sure, but I swear he has the same suit. Who knows, he could be."

Every time I looked out the window of the train, the man looked like he was staring at me. Then I saw him getting in line to board the train. I tried to see if he boarded, but he disappeared from view.

"Do you think he boarded the train?" Rachel whispered.

"I don't know," I whispered.

"Should we go check and see?"

"No, I really don't want to... what if he's looking for us.? I don't want to help him find us."

"Well, if he is looking for us... it looks like he just found us when he looked in the window and saw us."

"Rachel, did you have to go and say that? I was enjoying my birthday until you pointed the guy out to me."

"Well, the guy was staring at us."

"I know it looked like he was, but maybe he was looking at someone else."

Rachel stood up and looked up and down the aisle.

"Tara, we are the only two people sitting on this side of the train right now. There's no one sitting on this side of the car besides the two of us."

"Did you have to tell me that Rachel? You're creeping me out."

"Sorry, I know it's your birthday and we've been having such a good time, but it looks like we are back to reality now. We need to keep our eyes peeled for dangerous people at all times. We need to be ready for whoever tries to attack us."

"Yeah, I guess you're right, but I don't want to go see if the guy is on the train. Let's just stay here. Maybe he was just looking at the train."

The minute I said that, the door opened and the man in the gray suit stood in the doorway. He looked right at Rachel and me. I looked him in the eyes and a chill went down my spine.

The train started to move. Rachel and I sat, not moving. The man in the gray suit stood in the doorway not moving. I was scared. He looked mean.

"Rachel, let's go see if we can find Peggy," I whispered.

"Are you sure? We're going to have to walk by him."

"Yeah, he's giving me the creeps, but there are too many people in here now so I know he can't hurt us."

"Okay, let's go," Rachel whispered as she stood up.

We grabbed our stuff and walked quickly towards the door to the next car.

"Excuse me," Rachel said to the man as she squeezed by him.

"Excuse me," I said as I squeezed by him. He glared at me. My whole body shook with fear.

Rachel pushed the button to the breezeway, it opened, we went through the door, pushed the button to the next car, and went inside.

"Peggy is probably in the lounge car," I said to Rachel

"Okay," Rachel said as she headed through the car.

I turned around to see if I could see the man through the window of the breezeway, and saw he was following not far behind me.

"Rachel he's behind us."

"What?" she screamed.

We walked through the car into the breezeway and opened the door to the next car.

I looked over my shoulder as I followed her into the next car. The man was still behind us. It made the hairs on my neck stand up and gave me a chill. I put my hands on Rachel's back and pushed her to move faster.

"Rachel, he's following us, hurry!" I whispered.

We were walking so fast we were almost running. We picked up the pace and ran down the aisles. We headed into a breezeway and opened the door to another car. The train bounced along the track as we ran.

People stood in the aisleway talking to each other.

"Excuse me, coming through," Rachel screamed as she pushed and shoved and ran as fast as she could.

"Hey, watch where you're going!" a man yelled.

"Sorry," I yelled back at him as I kept running.

We ran by a conductor and he shouted, "Slow down girls, no running!"

"Sorry!" I screamed and then kept running.

"Is he still following us?" Rachel screamed.

"I don't know," I screamed.

We ran down the aisle and into the next car. We went through several more cars, and then we came to the lounge car. Peggy was nowhere in sight. We walked quickly through the car into the dining car.

"May I help you?" the waiter asked.

"Oh, no thanks. We're just passing through," Rachel said.

"Passing through? I'm sorry, but you can't go through this car. No one is allowed in the sleeper cars unless they've purchased sleeper car accommodations. Would you like to make reservations for lunch while you're here?"

"No thanks," Rachel said.

We turned around and headed back into the lounge car. I didn't see the man in the gray suit so I went down the stairs to the snack center. I looked around and saw the snack center sign said closed.

We had no place left to go and we were alone, it was not a good combination if the man in the gray suit wanted to kill us.

"Rachel, what should we do?" I whispered.

"Let's hide."

I turned around and looked at her.

"Where?"

"Do you want to go in there?" She pointed to the open door leading into the bathroom at the end of the aisle.

"Oh, you have to be kidding me," I sighed.

We ran into the bathroom and shut the door.

"I know, I know, it seems we're always ending up in the bathroom. Look at the bright side Tara. This is the best place to be stuck if you need to go," she smiled.

"I know, but I don't have to go," I shook my head.

The bathroom took up the whole width of the train, it was bigger than any bathroom we'd been stuck in so far.

"I guess this isn't so bad. It's nice and roomy. I guess it'll be fine for now," I said. "I just hope we don't have to stay in here the whole trip. Why did I come down here in the first place Rachel? It's a whole lot safer upstairs where people are watching and can make sure nothing bad happens to us."

"I guess you were scared like me. You're right, if we were upstairs... the guy really couldn't do anything to us until we get off the train. But, we came down here and there's no one around who's going to keep the guy from killing us now. No witnesses."

"I know," I shrieked. Rachel could tell by the look on my face I was scared.

"Oh, I know Tara, it's your birthday and things were going so well. I'm sorry the man had to ruin it for you." Rachel hugged me. "I'm scared too," Rachel cried.

We cried and hugged each other until we heard a knock on the door. Rachel's eyes opened wide and her mouth opened wider. We stood there, stunned not knowing what to do.

"Hey Abigail, let me in," the voice of a small child said.

Rachel and I stood there and didn't say a word.

Then I heard a longer knock and the sound of someone kicking the door.

"Abigail, let me in or I'm telling Mom," the voice yelled.

"Should we let the kid in?" Rachel whispered.

I shrugged my shoulders not knowing what to do.

"I'm telling on you," the voice said.

I listened for a moment and heard another voice outside the door.

"Is there a problem?" It sounded like an older man.

Rachel and I stood staring at the door. I wondered if the voice belonged to the man in the gray suit.

"Dad, Abigail won't let me in, and I have to go," the child yelled.

"Abigail's not in there, she went to the sleeper car Jack. Why don't you go tell Mom? She'll take you back to the sleeper car. You can use the bathroom in our room," the man said. "Here, I'll come with you," we heard him say.

"I can't wait. I need to go now!" the little boy said.

"Okay, okay, let's go now. There's another bathroom in the next car. Jack this one's full," the man said.

"I can't wait!" the little boy whined.

"Now, come on Jack. Let's go!"

"No, I have to go to the bathroom," the little boy said.

"Let's get out of here so he doesn't wet his pants. I'd feel bad if he wet his pants because we were in the bathroom so long," Rachel whispered.

"Me too. Rachel, what happens if the man wearing the gray suit is standing outside the door with them? He would have the perfect opportunity to grab us.

"He can't do anything to us while this little boy and his dad are here. It sounds like the kid really needs to use the bathroom."

"Okay, let's let him in," I said.

Rachel and I hugged one last time. Rachel opened the door just as the train bounced around on the tracks. The door flung open and smashed Rachel and me against the wall. Neither one of us said a word we just stood there in shock.

I heard a thud and the little boy started to cry. Rachel and I stepped from behind the door and saw a little brown-haired boy lying on the floor.

"Oh, you poor little man," Rachel said as we picked him up off the floor.

"Oh sorry, he was leaning up against the door. Did you hit your head Jack?" the brown haired man asked as he helped us pick the little boy off the floor. "Are you okay, Jack?"

"My head hurts," he sniveled as he rubbed the back of his head. "Who are you?" he asked as he looked at Rachel.

"I'm Rachel and this is my sister Tara," Rachel said.

"You're very pretty," he smiled.

"Why, thank you," Rachel and I said. We looked to see if the man wearing the gray suit was anywhere in the snack car, but he wasn't.

"Okay, Jack you can use the bathroom now," his dad said. "Hi, I'm Jackson," he smiled.

Jack went in the bathroom and shut the door.

"Nice to meet you Jackson," we said.

Rachel and I took a seat at a table and waited for Jack to leave the bathroom.

"Are you two having fun on the train?" Jackson asked.

Rachel and I looked at each other and didn't know what to say, we weren't having fun.

"Uh... yeah," Rachel said. Her face was glowing.

"It's fun," I said.

"So, where are you girls going?" he asked.

"We're heading to Seattle, how about you?" I asked.

"We're heading to Seattle too. We'll be in Washington State for a few days and then we're going up north to Canada. We're taking the kids zip-trekking in Whistler."

"Zip-trekking? What's zip-trekking?" Rachel asked.

"It's where we take a sky bridge up and there are ten different zip-lines, reaching over a mile, for a fun adventure of zip-lining down the mountain. They say we can reach speeds of up to fifty miles an hour," he said.

"That's fast. It sounds like fun. We were at Disneyland yesterday. We had a great time at the park," I said.

"Oh, I love Disneyland. We were there a few months ago. Jack needs to grow a little more before we go back. He was too short to ride a couple rides," Jackson laughed.

"Probably the Indiana Jones and Splash Mountain ride, am I right?" Rachel asked.

"You are correct," he smiled. "So you're heading home from Disneyland?" he asked.

"Yep, heading home," Rachel smiled.

I looked at her and she didn't turn red.

Jack came out the bathroom door and headed towards the stairs.

"Bye, see you later." He waved as he walked by us.

"It was nice meeting you girls," Jackson said.

"You too," we said.

They headed up the stairs and we headed back in the bathroom.

No sooner did we lock the door we heard another voice outside the bathroom.

"Jack, leave me alone. Go bother Mom," the girl yelled.

I heard the door jiggle and a girl sigh.

"That must be Abigail," I whispered.

"We better let her use the bathroom too." Rachel shook her head and rolled her eyes.

Rachel opened the bathroom door and there was a blonde girl sitting at the table we were sitting at a few minutes earlier. She appeared to be about eleven years old.

"Hi," she said.

"Hi," Rachel and I said.

She went into the bathroom and shut the door.

Rachel and I sat at the table and waited.

A few minutes later, the girl opened the bathroom door. She stood staring at Rachel and me for a minute.

"Hi, I'm Tara and this is Rachel," I said as she came out of the bathroom. "Are you Abigail?"

"How'd you know my name?" Abigail asked.

"We met your dad and little brother a few minutes ago. Your little brother was calling your name, looking for you," I said.

"Yeah, he's always looking for me. I try my best to hide from him. He's annoying," she laughed.

"Why are you girls sitting here? Isn't the snack store closed?" she asked.

"We can't say," Rachel said.

"Why can't you say?" she asked.

"Well, I guess we could tell you," I said.

"We're hiding out because we think someone's chasing us," Rachel said.

"Someone's chasing you? Who's chasing you?" Abigail asked.

"We think a guy in a gray suit is chasing us," I said. "Hey, maybe you can help us."

"Help you do what?" Abigail asked.

"Maybe, you can go upstairs and see if there's a guy wearing a gray suit sitting up there like he's waiting on someone."

"Why do you think the guy's chasing you anyway?"

"It's a long story," I said.

"Are you girls in trouble for some reason? Did you do something wrong? Does the guy want to kill you or something?"

"It's a long story Abigail. We don't know if he wants to kill us but we don't want to take any chances," Rachel said.

"Yeah, we don't want to take any chances," I said.

"You two must be paranoid if you think a guy is chasing you. Maybe he was just walking through the train to get to his seat or something and you just think he's chasing you."

"Maybe, all's I know is he was following us through the train and it scared us," I said. "He just gives me the creeps... that's all."

"You're right in the open area with no one around to save you. So, why are you hiding down here when it isn't a very good place to hide," she said as she looked around the room. "Oh, I see. You were hiding in the bathroom. That's not a bad place to hide. It's nice and roomy and there's no better place to be if you have to go."

"That's what I said." Rachel nodded her head and smiled.

Jack came down the stairs and stood in front of the table.

"Why are you still hanging out here Abigail? I was waiting upstairs for you. Are you waiting for the snack center to open?" he asked.

"No, we're just talking. You can leave now." Abigail looked at him.

Jack sat down on the seat next to her and smiled across the table at Rachel and me.

Abigail stared across the table at Rachel and me. "You two are very pretty," she smiled.

"Why thank you, so are you," I smiled.

"I can't tell the two of you apart. You must be identical twins." Abigail's eyes were moving back and forth from Rachel to me.

"Yep, we're identical." Rachel looked at me and smiled.

"Do you know where Mom went?" Jack asked.

"No, I don't. She was sitting upstairs on her tablet a few minutes ago. Why don't you go look for her?" Abigail sighed.

"Will you come with me?" Jack asked.

"Where's dad? Why don't you have him go with you?" she asked.

"Because... you're my favorite sissy in the whole wide world," Jack leaned up against Abigail, lifted his head, looked at her, and smiled.

"I'm your only sissy in the whole wide world," she said. "Okay, Jack let's go look for Mom," Abigail waited for Jack to get up from the table and then scooted out of the seat. "Hey, look... why don't Jack and I go up and have a look around the lounge car. I'll see if I can find the guy in the gray suit and see what he's up to. I'll take a video of him with my phone and show it to you. If you think the guy is really after you, I'll tell my mom and dad. If you decide he's harmless, and you imagined the whole thing then at least you'll stop being so paranoid and relax for a while. Does that sound like a plan?" Abigail asked.

Rachel and I looked at each other, we nodded.

"Okay, that would be great! Thanks Abigail," I said.

"Okay, then... if the guy isn't in the lounge car, we're going to walk through the train and we'll look in every car. You two stay right here we'll be back as soon as we can." Abigail stood up and headed towards the stairs. "I don't know how long it will take us to find the guy but we'll come back as soon as we can, okay?"

"Okay," Rachel and I said at the same time.

"Just sit here and don't move," Jack said as he followed Abigail up the stairs. "Abigail, what are we doing?"

"Never mind Jack, just come with me," Abigail said as she headed up the stairs.

"I wonder if he's upstairs in the lounge car. If he's not I wonder how long it's going to take them to search the train for this guy Tara."

"I don't know. It's a nice size train isn't it?"

104

"I think it is, but I wasn't paying attention. I was too busy being scared. Tara, what are we going to do if we find out the guy's after us?"

"I don't know. I really don't know," I sighed.

"We should go in the bathroom and lock the door," Rachel said.

"That's not a bad idea Rachel. I think I feel safe in there."

We went back into the bathroom.

"I hope no one else needs to use this." Rachel locked the door.

"Me either. Rachel do you think the guy was chasing us or do you think we're just a little paranoid like Abigail says?"

"Maybe we're both a little paranoid, I don't know. Maybe the guy was chasing us, maybe he wasn't. Better to hide and be safe than to be dead and sorry we didn't pay attention to our gut feeling."

"Yeah." I sat down on the floor.

"I think we should get off this train at the next stop and just take a hike in the wilderness," Rachel said as she sat on the floor across from me.

"Take a hike in the wilderness?" I asked. I had no idea what she was talking about for the first time since we met.

"Yeah, I think we should find a store that sells camping gear, buy some stuff, and head to the woods for a while. No one would think to look for us in the woods."

"Rachel have you ever been camping without your parents?"

"Yeah, I've been camping before I know how to start a fire, and how to keep warm in the cold.

I know a few things about safety and how to survive in the woods without food."

"I've only been camping with my parents and they were the ones who started the fires and kept me warm. I don't know if I want to be out in the wilderness foraging for food. It doesn't sound like fun to me."

"Tara, you might not like doing it at first, but it'll be funner than being dead. We won't be looking over our shoulders every minute of every day waiting for someone to grab us. Just think... it could be a great adventure for us. I know it would be fun just the two of us out communing with nature."

"Yeah? You think so Rachel?" I thought about Rachel and me hiking through the woods. I imagine the two of us as Snow White lost in the woods and stumbling across a small cottage with little dwarf people singing hi ho, hi ho, it's off to work we go. Then I imagine the dwarf people being Danny's brothers, Drake, Derek, Damian, and Devin. And Danny being my prince who comes riding up on his white horse to rescue me. Then I thought about Danny kissing me and waking me from a deep sleep. I thought of Danny and me riding to the castle on his white horse.

"Did you hear me Tara?" Rachel was moving her hand in front of my face. "Hello... anyone in there? Earth to Tara."

"What?" I asked.

"I said, I wonder if Abigail and Jack found the man in the gray suit. Where were you Tara? Thinking about Danny?"

"Yep," I laughed. "I was thinking about you and me being lost in the woods like Snow White. Danny's brothers all dwarfs and singing hi ho hi ho it's off to work we go. I was thinking about Danny

106

being my prince charming like Snow White's prince charming. I was thinking about him rescuing me and kissing me," I sighed. "I wonder if I'll ever see him again."

"You imagined all that stuff just from me saying we should hop off the train and head to the woods. Wow, that Fantasmic show at Disneyland sure has your imagination working overtime. Don't worry Tara you'll see Danny again. I don't know when, but I'm sure you'll see him again someday."

"Yeah? Someday my prince will come. It could take him a while to find me. I might have to wait a long time for him."

"Are you girls sitting in the bathroom again?" I heard the voice of Abigail say through the door and it startled me.

"Yeah, we're in here," I said as I stood up and opened the bathroom door.

Abigail sat at the table waiting for us to come out of the bathroom.

"Did you see the man we were talking about?" I asked.

"Yeah, he's the only guy on the train wearing a suit. I took a video of him with my phone for you to watch. He seems perfectly harmless to me." Abigail pulled her phone out of her pocket and touched it with her finger a few times then turned it around for Rachel and me to see. "Here's the video."

We watched the little movie of the man in the gray suit as he sat down next to an elderly woman who gave him a kiss on the cheek. He handed her an orange and pointed out the window showing the woman something. He talked to the woman, and they both laughed. As Rachel and I watched the video of the man in the gray suit, we could see he was harmless and was no threat to us at all. We were both relieved to know there was no one on the train wanting to hurt us.

"That makes me feel better," I said.

"Me too," Rachel smiled.

"I told you, you were just being paranoid," Abigail laughed.

"Well, my mom took Jack back to our room for a nap. I think my dad is taking a nap already. I'm going to head back too. So, what do you girls want to do? Do you want to sit down here, and be scared? Or... do you want to go upstairs and relax?" she questioned.

"I think we're going to go sit upstairs in the lounge car and relax for a while," I said.

"Yeah," Rachel said.

"Okay then, I'm going to go to my room. Maybe I'll see you two later," Abigail said.

"It was nice meeting you Abigail and we really appreciate all you've done for us. Thank you," I said.

"You're welcome. I'll find you later before we get to Seattle," Abigail said as she headed up the stairs.

"Okay," Rachel and I said.

I followed Abigail up the stairs with Rachel following behind me.

I sat in a seat facing the window and Rachel sat next to me.

"I guess the man in the gray suit is harmless. That's good isn't it?" I whispered.

"Yeah, I was starting to wonder if we'd be climbing on the top of the train like you see people do in the movies."

"I know. I was wondering if they really have ladders for people to climb attached outside the train, or is it just a movie thing."

"We'll need to take a closer look when we leave the train," Rachel laughed.

I watched out the window at the scenery. Rachel tapped me on the shoulder. I turned and looked at her. She was looking over at Peggy who just came into the car. I watched as she sat down at a table on the other side of the car, opened up her laptop and began typing.

I nodded my head at Rachel and went back to looking out the window.

We traveled through towns and stopped at others. Rachel and I stared out the window the whole time. I fell asleep awhile and woke up when I heard the conductor over the speaker say we were stopping in Santa Barbara.

I looked over at Rachel and she wasn't in the seat beside me. I felt a queasy feeling in my stomach wondering where she went.

I looked around the car and there was no sight of her. Peggy was sitting in the same place working on her laptop. She saw the look in my eyes, smiled and nodded her head.

I felt better. I knew Rachel was okay.

I watched out the window as people left while others stood in line to board the train. A few minutes later we were on our way again.

I caught a glimpse of what Santa Barbara looked like when we departed from the station. It looked like a nice place from what I could see.

A few minutes later Rachel came up the stairs with a couple of sandwiches in her hand.

"Here, I brought you a sandwich. I figured you'd be hungry," she said.

"I'm not hungry right this second, but I'm sure I will be as soon as I wake up a little more," I grabbed the sandwich she held out for me. "Thank you."

"You know you were snoring so loud I had to get up and leave," Rachel said as she sat in the seat next to me.

"I was? I didn't realize I snored," I laughed.

"No, you weren't snoring. I'm just joking," she laughed.

I looked over to see what Peggy was doing, and she was still working on her computer. I wanted to talk to her, but I knew I shouldn't.

"I want to talk to Peggy, but I don't think I should," Rachel whispered.

"I was thinking the same thing. We'll have to wait until we get to her house," I whispered. "What time is it, Rachel?"

"The train stopped in Santa Barbara at twelve-forty, so I'm sure it's almost one."

"What time do we get to Tacoma Washington do you know?"

Rachel pulled the train schedule out of the backpack, opened it, and looked for the time.

"We're not going to get to Tacoma until tomorrow night at seven-o-three pm."

"That's... uh... let's see, one to two, two to three, three to four, four to five, five to six, six to seven, so that's five, six plus twenty-four more hours. So thirty hours, and a few minutes from now we'll be there," I said.

"That's a long time from now. It's almost like riding the bus."

"Yeah, but I like the view from these seats way better than the view from the bus seats."

"Me too."

"Where's our next stop Rachel?"

Rachel looked at the schedule to see where our next stop was.

"Let's see, our next stop is San Luis Obispo, I think that's how you say it. We get there around three-thirty-five p.m."

"San Luis Obispo... um... okay," I said. "I wonder what that's like."

"I don't know, I guess we'll see when we get there."

We stared out the window as we went by the trees, houses, and water. It was a great view from where we sat and I was enjoying the train ride.

As we approached San Luis Obispo, the conductor announced it.

"Oh, that's how you pronounce it," Rachel said.

We both laughed because we were pronouncing it wrong.

We stopped at San Luis Obispo for a minute and we headed down the track again.

"What's the next place we're going to Rachel?"

"Paso Robles."

"Paso Robles?" I asked. "Huh, I wonder if that's the way you pronounce it."

I don't know but we're going to find out when we get there," Rachel laughed.

"What's the next town after that?"

"It's Salinas, I hope I pronounced it right. San Jose, and... hey look Tara." She pointed at the schedule. "We're going to be stopping in Oakland. Do you remember when we stopped in Oakland? We sat in the bathroom for what seemed like forever... waiting."

"Yeah, it was scary. I remember the police putting a guy in the backseat of his squad car. I hope we don't need to get off the train there."

"That wasn't Oakland Tara... that was Reno."

"It was?

"Yeah, Oakland was where we bought our makeup and had lunch at the Mexican restaurant."

"Oh, yeah, now I remember. We've spent so much time in the bathrooms I can't remember which town is which," I laughed.

Rachel looked at the schedule.

"Well, we have a few more stops before we get to Oakland," she said.

When we arrived in Paso Robles, the conductor announced it over the loudspeaker.

"Boy, I had that wrong too," Rachel laughed.

"Yeah, you weren't too far off though," I nodded and smiled.

The train continued to Salinas. We arrived at the station and it was already nightfall. Rachel was happy to hear she had pronounced the town's name right. After a quick stop, we were on our way to San Jose. When we arrived there, the announcement said this stop was a rest break and passengers could leave the train and stretch their legs if they wanted.

Rachel looked at the schedule. "It says we're going to be here twelve minutes. The next three stops are longer ones. Let's see... Oakland is after this and it look like we'll be there for fifteen minutes. We'll be staying in Emeryville for ten minutes. Do you want to leave the train and stretch your legs here in San Jose or do you want to wait and stretch your legs at a different stop?"

"Hum, well let's hop off here."

"Okay, it's eight-eleven, and the train is leaving at eight-twenty-three p.m. let's go look around."

We jumped off the train and took a walk around the building to the parking lot. There were people hugging and kissing and saying good-bye to their loved ones.

We crossed the street and walked a block turned around and walked back to the station.

"This looks like a nice little town. I could live here," Rachel said.

"Me too," I said.

"Maybe we should go sit in our assigned seats for a while. It's dark outside and there's nothing to see except city lights," Rachel said.

"Okay, do you remember which car we were in?"

"Yeah, follow me."

We climbed back on the train and headed to our assigned seats.

I walked slowly down the aisle behind Rachel. We found ourselves waiting for this passenger and that passenger to put their bags in the overhead compartments and sit before we could make it to our seats.

We finally made it to our seats. I sat down, leaned back, and put up the footrest.

"You know these reclining seats aren't bad. I should have taken a nap here," I said.

"Yeah, they are comfortable aren't they?"

"I think I'll sleep here tonight," I sighed.

"Hey Tara, I'm getting hungry. Will you go to the lounge car and get me something to eat? I'm too tired to get up and go there myself," she laughed.

"All right, give me some money." I held out my hand and waited for Rachel to dig the money out of the backpack and hand me a ten-dollar bill. "Thanks, I'll be back in a few minutes."

I headed out the car through the breezeway into another car. I notice the train was crowded. By the time I reached the snack car, the train was on its way bouncing down the track. I bought a sandwich, a bag of chips and lemonade, and headed back to the coach car. By the time I reached our car, Rachel was asleep with the backpack sitting in my seat. I shook her and woke her.

"Here Rachel, hold this," I handed her the sandwich, chips, and lemonade then took the backpack, opened it, put our pictures inside, put it in the overhead compartment, and sat in my seat. I tilted the seat back and put the footrest up so I could relax.

"Thanks Tara. I can't believe I fell asleep so quickly." She took half the sandwich and handed me the other half.

"I'm getting a little tired myself," I said.

We ate our sandwich half, shared the chips and lemonade.

"Hey Rachel, what time do we get to Oakland?"

"Nine-thirty p.m."

We sat and enjoyed the train ride as we went over bridges, near water, trees, vineyards, and towns. We watched out the window and saw the moon as it followed us on our journey.

By the time the conductor announced we were coming into Oakland, I could feel myself nodding off but kept myself from falling asleep. I looked over to see what Rachel was doing, and she was looking out the window.

We watched as the people left and boarded the train in Oakland.

"I can't believe I was mixed up between Oakland and Reno. Oakland looks a lot nicer than Reno," I said.

"I'm sure Reno's not a bad place. It was probably just a bad neighborhood. Even in my hometown of Cooper there's a bad part of town where you wouldn't want to be walking around late at night."

"Really? That little town has a bad part?"

"Well, not really bad but the cemetery is over there and it's very scary at night."

"Yeah, the cemetery back home is a creepy place too. My brother Zach used to tease me and tell me he was going to take me to the cemetery and make me get out of the car. I'd start crying and my dad would yell at him for making me cry," I laughed.

I watched the twinkling lights out the window of the train as we went through little towns.

The time we spent on the train seemed to pass quickly, there were still things to see in the darkness of night as we travel across the country. The scenery alone kept us amused.

I heard the conductor announce we would be stopping in Emeryville.

"What time is it Rachel?" I asked.

Rachel didn't answer. I looked over to see, she had fallen asleep with her head leaned over to one side. I picked up the schedule that was laying in her lap and found Emeryville. It showed we would be at the station at nine-fifty-four p.m. and leaving at ten-o-four p.m. I put the schedule back on Rachel's lap and watched as the train slowed to a stop.

I thought about Danny and wondered if he was okay. I said a prayer and hoped he and the rest of his family would be safe. I thought about the time we spent on the boat together and remembered how well he knew me.

The train pulled in and stopped, ten minutes later we went on our way.

I kept thinking about Danny and how the last time I saw him we said we loved each other. I prayed Danny and I would see each other again someday.

The more I thought about him the more it made me smile. I was thinking about the two of us kissing on the beach as I drifted off to sleep.

The next think I heard was the conductor saying Redding. I opened my eyes and looked out the window. I saw it was still dark, but I had no idea what time it was. I looked over at Rachel and she was still sleeping so I closed my eyes and went back to sleep.

The next time I woke up the conductor was saying we were in Klamath Falls. I sat up, stretched, looked over at Rachel. She was awake and looking out the window.

"Hey Rachel, we're in Klamath Falls can you look at the schedule and see what time it is.

Rachel grabbed the schedule and looked. "It's eight-seventeen a.m.," she said. "Did you sleep well?"

"Yeah... did you?"

116

"Yeah, I slept really well. I was dreaming about Paul," she smiled.

"Really? What did you dream?" I asked.

"I dreamed Paul and I were kissing on the Ferris wheel. We did that once when we went to the carnival together," Rachel sighed.

"I was dreaming about Danny too, I dreamed we were kissing on the beach," I sighed.

"We have some dreamy boyfriends don't we," Rachel smiled.

"Yeah we do," I smiled.

I heard my stomach growl. Rachel looked at me and smiled. It growled so loud she heard it too.

"Rachel, I'm hungry. Do you want to go get something to eat with me?"

"Yeah, let's go to the dining car and have breakfast. My stomach isn't yelling as loud as yours, but if I don't eat soon it will be," she laughed.

I followed Rachel as she headed towards the dining car. The train bounced on the track. We held on to the seats to keep from falling as we walked down the aisle.

We sat down and a server handed us each a menu.

"I'll be back to take your order in a minute," he said as he moved on to the next table.

He was back a minute later.

"Here you are. You can join these girls at this table," he said as he pointed to our table. An elderly man and woman looked at Rachel and me.

"Well, look what we have here, twins," he smiled. "Do you mind if we switch seats? I would

117

like to sit next to my wife," the elderly man asked me. It sounded like he had an English accent.

"Oh no, not at all," I smiled and scooted from the seat. I went over and sat next to Rachel as the man and woman took the seat across from us and looked at the menu.

"You girls are very pretty," the elderly woman said.

"Thank you," Rachel and I said.

"Is that an English accent I hear?" I asked.

"Yes it is. We're on holiday. It's our first time to the States. It's very lovely here," the woman said.

"It is very lovely isn't it," I smiled.

"I'm Agnes and this is my husband Bernard, and what are your names?"

"I'm Martha and this is Rita," Rachel said.

"Well, it's nice to meet you girls," the man said.

"Are you ready to order?" the server asked as he held onto the table for support as the train bounced.

"I think I'll have the eggs and hash browns and a glass of orange juice please."

"Me too," Rachel said.

"What would you like for breakfast this morning?" he asked the couple.

"We'll each have the eggs and hash browns and a cup of tea please," Bernard said.

"Okay, I'll bring the tea right out for you and the breakfasts will be done shortly," the server said. "Can I bring you anything else?"

Rachel and I looked at each other, I shook my head.

"No, we're good, thank you," Rachel said.

"Thank you," I said.

"Yes, thank you," the couple said.

"Are you girls on holiday?" Agnes asked.

"Holiday?" Rachel said.

She looked at me and I shrugged my shoulders.

"Uh, we're going to our Aunts house. She lives in Washington," Rachel said.

She looked at me. I could tell by the look in her eyes she wanted to know if her face was turning red.

I shook my head no.

"Where are you traveling today?" Rachel asked.

"We're heading to Seattle. We're going to stay a few days, take in the sights, and then we're heading to Vancouver Canada," Bernard said.

"Oh, that sounds like fun," I said.

"So, it's your first time in the States? How long have you been traveling?" Rachel asked.

"This is our third week," Bernard said.

"Yes, my brother, and his family live in Colorado, so we flew in to see them. We stayed about a week then we took the train and headed to California. We went through New Mexico and Arizona. We decided to get off the train in Flagstaff and rent a car so we could drive up to see the Grand Canyon, it was fantastic. Then we drove to Sedona and spent some time there. We drove all over the place looking at sights," Agnes said.

The server interrupted her.

"Here's your tea. Can I bring you anything else?" he asked.

We shook our heads no, and Agnes continued.

119

"We drove to Lake Mead and Hoover Dam. We drove down to Needle's California, stayed a night, and caught the train to Los Angeles. We rented a car and went to Disneyland. It was lovely. We decided we wanted to drive up the coast, so we did. We stayed in Santa Barbara and then went to Morro Bay and stayed there. We went and visited the Hearst Castle and then stayed in Santa Cruz. We crossed the Golden Gate Bridge and then went inland to Sacramento and caught the train last night. It's all been quite lovely," Agnes said.

"Wow, it sounds like it's been a nice holiday for you," I said.

"It's been quite nice my dear. We've met all sorts of wonderful people. Everyone has been very nice," Bernard said.

The waiter brought our breakfasts.

"Do you need anything else?" he asked.

Everyone shook their heads and told him thank you.

"Okay, enjoy your meal," he said and left the table.

"We were in Disneyland too," I said.

"Yeah, it's the happiest place on earth," Rachel said.

"Yes, well I suppose it is. Isn't it my dear," Bernard looked at Agnes.

"Well, indeed it is," Agnes smiled.

"We rode a lot of rides. I had the most fun I've ever had in my entire life," I said.

"Me too," Rachel said.

We ate our breakfasts and swapped stories about our trips to Disneyland. Bernard and Agnes finished eating before us.

"It's lovely to meet the two of you girls. You girls are charming," Bernard said as he stood up from the table.

"Yes girls, you are delightful. Have a safe trip," Agnes said as she scooted out of her seat and stood in the aisle.

They both grabbed the table when the train bounced.

"It was nice meeting the both of you too," I said.

"Yeah, thanks for sharing a meal with us," Rachel said as they headed out of the car.

We finished our breakfast and paid for our meals.

"Where do you want to go now, Rachel?" I asked.

"Do you want to go to the lounge car?"

"Okay."

We went to the lounge car, and it was half-full. We found two seats next to each other facing out the window and sat there.

"I wonder what time it is," I said.

"Well, we were in Klamath Falls at eight-seventeen so I'm thinking it was about an hour ago."

Just as Rachel finished her sentence, the conductor announced we were stopping in Chemult. Rachel pulled the schedule out of the backpack and looked.

"Okay, it's nine-thirty-two a.m. right now."

"Rachel, I wonder how Danny is doing."

"Yeah, I was wondering the same thing. I wonder if they're out of the hospital."

"I don't know, but I would sure like to see him."

"Tara, do you still have Danny's phone number?"

"Well, of course I do Rachel. Do you think I would forget his number? No. It's etched in my mind forever," I laughed.

"Yeah, Paul's number is etched in mine too," Rachel smiled.

"When we get off the train in Tacoma we should call them."

"Rachel, I don't think it's a good idea to call either one of them. Their phones are probably bugged and they would know exactly where we were calling from."

"I know, but maybe what we should do is get one of those disposable phones like Drake bought. Maybe Peggy could get us one so we could call the boys. We could throw it away right after we use it."

"I don't know, they tracked the disposable phone to the cabana and if we would have been in it, we would have been killed," I said. "Let's talk to Peggy about it and see what she says. Maybe she knows how we could call someone without being traced. I really want to talk to Danny. I want to know how he's doing. I miss him."

"I miss Paul too," Rachel sighed.

We watched out the window as the train kept going. The next stop was Eugene. Then we headed on to Albany, then Salem, then Portland. It didn't seem long before we heard the conductor say we would be stopping in Vancouver Washington. He also announced they would be taking dinner reservations.

"What time is it Rachel?"

"It will be four-twenty-eight p.m. when we stop in Vancouver."

"I'm getting hungry how about you?"

"Yeah, I'm hungry too."

"Let's make reservations for the dining car when the conductor comes by again."

"I don't know if I can wait that long. I'm starving."

"Let's go downstairs and get something to eat."

We went down into the snack car and we each bought a hot dog and a bag of chips.

As soon as we were finished, we went upstairs to the lounge area. Peggy was sitting in the same spot she was sitting in earlier. She was still working on her computer.

The lounge car was fairly empty and we had our pick of seats. We sat next to each other, relaxed, and looked out the window.

"I think this car's my favorite," Rachel said.

"Me too."

We stopped in a town called Kelso and were on our way again.

The conductor announced the stop in Centralia. Rachel and I looked at each other.

"Didn't we go through here on the Motorcycle?" I asked.

"Yeah, this town's right before the little town where we filled the tank and headed to the beach. I can't remember what that town was called?"

"I think it was Chehalis wasn't it?"

"Yeah, that's it. Some famous author lives there but I can't remember what her name is for the life of me."

"Hum, I didn't know that."

"Well, you'd probably know her name if you've read her books, but I can't think of it right now. I read her books though."

The next stop was Olympia.

"I remember going through this town too," Rachel said.

"Yeah, I remember learning this is the state capital of Washington State."

"I always used to get Washington State mixed up with Washington D.C."

"Yeah, me too... hey, what time is it Rachel?"

Rachel pulled out the schedule. "It's six-fourteen p.m. we have less than an hour before we get to Tacoma."

"I've really enjoyed this trip Rachel, but I'm ready to sleep in a bed. I want off the train."

"Me too."

It didn't take long, and we heard the conductor say we would be stopping in Tacoma. Rachel and I looked over at Peggy. She was packing up her laptop and getting ready to go.

Rachel and I walked downstairs to the door. I looked over my shoulder and saw Peggy. She smiled and nodded at me as she followed a little ways behind us.

We stood waiting for the train to stop and the doors to open.

As soon as the doors opened, we walked out into the cold rainy air.

CHAPTER 5

Staying at Peggy's

"Burr, it's cold here," I said.

"Yeah, it's a lot colder than it was in California," Rachel said.

We stood there in the rain a minute, zipped up our hoodies and watched as Peggy went into the station. We followed but stayed far enough away so no one could tell we were going with her.

Peggy walked through the small station and went out the door on the far side of the building into the parking lot. Rachel and I kept our distance as we headed out the door.

Peggy crossed the street and headed towards a parking garage. Rachel and I walked up the street until we were in front of the garage, looked around to see no one was watching, then crossed the street and followed Peggy inside the garage.

Peggy was standing just inside waiting for us. There was no one around to see us with her.

"Come on girls. My car is right over here."

We followed Peggy to her car. Rachel sat up front with Peggy and I climbed in the backseat.

"Okay girls, as soon as we reach my house we can talk about everything. I was dying to talk to you on the train, but I didn't think it would be a good idea." Peggy started the car and backed out of the parking space.

"We're dying to talk to you too, but we knew it wasn't a good idea either. Peggy... we found out we're clones."

"Clones? You're clones? That's hard to swallow. I'm still in shock over the two of you looking like my niece. I would have never guessed in a million years, the three of you are clones. You two seem to be fine with the whole thing." Peggy pulled out the garage and drove down the street.

"Well, it took us awhile to get use to it. I was in shock at first," I said.

"Before we found out we were clones we thought we were triplets," Rachel said.

"Triplets? Why would you think you were triplets?"

"We thought there were only three of us. We thought our mother gave us up to three different couples so it wouldn't be a burden for anyone to raise us," I said.

"Boy, did we get that wrong." Rachel shook her head.

"Where's the girl you thought was your sister?"

"We left her on a boat in San Diego. She didn't want to come with us," I said.

"We don't know where she is now," Rachel said.

"You left her on a boat in San Diego?"

"Yeah, we were scared, so we left her on the boat because she didn't want to come with us. We tried to get her to come, but she wouldn't," I said.

"I'm so confused. You'll need to start from the beginning and tell me everything, but let's wait until we're at my place. I think I need to write it down."

I looked out the window just in time to see the moon reflecting off the water as we drove on a road next to the water.

"Wow, look how the moon hits the water isn't it pretty. Am I looking at the ocean or a big lake?" Rachel asked.

"Well, it's the ocean, but technically they call it the sound. It's Puget Sound, it's an inlet from the ocean. So we aren't directly on the ocean, but it's seawater."

"I see," I said.

When we arrived at Peggy's house, she pulled into the driveway and pressed the button to open the garage door. The lights came on automatically as she pulled the car in, turned off the motor, and pushed the button to close the door.

We hopped out of the car and followed Peggy into her house. I didn't realize how big the house was until we were inside. The house was huge with great big windows overlooking the water.

"Wow... what a beautiful view you have," I said.

"Wow... this is nice." Rachel and I looked out the window.

I heard a knock at the door. Rachel and I looked at each other. I could tell she was as scared as I was.

"Girls it's okay. Nobody followed us. It's probably my neighbor. He probably saw me pull up. He has my dog. Why don't you two go down the hall and sit in the dining room while I talk to him for a minute. I don't want him to know you're here," Peggy whispered as she pointed towards the dining room.

"Okay," Rachel and I whispered.

We walked down the hall into the huge dining area with a big glass door, which opened onto a deck overlooking the water. We sat at the table and waited quietly.

We could hear the muffled sounds of Peggy talking and laughing with her neighbor but we couldn't hear what they were saying.

"They sure are laughing a lot," I whispered.

"Yeah, I know. Do you think she likes him?" Rachel whispered.

"I don't know. I can't tell. It's too muffled."

Rachel went over, stood in the archway, and listened.

"It sounds like they're flirting. Listen to their voices." Rachel covered her mouth to keep from laughing.

Then the sound of a big dog barking made me jump. Rachel jumped too. She peeked around the corner and then headed straight towards me with a panicked look on her face.

By the time, she reached me a big Saint Bernard came out of nowhere, pounced on her back, and knocked her down on top of me. The big dog licked me across the face a couple of times then licked Rachel as she rolled over onto the floor.

Peggy came running into the room. "Jomba no! Sit!" She yelled, "Are you okay girls?" She grabbed the dog by the collar and pulled him off me.

"Nice dog Peggy," I laughed.

"Yeah, well he can be a real pain sometimes. He's just a big baby."

"How old is he?" Rachel asked.

"He's almost two." She held him by the collar for as long as she could then he pulled away from her, pounced on me, knocked me down, and licked me in the face again.

"Jomba no!" Peggy screamed, "Doggone it! Stop!" She grabbed him by the collar and pulled him off me again. "You're going in your kennel," she scolded as she drug him by the collar out of the dining room.

Rachel gave me her hand and pulled me to my feet.

"That dog really likes you Tara."

"Yeah, I can see that, I must have hot dog flavor on my face," I laughed.

Peggy was back a few minutes later.

"Sorry Tara. I don't know what to tell you. He's normally just a good quiet dog. He doesn't usually do that to people. I can't believe the minute he sees the two of you girls he's barking and jumping all over you. I don't know what is wrong with him. I don't know what to tell you girls. He must really like you."

"It's okay. I like him too," Rachel and I laughed.

"Where did you take him?" I asked.

"I put him in his kennel in the garage he's been sleeping out there since he was a puppy. I'll bring him back in the house in a little while he's a little too wound up right now," Peggy shook her head. "Hey, why don't you girls go into the living room and have a seat? I'm going to run upstairs and take a quick shower. If you want something to eat or drink, I have snacks in the cupboards. There's water, pop, and juice in the refrigerator. The kitchen's off to your left. I'll be out in ten minutes."

"Okay," Rachel and I said at the same time.

We went into the living room, stood by the window and stared out at the water. The moonlight beamed off the water and I thought it was very pretty.

"I can't believe this view," Rachel said.

I went over and sat on the couch the view was just as beautiful sitting there.

Peggy came down the stairs in her pajamas. "Hey girls, did you find something to eat or get something to drink?"

"No, we didn't, we're good," Rachel said.

"Are you sure you're not hungry or thirsty?"

"No, we're fine. We just ate a couple of hours ago on the train," I said.

"Okay, well if you get hungry at all, just let me know. I'd be happy to fix you something to eat."

"Okay, we will," I said.

"So girls, why don't we go into the dining room and talk about what's going on with everything? I'll grab a pen and paper so I can take notes." She disappeared into the kitchen. She came out a minute later with a pad of paper and a pen. "Girls follow me," she motioned to us to come.

Rachel and I followed her into the dining area.

Peggy sat at the end of the table and motioned for Rachel and me to sit next to her.

"You know girls I'm still in shock. I can't wrap my brain around the fact you girls are identical to my niece. It's as if I have two Selena's sitting beside me. I don't even know where to begin to deal with this situation. So tell me everything you know and I'll see what I can do."

"Okay," I said. "We'll do the best we can. We don't know everything, but we do know, they are looking for us and we're not safe no matter where we go."

"Who's looking for you girls?"

"The government is looking for us," Rachel said.

"The government is looking for you?"

"Yeah, the government is looking for us," I said.

"Why would the government be looking for you?" Peggy questioned.

"We're clones. We're part of a government experiment."

"Hold that thought," Peggy said. She grabbed her laptop, typed something. She waited. "That's another thing I have a problem wrapping my brain around. I spent plenty of time with my sister during her pregnancy. I was in the delivery room with my sister and her husband when Selena was born. I just don't know why my sister wouldn't tell me something as big as this. My sister and I are very close. I just can't believe my sister has a clone for a daughter and she didn't tell me. I mean, who does that anyways? Wow, my sister has a clone daughter." Peggy sat back in her chair and stared at the ceiling for a minute. Peggy looked at her computer screen. "Ah there we are. Let's see... what does this say. Let's see cloning."

Peggy read the definition of cloning aloud to us.

"A. The aggregate of genetically identical cells or organisms asexually produced by a single progenitor cell or organism. B. An individual grown from a single somatic cell or cell nucleus and genetically identical to it. C: A group of replicas of all or part of a macromolecule and especially DNA. 1. Clones of identical recombinant DNA sequences. 2. One that appears to be a copy of an original form... duplicate.

When she finished reading, she sat there for a minute and didn't say a word. Then she looked at Rachel and me.

"Okay, girls tell me from the beginning everything you know and I will tell you if I can help you or not."

Rachel looked at me.

"Okay, Tara you start since you know from the beginning how this all started. So you can tell Peggy."

I looked at Rachel, nodded my head and began to tell Peggy the story of me waking up on the island and me swimming off the island. I told her about Danny saving me from drowning and about meeting Billy and finding out I looked like his sister Amanda. Then meeting Kate and Trevor and seeing the pictures of Isabella. I told her about Billy and me going to the island, thinking we found Amanda the discovering it was Rachel. I told her about our bus ride, and hiding in Paul's basement. I told her how Rachel's parents were acting strangely. I told her about taking the motorcycle back to Windyn and staying in Danny's family cabin. I told her about going to the island, witnessing the death of Dillon, and going on the boat with Danny, Drake, Derek, Damian, Devin. I told her, Amanda was the one who told us we were clones, her telling us the story about Nichole dying, and Malory wanting Amanda to live with her. I told her how we ran from the boat and went to Danny's dad's office. I told her about the phones being bugged and tracked and having someone showing people our picture looking for us. I told her about meeting Jess, the cabana getting shot up, and dressing like Danny's grandma to get into the hospital to see Danny. I told her how we were being followed to the train station and how we ran for our lives when we boarded the train. I told her about being scared the whole time and how lucky we were running into her.

"Did I leave anything out Rachel?"

"You left a lot out, but nothing really important," Rachel nodded her head.

"That's quite a story girls." Peggy put her pen down, shook her head, and didn't say another word. She looked back and forth at Rachel and me. We knew she was thinking.

After a few minutes she said, "I wonder how many girls there are. I think we need to write a list starting with the ones we know. So there's the two of you." Peggy turned to a new sheet of paper, picked up her pen and wrote our names on it. "There's Salina... and can you tell me the other girl's names again?"

"There's Amanda, Nichole, and Isabella," Rachel said.

"Now, Isabella is the youngest one you know of right?"

"Yes, as far as we know," I said.

"And how old did you say she was?"

She's nine," I said.

"Well, I can almost guarantee you, all of your parents believe they're a small select group of individuals who were chosen to be part of the experiment. And the agency knew exactly what they were doing when they selected your parents. Your parents don't realize just how many of you there actually are. I'm sure they were all told there were only a few clone embryos. I'm sure they were selected for this program because of some specific reason."

"What do you think the reason was?" Rachel asked.

"I don't know why your parents were selected to participate in this program. I'm sure they told your parents why. Maybe your parents filled out an application somewhere and were selected because they fit the profile the government was looking for."

"I don't understand why my parents would want a clone. My parents are law-abiding citizens. Experimenting with human clones is against-the-law in all states my parents could go to jail for creating me. I mean, don't get me wrong. I'm glad they did what they did, or I might have never been born, but my parents would never do anything that was against the law. I just don't get it," Rachel said.

"I don't know. I hope I can help get this mess straightened out. I don't know why my sister did it either. She's a police officer. Who would have figured she was walking on the wrong side of the law?" Peggy shook her head. "Your parents can't tell anyone because your parents would end up going to jail because producing human clones is against the law. Your parents know this and the government agency probably holds it over their heads. Your parents won't tell. It's sad when something like this happens to good people like your parents. There isn't a winning situation for them."

"I don't understand how the government can start up a clone program and nobody knows about it," I said.

"I don't know how the government gets away with a lot of things they do, but they do. Okay now, you said you girls were all born on the eleventh day of the month, but you're born in a different month, so what are your birthdays?"

"My birthday is October eleventh," I said.

"Your birthday was yesterday? Well happy belated birthday to you," Peggy smiled.

"My birthday is November eleventh," Rachel said.

"Okay, do you know when any of the other girl's birthdays are?"

"Amanda's birthday is December eleventh and I'm not sure what month Nichole or Isabella were born," I said.

Peggy wrote down birthdays next to our names.

"And Selena's birthday is March eleventh. So, she's a few months younger than the two of you. We'll have to call Kate and find out when Isabella's birthday is."

"I don't think that's a good idea. They are probably watching her," I said.

"Yeah, her phone is probably bugged," Rachel said. "We can't call anyone we know. All their phones are probably bugged."

"Yeah, because they are hoping we get into trouble and call someone for help. Then they can find us and kill us."

"Oh, that sounds so awful when you say it like that," Peggy shook her head. "Let's talk about Kate. You said she worked at the hospital."

"No, she didn't work *at* the hospital. She worked *for* the hospital," I said.

"Yeah, she scanned in patient records or something like that, but it was at an office in Windyn."

"Okay, so Kate needs a job right?"

"Yes, she was let go because the hospital closed."

"So, she needs a job if she didn't get one already. Well, I will have to call her with a job opportunity," Peggy smiled.

"Job opportunity?" Rachel and I asked at the same time.

"I'm going to call her and schedule a job interview with her. Do either one of you know her

135

phone number or last name so I can get ahold of her?"

"I have Kate's phone number. I memorized it," I said.

"What is it?"

I gave Peggy Kate's phone number, and she wrote it at the top of the sheet of paper.

"I own a company call Consolidated Finance, and it just so happens we are looking for a secretary out of our California branch office. I'm going to give her a call and set up an interview with her. That way I can talk to her in private without anyone knowing," Peggy smiled.

"Wow, that's a great idea," Rachel said.

"Yeah, I think so too," I said.

"Well, I'm glad you like my idea girls. Now it's time to go to bed. I am exhausted from the train ride," she stood up and stretched. "Let me show you where you'll be sleeping tonight. Would you like separate rooms or would you like to share a room tonight?"

Rachel and I looked at each other.

"I think we'd like to share a room," I said.

"Yeah," Rachel said.

"Okay, let me show you where your room is."

We walked through the big house and up the stairs. We followed Peggy down the open hall to a huge room with a big king-size bed in it.

"Here you go girls. You girls can sleep in this room until we can figure things out. My room is right down the hall on your left. If you need anything to eat just go downstairs, there are plenty of things in the refrigerator, eat whatever you want. You have your own bathroom and a shower right through that door," she pointed to the open door at the end of the room. "Shower if you want. Make yourselves at home. You girls get a good night sleep. I'm tired and I need to go to bed," she walked down the hall towards her room. "Good night girls."

"Night Peggy," we said.

"And thanks," I said.

"Yeah thanks," Rachel said.

"You're welcome girls. You know it was really nice to meet you two. See you in the morning."

"You too Peggy," Rachel and I said.

Rachel and I looked around the room. It was a very nice room with big thick curtains. Rachel and I looked at each other and smiled. We both walked over to the curtains, grabbed a curtain pole, and pulled the curtains open. The view looking from the window was just as nice as the view looking from the living room.

"Oh Rachel, look at the view."

"Yeah, it's beautiful. Let's leave the curtains open all night."

"Okay, what did Peggy call this water?"

"I think she said it was the Puget Sound."

"Oh yeah, that's right the Puget Sound. I remember studying about that. I never thought I'd see it."

"Me either. Of course, there are lots of things I never thought I'd see. And I've seen a lot since I met you Tara."

"I know we have seen a lot haven't we."

"Yes we have."

"And this view is really beautiful isn't it."

"Yes it is."

"I sure am tired."

"So am I."

Rachel pulled our pajamas out of the backpack and handed me a pair. We put our pajamas on, climbed into bed, said good night to each other, and we went to sleep.

As I slept, I dreamed about Danny. We were in San Diego and he took me to dinner on the boat out on the water.

"Tara... I love you," he said.

"Danny... I love you, too," I said.

We stared into each other's eyes and we kissed.

The next morning when I awoke Rachel was lying on her side facing me with her head propped up by her hand. She was looking at me and smiling.

"Oh Danny, oh Danny," she laughed. "You were dreaming about Danny all night long. You woke me up at least three times talking about him or talking to him... mainly talking to him."

"Really, are you joking with me?"

"No, I'm serious. That's the first night you were loud enough to wake me up," she laughed.

"Well, I did have a good dream about him. Remember the boat in San Diego. The one he said he would take me to dinner on someday?"

"Yeah."

"I dreamed we were on the boat having dinner together. He told me he loved me and I told him I loved him. Then we kissed. That's all I remember. I don't remember anything else."

"Well, you must have been dreaming it over, and over, and over, again. Because you woke me up every time. That's funny."

"Rachel, I miss Danny so much. I hope he's okay."

"I hope he's okay too, Tara. I'm sure the hospital is taking good care of him and Drake. The hospital is probably the safest place for them right now."

"Yeah, it is."

"I guess we should hop out of bed, Tara," Rachel yawned and stretched.

"Yeah, what time is it?"

"It's nine-thirty."

"Wow, nine-thirty already! I must have been really tired. The train ride must have worn me out."

"Yeah, me too, It was a nice train ride. I really liked it."

"Me too."

"I'm first in the shower." Rachel jumped off the bed, went into the bathroom and closed the door.

I closed my eyes and pictured Danny and me walking on the beach together holding hands and I drifted back to sleep.

"Tara," Rachel whispered.

I opened my eyes and looked at her. She was standing next to the bed in a towel.

"Your turn, Sleepyhead."

"I was dreaming about Danny again."

"It figures," she laughed.

I climbed out of bed and headed into the bathroom to take a shower. I showered, dried my hair, and headed out of the bathroom in my towel. Rachel put clothes on the bed for me and headed downstairs.

"Thanks Rachel," I shouted out the door.

I dressed and went downstairs to the kitchen.

Rachel and Peggy were sitting at the kitchen table looking out the window at the rain. I pulled out a chair next to Rachel and sat in it.

"I don't know about you girls, but I'm still a little tired from the train ride. It may take me a few days to recuperate," Peggy laughed.

"Yeah, I'm still feeling a little tired," I smiled.

"I don't know if I'm tired from the train ride or from being woke up last night," Rachel laughed.

"What woke you up Rachel?" Peggy asked.

"Tara was dreaming about her boyfriend all night. She was talking in her sleep. She was pretty loud," Rachel shook her head and laughed.

"His name is Danny, right?"

"Yes, his name is Danny," I smiled.

"You're awfully young to have a boyfriend, aren't you?"

"I know, my mom would say so, she says I can't date until I'm sixteen, but I really like him. I'm fifteen now. I don't think I'm too young."

"I guess you're not too young for puppy love," Peggy smiled.

"Puppy love?" I asked.

"Yes, infatuation... a crush."

"I can tell you Peggy, this is no infatuation or crush. I really love Danny and he loves me."

"Oh, you're that serious about the boy?"

"Yes," I nodded my head.

"Well, let's figure this mess out so you can see your guy. I'm not one to stand in the way of true love." Peggy smiled and winked at me. "Are you ready for breakfast? I make a mean omelet."

140

"An omelet sounds great," Rachel and I said at the same time.

"Wow, girls how do you do that?" She shook her finger at both of us and laughed.

"It's funny. People we meet who don't know we're not twins always tell us we have that twin thing going on," Rachel laughed.

"Well, if you didn't look exactly like Selena I would think the same thing. The overwhelming feeling of shock has finally worn off a little." Peggy grabbed the eggs out of the refrigerator, put a pan on the stove, and went to work making breakfast.

"Is there anything you need us to do Peggy?" I asked.

"No, just sit back and relax. I love to cook," she said as she pulled an onion and couple of tomatoes out of the refrigerator and continued looking for more items. "You know I was lying in bed thinking about you two this morning. I wonder how many clones there are we don't know about. If they're making clones, why stop with one person. Who knows, the government could make lots of different clone children and we'd never know," she gasped. "I wonder if my nephew's a clone too." She grabbed a block of cheese and set it on the counter.

"Who knows...Maybe... Yeah, we wouldn't even know it," I said.

"Well, I was thinking... from what it sounds like... and mind you, I could be wrong but, what I was thinking is... it sounds like they're making clones on the island." She grated the cheese into a bowl.

"Are you sure you don't want us to help you Peggy?"

"No, I'm fine. I love to cook," she finished grating and wrapped the cheese block in plastic

141

wrap and put it in the refrigerator, grabbed the tomato and diced it. "So if they're making clones on the island, that's against the law. The government is supposed to obey the law just like the rest of us. If they don't, they could be in serious trouble."

Rachel and I looked at each other and nodded our heads.

"That's what Jess said too," I said.

"He did? Well, you left that part out," Peggy looked at me.

"Yeah Tara, you left that part out," Rachel said.

"Oh, sorry, I didn't mean too."

"Well, it was sort of an important detail. Can you think of anything else important you might have forgotten to tell me?"

Peggy cracked the eggs and mixed them in a bowl.

"No, I can't think of anything, Rachel can you think of anything I left out?" I asked.

"No, but if I remember anything important I'll let you know," Rachel said.

"Good." Peggy tossed all the ingredients on top of the cooking eggs.

"You're really smart Peggy," I said.

"Why thank you Tara," she laughed.

"Yeah, Jess said that's why they plan to exterminate us so they don't get into trouble," I said.

"Exterminate? What do you mean exterminate?" Peggy gasped as she cut the huge omelet into three and slid them onto three plates.

"Oh, did I leave that part out too, Rachel?"

"I was so tired last night I don't know. I don't remember."

"Well, you must have left it out, because you never told me that either."

"I told you about finding Amanda, right?" I asked.

"Yes you did. You told me Amanda told you you're clones. You told me Drake and Derek were missing and you were scared so you left Amanda on the boat and ran."

"Oh, well I must have left that part out," I said.

"I'll tell you what Amanda told us about the government contract each of our parents have. It says *If for any reason this experiment does not fulfill government expectations, the human clone specimens will be terminated.*" That means exterminated," "Rachel said.

"Yeah, Danny's dad said he found out the government agency who produced us plans to exterminate us. They feel we could be a threat to the whole project. They told Malory we would have to be terminated as soon as they find us," I said.

"I can't believe they would want to exterminate you." Peggy set the plates on the table in front of us, handed us each a fork, "dig in."

"Well, from what Amanda told us, our parents signed the same contract."

"You girls have been running for quite a while. I feel bad for you. You can stay here as long as you want."

"Peggy, it's very nice of you, but they know we were on the train and it's only a matter of time before they find us again," I said.

"It didn't take them long to figure out we were in the cabana and they destroyed it with gunshots.

143

Our friend Jess is probably in a lot of trouble right now, just because he helped us. We don't want to stay here too long. We don't want to cause you any problems."

"That's awfully sweet of you girls, but I'm not going to let this go. My niece is involved and even though she's a clone, she's still my niece and I love her."

"This omelet is really good," I said.

"Yeah, you're a very good cook," Rachel said.

"Why, thank you girls," Peggy smiled. "Today is Saturday, I have laundry and a few other things around the house to do. Do you girls have any clothes you need washed? I'll run a load as soon as we're done eating."

"I think we have a few things we need to have washed. I'll go get them." Rachel finished her omelet and headed upstairs to grab the dirty clothes out of the room.

"Tara, are you sure you've told me everything? Can you remember if you've forgotten to tell me any small details?"

"No, I'm sure that was it." I finished my omelet and took mine and Rachel's plates, rinsed them off and put them in the dishwasher.

"That really irritates me! The government considers you specimens and they feel they can terminate you just because they're doing something they shouldn't be doing in the first place. There are laws to protect us against human cloning. So, who do they think they are, having their own top secret little clone experiment going on? I wonder which agency it is." Peggy rinsed her plate and put it in the dishwasher.

"Here's our clothes Peggy," Rachel said as she handed them to Peggy.

"Where did you get these clothes?" Peggy asked.

"These were Jess' daughter's clothes. His daughter left them in her room when she moved out."

"How many years ago did she move out?" Peggy smiled.

"I don't know, why?" I asked.

"They look a little outdated. I'm going to pick up a few new clothes for you today."

"Peggy, you don't have to do that. We're fine with these clothes," I said.

"I know I don't have to but I want to. You girls need warmer clothes. You girls aren't in California and it's a few degrees colder here. I'm going to wash these clothes for you and then I'll head to the store. There are games and the television set downstairs in the family room. Why don't you go down and make yourselves comfortable?" Peggy took the clothes and headed to the washing machine.

"There's another level?" Rachel asked.

"Yes, this is a three-story house," Peggy shouted from the laundry room.

"I don't remember it looking very big from the outside, of course it was dark out," I shouted.

"There's another level, and a basement carved into the hillside. You can't see the bottom story from the street you have to go around to the waterside of the house to see the lower level. And you can't see the basement at all. Go ahead girls go check it out. I'm going to take Jomba for a walk. I'll be back shortly," Peggy shouted.

"Okay, see you later," Rachel and I said.

We walked down the stairs to the bottom level.

"This house is very nice. Look Tara even the family room has a view of the water."

"I see and look at the yard."

There were flowers and sculptured shrubs on the neatly mowed lawn. We stared out the window for the longest time. Looking at the ocean had a calming effect on me.

"Look, there's Peggy down on the street below walking Jomba," Rachel pointed.

"She's not walking him. He's walking her. Look he's pulling her all over the place," I laughed.

"That's a big dog," Rachel nodded her head and laughed.

We watched as Jomba pulled Peggy around from tree to tree. He would lift his leg and move on to the next.

"I've always wanted a big dog like Jomba. One day I'm going to get one," I said.

"Yeah, I always wanted a dog too. One day we'll have one," Rachel said.

"Wouldn't it feel great to take a walk by the waterfront?" I said.

"When Peggy gets home we should ask her if we can go for a walk there."

"Yeah," I watched out the window as Peggy dragged Jomba back up the street by the collar.

A few minutes later, we heard the door open and close.

"Hey Peggy, can we go outside?" I walked up the steps and shouted.

"Huh, I think you should stay in the house girls. The neighbors have security cameras. I would rather no one see you here," Peggy shouted.

"Okay, we'll stay in the house," I shouted.

"Hey girls, I'm going to run to the mall. I put Jomba in his kennel. See you in a little while," Peggy shouted.

"Okay, Bye," I shouted.

I heard the door shut.

I walked back downstairs. Rachel turned the TV on and surfed the channels.

"That's a huge TV. I don't think I've ever seen one so big," I said.

"Me either. Look there's an endless supply of channels to watch too. There are so many channels I don't know which channel to watch," Rachel laughed.

"Find the cartoon channel. I haven't seen any cartoons in a while."

"Yeah, me either."

I stood by the French door, and watched out the window as the boats moved across the water. I thought about Danny, and the fun we had jumping off the sailboat and swimming in the ocean.

"I want to call Danny's house and see if he's all right," I said.

"Yeah, I want to call Paul's house too. But I can't." Rachel was still channel surfing.

"What are we going to do Rachel? It's just a matter of time before we have to leave this place. I'm getting tired of running."

"I know, we don't seem to have a lot of choices, we run or we die... that's it, there are no other choices."

"Run or die," I shook my head. "I guess we keep running." I watched out the window as a big black cloud came out of nowhere, and the rain came pouring out of it. "Look at this Rachel. It was sunny and beautiful a minute ago now look it's raining again."

Rachel stopped surfing as soon as she found the cartoon channel and came over to look out the window.

"Ick, I'm glad we didn't go out, we would have been drenched."

We stood watching out the window as it rained. The rain came down in buckets.

CHAPTER 6

Walking Jomba

"I can't believe Peggy is out in this rain," I said.

We watched the rain pour a little longer then went and sat on the couch and watched cartoons.

"Tara, what if Peggy's right and we're not the only clone children? What if her nephew's a clone?" Rachel gasped. "Tara, what if Robert's a clone?"

"I don't know Rachel. How could you tell? We didn't know we were clones... how would anyone know unless they were told?"

"Yeah, that's true."

"I don't think they're going to keep us alive though. I'm scared Rachel."

"I know, I'm scared too," Rachel nodded then she was quiet for a moment. "Tara, have you ever thought about death before?"

"Yeah," I nodded. "When I was on the island, I was lying on the hill and I couldn't move my legs. I thought I was going to die. I thought about death then. I wondered what it's like to be dead. I imagined floating above my body and looking at myself lying in the daisy field. I wondered what it would be like to meet God and stand in his presence."

"Do you think he would let us in the pearly gates? I mean. We aren't his creations. I didn't find the manufacturing stamp on my butt, but I know it's there," Rachel laughed. "But seriously Tara...we're man-made. How do you think he feels about that?"

"Of course he would let us in the pearly gates Rachel. We're still his creations. No man could figure out how to create us without his divine inspiration," I said. "He loves us no matter who made us," I smiled.

"Yeah... he does, doesn't he," Rachel smiled as she sat down next to me on the couch.

We hugged each other.

"I wonder if they'll ever stop chasing us," I said.

"I don't know. I sure wish they would. I would like to stay in one place."

"You know Rachel, we've been very blessed. All the nice people we've run into who have helped us and kept us safe, dry, and warm. You know we couldn't have done any of this by ourselves. The people who've helped us have been good to us. We are very fortunate to meet people who truly care about us. We have made good friends along the way, haven't we Rachel."

"Yeah, people are pretty nice aren't they Tara. It's amazing how many people have gone out of their way to help us, giving us money and places to stay. We have met some true angels."

"Yeah, angels... they're truly angels."

We heard the door open and close.

"Hey girls, I'm back," Peggy shouted from upstairs.

Rachel and I turned the TV off and headed upstairs.

"I found some cute clothes for the two of you." She put the bags she was carrying on the kitchen table and went out to her car. She was back a few minutes later with three more bags.

"Okay girls, have at it," she said.

I counted seven bags total.

"Are these seven bags of clothes for us?" Rachel asked.

"I think there's an outfit for me in one of those bags," She looked around until she found the bag she wanted and grabbed it off the table. "Okay, the rest of the bags are for you girls," she smiled.

"Wow, Peggy you didn't have to do this for us," I said.

"I know, I know, but I wanted to. I don't have kids to spoil with the exception of nieces and nephews. It's fun shopping for the two of you. Now, go upstairs and try the stuff on. If it doesn't fit I'll take it to the store tomorrow and exchange it," she smiled.

"Thanks Peggy, you don't know how much this means to us," Rachel said as she took two bags and headed up the stairs to the bedroom.

"Peggy you're an angel," I said as I grabbed two bags and followed Rachel up the stairs.

"Oh, I'm an angel?" Peggy laughed.

"That's right. Rachel and I have decided you are an angel sent by God," I shouted from the top of the stairs.

"An angel... No one's ever called me an angel before. They've called me a few other choice words, but never an angel. Thanks girls," she laughed.

"You're welcome," Rachel and I shouted from the bedroom.

We tried the clothes on and they fit perfectly. Rachel went downstairs to get the other bags. She brought them upstairs, set them on the bed and we looked through them. There were more clothes, socks, underwear, and tennis shoes.

"Look at all this stuff, Rachel. There's a coat and pair of shoes for each of us. There's five pairs of pants, five shirts, five pairs of socks and underwear for each of us too. She spent a ton of money on this stuff for us. I hope we don't have to run off and leave this stuff behind like we've had to everyplace else we've been."

"Well, we have to do what we have to do Tara. We can't help it."

"I know, it would be nice to stay awhile, that's all."

We folded the clothes and stacked them in two piles on the bed, then headed downstairs.

"Can we go out into the garage and pet Jomba?" I asked Peggy.

"Sure, maybe he won't go so crazy over the two of you now," Peggy laughed.

Rachel and I went out into the garage to Jomba's kennel. I knelt beside the kennel and looked in at him. He was lying on a big pillow with his eyes closed.

"Hi Jomba," I said as I put my hand next to the kennel.

Jomba opened his eyes, lay there, and thumped his tail on the floor.

"Hey Jomba," Rachel said as she reached in the kennel and scratched Jomba's head.

"He's a lot calmer now," I said.

"Yeah, you're a good dog aren't you boy," Rachel said.

I reached my hand in the kennel and patted Jomba on the head too. His tail wagged.

"You're a good doggy. We'd like to take you for a walk, but we can't boy. Maybe one day we'll be able to," I said. "Your big brown eyes are amazing. I'm going to have a big dog like you one day."

"Yeah, me too."

We sat in the garage and petted Jomba for a long time, then went in the house to see what Peggy was doing.

"So, do you like your new clothes girls?"

"Yes, thank you very much Peggy. We really appreciate you buying them for us," I said.

"Thank you Peggy," Rachel said.

"So, did you like the workout clothes I found for you?"

"Workout clothes?" Rachel and I asked at the same time.

"Yes, I bought you each an outfit so you can join me while I do my P90X workout. I usually do my workout downstairs in front of the TV on Saturdays. That's the only day I have for a good workout," Peggy said.

"Oh, that sounds like fun," Rachel said.

"Let me check and see if I left a sack in the car." Peggy went in the garage and returned with a sack. "I left it in the trunk. Here girls, there's a cute workout shirt and leggings in the bag for each of you."

"Thanks Peggy," I said as she handed me the sack.

"Okay, go upstairs and change. Meet me downstairs. We're going to do a full routine," she said.

"That sounds like fun," Rachel and I said.

Rachel and I headed upstairs, changed into the spandex leggings, an exercise shirt, and headed downstairs.

Peggy was stretching, getting ready for the workout.

"What did you call this workout?" I asked as I followed Peggy's lead and stretched.

"It's the P90X," Peggy said.

What does P90X stand for?" Rachel asked as she stretched her arm over her head.

"It stands for Performance ninety minute extra hard," Peggy said as she grabbed the remote and turned on the TV.

She pressed another button and turned on the DVD player. She took her place in the center of the room and faced the TV with Rachel standing on one side and me standing on the other.

"Performance ninety minute extra hard?" Rachel looked at me.

"Yes," Peggy said

I shrugged my shoulders and shook my head.

"Ninety minutes?" Rachel mouthed to me.

"Extra hard?" I mouthed and shook my head.

Rachel and I kept stretching. We weren't sure exactly what we were going to be doing, but the ninety minutes extra hard part didn't sound like fun.

"We're going to do the Plyometrics workout today. It's one of the hardest workouts of the P90X program. It's a cardio routine. Try and keep up," Peggy said.

We started with Jump Squats. We did a normal squat when we were at the lowest point, we exploded upward with our arms in the air, by jumping off the ground. Then we did Run Stance Squats. We started in the running stance with one foot in front of the other. Then we did four squats and on the fourth one, we jumped in the air, turned and landed with the opposite leg in front. Then we were on to the Airborne Heisman, which we started jumping sideways, into the Heisman Trophy pose, bringing our inside knee up to our chests. After those, we did Swing Kicks. We swung each leg over Peggy's stools and went from one-side to the other.

I was feeling good about the workout, so far I hadn't worked up a sweat yet. I looked over at Rachel and Peggy. They weren't sweating either.

Next, we did Squat Reach Jumps. We squatted with our fingers touching the floor and then we exploded up, with our arms raised over our heads. Then on to the Run Stance Squat Switch Pick Ups. We started in a running stance with our front heel close to our back foot. We did four squats, jumped and turned. Then did a Double Airborne Heisman, where we pretend to jump laterally through two tires, and end in the Heisman Trophy pose, with our knee in the air. After that came the Circle Runs. We put a towel on the floor then ran in small circles, around the towel keeping our heads and shoulders in the same spot.

I was doing fine and so was Rachel. Peggy was doing fine too, but I could see the sweat on the back of her workout shirt and she was breathing hard.

We went on to the Jump Knee Tucks. We jumped up while bringing our knees to our chest. Then we did something called the Mary Katherine Lunges. We went into a forward lunge, then jumped up and landed with our opposite leg in front. Then came the Leapfrog Squats where we did a wide leg squat and jumped up in the air. Next came the Twist Combos. We jumped up and turned our body one-hundred-eighty degrees by the time our feet hit the floor.

"Boy, I'm tired," Peggy puffed.

"Peggy, we're not quite halfway through yet," Rachel said.

Rachel and I kept the pace of the instructor with no hesitation.

Next came the Rock Star Hops. We played air guitar while we jumped up with our heels touching our butts. I remembered doing something like it while we were at Danny's family cabin.

Then we did the Gap Jumps. We leaped forward and then backwards. Next, we did the Squat Jacks. We did Jumping Jacks, landing in a squat position. Then the Military Marches where we marched in place by lifting one leg as high as possible while we raised up the opposite arm in front of us.

At one point, I wasn't sure if Peggy was going to make it through the whole ninety minutes, but she kept going.

Rachel and I kept moving as if it was nothing.

I couldn't believe I wasn't working out hard enough to break a sweat. It's not like I worked out every day. The only time I worked out was in the school gym class.

Then we did the Run Squat one-eighty degree Jump Switches. First, we squatted, then leaped up, turned one-eighty degrees, and landed in another squat. Then the Lateral Leapfrog Squats. We leaped sideways in wide-legged squats. Next came the Monster Truck Tire Jumps. We imagined we had eight tires in front of us with four to the left and four to the right. We jumped in imaginary tires one leg at a time, back and forth. After those came the Hot Foot Jumps. We hopped on one foot then held still awhile before hopping on the other foot.

Peggy was breathing heavy by now, she was getting a good work out. She barely kept up with the trainer on the video. Rachel and I didn't look or sound winded at all.

Next, we were on to the Pitch & Catch. We pretended to pitch and catch a baseball. After we did that we did the Jump Shots. We pretended to catch and shoot a basketball. Then the final exercise was the Football Hero. Where we stepped quickly four times forward and six high steps back.

By the time we finished I was feeling like I could still do another ninety minutes. It felt great.

"Girls, you're in really good shape," Peggy said as she collapsed on the couch from exhaustion.

"Thanks Peggy," we said.

"I don't know how we're in such good shape. It's not like we do this regularly," Rachel laughed.

"I'm beat. Ten more minutes of this and you would've had to take me to the emergency room," Peggy moaned.

"Aw, come on Peggy, that didn't wear you out... did it?"

"Yeah, I'm worn out," Peggy said.

Rachel and I laughed.

"Neither one of you girls broke a sweat. I'm amazed... you're in such good shape. Do you work out at home?"

"No," Rachel and I shook our heads.

"Wow, that's amazing," Peggy shook her head. "I'll chalk it up to youth," she laughed.

"Are either of you girls hungry? Are you ready for dinner?" Peggy asked.

"No, not really... well, maybe a little," I said.

"Maybe just a little," Rachel said.

"Well, I'll head upstairs and fix us something to eat," Peggy said as she pulled herself off the couch and went up the stairs.

We followed her upstairs, sat at the table and watched as Peggy took containers out of the refrigerator, and put them on the counter.

"Can we help Peggy?" Rachel asked.

"No, that's okay. You two just relax. I really enjoy cooking. It helps me to relax."

"I think the workout was a stress release for Tara and me," Rachel sighed.

"Yes, the workout releases stress and cooking is very relaxing for me," Peggy nodded.

"Is there something you would like us to do, Peggy?"

"Yes girls, as a matter of fact, you two could put the clothes in the dryer for me. The laundry room is around the corner to your left," Peggy said.

"I'll do it," I said.

I went down the hall around the corner to the laundry room. I realize the house was even bigger than I thought it was. I put the clothes in the dryer, went to the kitchen and sat at the table.

"So, what would you girls say is the worst part of this mess for you two?" Peggy asked as she put a pot of water on the stove to boil.

"The worst part?" I thought for a minute.

Rachel and I looked at each other.

"Well, running and hiding... being scared all the time," we both said at the same time.

"Yes, I guess running and hiding and being scared wouldn't be fun," Peggy nodded. "We need to do something to stop it. You girls are much too young to be spending your time hiding away. We need to figure out a way to put your lives back together for you."

The smell of garlic filled the air.

"Oh Peggy, that smells good. What are you making?" Rachel asked.

"I'm making chicken fettuccine alfredo. Are you girls hungry now?"

"I wasn't, but now I am. It smells so good," I nodded.

"Why don't you two go downstairs and see if you can't find something to watch on TV. I'll call you when dinner is ready," Peggy smiled.

"Okay," Rachel and I said.

We went downstairs, sat on the couch. Rachel grabbed the remote and turned on the TV.

"What do you want to watch?" she asked.

"Hey, let's find the news. I want to see if they say anything about how Danny and Drake are doing."

"Do you think they would show them on the news?"

"They might give an update. The last time we saw them on the news was when they first went into the hospital. That's been days ago."

Rachel surfed the channels looking for the news.

"That one looked like a news channel Rachel," I pointed.

Rachel was already a few channels farther ahead before she stopped pressing the button.

"Can you back up a few channels, please," I asked.

Rachel pushed the button slowly.

"There... that one," I said.

Rachel turned up the volume.

"Any news about Danny and Drake will show up on the national news, right?"

"I think so, since we're in a different state."

We sat and watched the local news.

"I don't like watching the news. It's depressing." Rachel shook her head.

"Yeah, I don't like watching it either. We'll probably sit through all the news shows and there won't be a thing about Danny and Drake. They're probably out of the hospital sitting at home. If they're not I'm sure they're out of ICU. Danny was awake and talking when I saw him on Tuesday."

"Yeah, that was five days ago. People can get well in five days. He's probably sitting at home worried about you by now."

"You think so?"

"Yep."

"You're right. He probably is worrying about me. I wish I could call him. He told me I needed to get as far away from that place as I could. He told me they will kill me when they find me. They tried to get Danny and Drake to talk but they wouldn't. Those thugs left them for dead. Danny told me they're not going to stop until I'm dead. Then Danny told me he loved me and didn't want anything to happen to me," I smiled. "I just wish I could call him and tell him I'm okay."

"Listen to you Tara. You're all bubbly sounding," Rachel laughed.

"I know, It's funny how Danny makes me feel that way," I smiled.

We watched the state news and waited to watch the world news.

"I think they need to liven up the news shows. Put more happy things on, like ducks and chickens. Maybe throw in a few little kids on ponies. I don't know how much more I can take of this depressing stuff. I'm ready to stick my fingers in my ears if I listen to more bad news about who died and who's going to be running for office," Rachel sighed.

"I know, you don't realize how good you have it until you sit down, watch the news, and see how bad everyone else in the state is doing. Not to mention, next we get to see just how bad the rest of the world is doing."

"Oh, did you have to tell me that Tara? I can't take much more," Rachel laughed.

We sat through the world news, and saw nothing about Danny, Drake, or anyone else we knew.

"See, I told you Tara, there was nothing on the news. I know Danny and Drake are probably out of the hospital already," Rachel smiled.

"Yeah, you're probably right."

"Hey girls, it's time to eat," Peggy yelled from upstairs.

"Okay, were coming," Rachel yelled as she turned off the TV. "To bad you can't call his house."

"I know, I want to talk to him so bad," I said as I went up the stairs.

"Oh, that smells delicious," Rachel said.

"Well, it's on the table girls. Dig in," Peggy said as she opened the refrigerator. "What would you like to drink?"

"Water would be good," I said.

"Yeah, water would be good," Rachel said.

"Okay, water it is," Peggy brought us each a glass of water and sat at the table beside us. "I need to take Jomba for a walk after we're finished eating."

"I wish we could take him for a walk with you," Rachel said.

"Yeah, that would be fun," I said.

"I know girls, but I don't want my neighbors to see the two of you here. It would really disturb them," she laughed. "They've all seen Selena many times over the years. Can you imagine how they would react if they saw two Selenas walking around the neighborhood. I think it would cause a few of them to have major heart attacks. No... I can't do it to my neighbors. A lot of them are too old to be shocked like that," she shook her head and smiled.

"So, if they've met Selena then we could be Selena," Rachel said.

"Yeah, we could go out with you one at a time and be Selena," I said.

"You girls are brilliant. Why didn't I think of it," Peggy laughed, "Okay who wants to be Selena first?"

"I do, I do," Rachel raised her hand as if she were in school.

We ate the delicious meal Peggy fixed and watched out the window as it rained.

Rachel finished eating, rinsed her dish, and put it in the dishwasher.

"Okay Rachel, go upstairs and get your coat, it's cold and rainy out there. Meet me in the garage," Peggy said.

"Okay," Rachel said as she went upstairs.

"This will be fun," Peggy laughed as she took her plate and put it in the dishwasher. "It will be your turn next," she said as she headed out the door into the garage.

"I'll see you in a little while Tara," Rachel said as she came down the stairs and headed out the garage door.

"I'll be watching you," I said as I put my dish in the dishwasher.

I went to the living room and watched from the window as the rain poured from the sky. I was glad Rachel wanted to walk Jomba in the cold rainy, weather so I could stay in the house, warm and dry.

It seemed to take Rachel and Peggy longer to walk Jomba to the waterfront, than it took Peggy to walk him by herself.

I waited and watched, but still no sign of them. About twenty minutes later, I saw them on the sidewalk below me. They had a boy with them who looked close to our age.

He seemed to be talking to Rachel as they walked. I watched until they went out of sight. I watched and waited for them to walk back. After about forty minutes, I saw them appear. They walked back the way they came. The boy was still deep in conversation with Rachel. He was walking backwards while he talked to her. At one point Peggy stopped for Jomba to pee on a tree. Rachel and the boy kept walking. I watched as the boy tripped over the leash and fell on the grass. Peggy and Rachel helped him to his feet. Peggy switched places with Rachel and the boy, and they kept walking.

A few minutes later, they were out of sight again.

I went upstairs to the bedroom to see if I could get a glimpse of them coming up the hill towards the house, but I couldn't see them at all.

I went into the living room and waited.

I closed my eyes for just a minute.

"Did you have a nice nap?" Rachel asked.

"What?" Rachel startled me. I opened my eyes, and she was standing in front of me. Her hair was soaking wet.

"Did you sleep the whole time we were gone?" Rachel laughed.

"No, I must have dozed off a few minutes ago. I watched you until I couldn't see you anymore," I said, "Rachel, who's the boy you were talking too?"

"Oh, that's Owen. He has a mad crush on Selena," Peggy laughed.

"Oh, I bet that was fun," I laughed.

"Yeah, he kept asking me 'Do you remember the time we did this' and 'do you remember the time we did that,'" Rachel laughed. "Lucky for me Peggy would jump in and say, 'Yes, I remember Selena did this or Selena did that,' I just nodded my head a lot and listened," she laughed.

"I saw him trip over the leash," I said.

"Oh yeah, he was so embarrassed," Peggy said.

"His pants were soaking wet from falling in the grass. Poor guy," Rachel said. "He is really cute too."

"I hope we don't run into him again when it's your turn Tara, that could be a disaster," Peggy laughed.

"She would do fine. He talks a lot. I mean *a lot*. You just have to nod your head and say 'uh-huh,' 'yep,' and 'that's nice,' and you'll be fine," Rachel laughed.

"Yes, I guess you're right Rachel. He did do most of the talking. I only had to save her a couple of times," Peggy laughed.

"He really likes Selena," Rachel said.

"No, he doesn't," I laughed.

"Why do you say that?" Peggy asked.

"If he really liked Selena he would know Rachel wasn't Selena," I said.

"How would he know Rachel wasn't Selena, they're identical," Peggy said.

"We're not identical, we are all different. I know we look identical, we think along the same lines, and we feel the same way about different things, but we're different in lots of ways. People who love us know the difference between us," I said.

"Yeah, they do," Rachel said.

"I can see the differences when I'm around the two of you. But, when you girls first come down the stairs in the morning I still need to ask you who you are. I tell you apart by what you're wearing," Peggy said.

"After a while you won't even have to ask," Rachel smiled, "Tara's boyfriend, Danny, knows her so well, he can pick her out from the two of us without her saying a word," Rachel said.

"You're kidding? He knows her so well he can just look at the two of you and know which one is Tara?"

"Yeah, he can," I nodded.

"That's a deep love the boy has for you if he knows you that well," Peggy nodded. "He knows the spirit within you and that's a far greater love than any other love that exists." Peggy looked at me. "You're a lucky girl Tara."

"I feel lucky," I smiled.

"That's a great feeling to have, knowing someone loves you that much especially since you girls have been through so much lately. What do you say we play a board game or a card game?" Peggy asked.

"Yeah, that would be fun, what games do you have?"

"I have Uno, Monopoly, Scrabble, and Yahtzee. I haven't played since my nieces and nephews were here last summer. What do you girls like to play?" Peggy asked.

"I like all of those games," I said.

"Me too," Rachel said.

Peggy wiped her hands on the dishcloth, walked around the counter, opened a cabinet and looked inside.

"Which game do you want to play, girls?" she asked.

"How about Monopoly?" Rachel said.

"Yeah, let's play Monopoly," I said.

"Okay we'll play Monopoly." Peggy pulled the game out and set it on the counter. "Why don't we take this in the dining room and play, the table's bigger in there?"

"Okay," Rachel and I said as we headed towards the dining room.

We set up the game at the table and started playing.

"I'll be the banker since that's what I do for a living. Help people manage their money," Peggy smiled.

"Really, and how did you decide that's what you wanted to do?" Rachel asked.

"Well, I went to culinary school and was going to be a chef. Then I decided I wanted to do more with my life than just cook for other people, so I went into business for myself. Now I help people save money," Peggy smiled. "What do you girls want to be when you get older?"

"I've always wanted to be a surgeon who does surgery on babies before they're born," Rachel said.

"I've always wanted to be a neonatal doctor caring for tiny babies after they're born," I said.

"A surgeon and a neonatal doctor... those are noble professions girls. What made you girls choose those?"

"I saw a picture once of an unborn baby reaching out of the womb and holding the doctor's finger, it touched my heart so much I decided that's what I want to do," Rachel said.

"I saw the same picture. That picture is the reason I want to help tiny little babies who are just starting out in life. It warms my heart just thinking about it," I said.

"Those are very similar type professions. I know you girls say the same thing at the same time a lot and of course you look alike, but do you girls find you have a lot of other things in common?"

"Yeah, we do have a lot in common. We like the same foods, the same clothes, and the same music," Rachel said.

"Neither one of us can carry a tune," I laughed.

"That's amazing since you both grew up in two different spots."

"Yeah, it is pretty amazing. I wonder how much we're like the other girls," I said as I rolled the dice and moved my boot to Vermont Avenue. "I'll buy it."

"I don't know, it will be interesting to find out," Rachel said as she took her turn rolling the dice and moved her iron to Connecticut Avenue.

"You two do remind me a lot of Selena. You have similar mannerisms," Peggy said as she moved her wheelbarrow to States Avenue. "What's going to be interesting is when Selena meets the two of you."

"The first meeting is the hardest. After the shock wears off, you realize you have a new friend who's a lot like you, then everything's fine," Rachel said.

I nodded my head and smiled at Rachel. I picked up the dice and rolled it. I moved my boot to St. James Place.

"I'll buy it," I said.

We sat up until three-thirty a.m. playing Monopoly.

"Well, girls it looks like I'm out," Peggy said. "Rachel you cleaned me out. I only have five dollars left after paying you rent. I'm done."

"I'm done too Rachel you win. I don't have enough money to make it through your side of the board. All your hotels will wipe me out."

"Yes! I win," Rachel smiled. "I'm too tired to care," she laughed.

"Okay girls, I'm heading to bed. I'll see you in the morning," Peggy yawned, stretched, and headed out of the dining room. "Just leave the game girls we can clean it up tomorrow, goodnight."

"Night Peggy," Rachel and I said as we cleaned up the game and put it away. We went upstairs and went straight to bed.

The next morning I woke up and rolled out of bed. Rachel was still sleeping.

I went into the bathroom and took a shower. By the time I was getting dressed. I heard Rachel moving around in the bedroom.

"I hope you saved me some hot water," she shouted.

"I did. There's plenty of hot water for you," I said as I came out of the bathroom. "I'm going to go downstairs now. I'll see you in a few."

"Okay, I'll be down later."

Peggy had breakfast ready and on the table for us by the time, I came downstairs.

"Tara... or Rachel?" she asked.

"Tara," I said.

"Like I told you last night, I can't tell you apart until I know what you're wearing for the day," Peggy laughed. "Breakfast is ready and we'll consider this brunch since it's almost noon. Dig in Tara."

I pulled out a chair and sat at the table. There were plenty of hash browns, sausage, and eggs, so I loaded up my plate.

"Wow, we slept late didn't we," I said.

"Yep, that's what happens when you stay up half the night losing at Monopoly, and then you can't sleep because your whole body hurts," Peggy said.

"It does? Why?" I asked.

"I think I overdid it on the workout yesterday."

"Oh, that's not good," I said.

"Yes, I thought I was in pretty good shape but I haven't done the P90X since the day I left on vacation," she laughed. "Good morning... afternoon Rachel."

"Good afternoon?" Rachel questioned as she came down and sat at the table beside me. She grabbed a plate, piled it with food, grabbed a glass, and filled it with orange juice.

"Yep, it's afternoon," Peggy said.

"Want some?" Rachel asked as she held up her glass of juice.

"Sure," I said.

She grabbed a glass, filled it full of juice, and handed it to me.

"Here Jomba," Peggy called. Jomba came out of the living room and sat next to Peggy by the table. He was calm and well behaved. "I figured I'd let him out of his kennel he's not used to being cooped up in there for so long. Poor baby." She patted him on the head.

"He's a good boy," I said.

We ate breakfast with Jomba staring at every bite of food we ate.

"He sure is funny." Rachel took a piece of bacon and moved it up and down in the air. Jomba's head followed her every move.

We finished breakfast and put our plates in the dishwasher.

CHAPTER 7

The Trouble with Owen

"Tara, it's your turn to go for a walk with Jomba and me. You better grab your coat it's still raining out there," Peggy said.

"Okay," I said as I headed upstairs to grab my coat.

Peggy and Jomba were standing by the door waiting for me when I came down the stairs.

"Okay Rachel, we'll be back in a while," Peggy said.

"Enjoy your walk," Rachel said.

We headed into the garage and went out the garage door to the street.

One of Peggy's neighbors waved at us as they backed out of their driveway.

"That's Mr. Omosi, he's very old, and I'm surprised he still has a driver's license. He has taken out more than his fair share of garbage cans," Peggy shook her head. "I think he's in his late nineties."

"That's old," I said.

We walked up the hill and down the next street.

"Be on the lookout for Owen, he's probably watching out his window waiting to see if we come by again," Peggy whispered.

"Oh yeah? Where does he live?"

"See the big blue house over there." Peggy moved her head in the direction of the house, trying not to look to obvious she was pointing just in case

Owen was watching out the window. "Don't turn your head just look with your eyes," she said.

"Okay," I said as I glanced in the direction of the house. "Here comes someone," I whispered.

"Oh darn, he saw us," Peggy laughed.

"He must really want to get to know Selena," I whispered.

"I don't know why. She lives in Texas and it's a long ways from here."

"How long have they known each other?"

"Well, I moved here five years ago. So they've known each other for five years I'd say."

"Here he comes," I whispered.

"Hey Selena, how's it going? Hi Peggy. Hi Jomba," Owen said as he patted Jomba on the head.

"It's going great. Same as yesterday," I smiled.

Rachel was right. He was a cute boy.

We walked down and around the corner, crossed the railroad tracks, then crossed the street onto the sidewalk.

"So, where you three walking today?" Owen asked.

"The same place we walked yesterday Owen. Just down the street and back," Peggy smiled.

"Mind if I tag along again? I could use the exercise and the company."

"Sure Owen," Peggy said." So, how are things going today after your mom yelled at you?"

"Oh, you heard that? Oh, things are just fine, couldn't be better," Owen laughed. "My mom yelled at me about my pants being soaked. She said I shouldn't be out in the rain getting soaking wet.

I told her I didn't mind at all, because I was in the company of a beautiful girl." Owen looked at me and smiled.

I smiled at him but didn't say a word. If he only knew he was talking about three different girls and the last two were not who he thought... he would freak out.

"We could hear your mom yelling all the way up the block," Peggy laughed.

"Yep, that's my momma," he smiled. "So Selena, how long are you staying? Don't you have to go to school tomorrow?"

I looked at him and didn't know what to say. Rachel said Owen did all the talking, now it sounded like I was going to be stuck with all the questions.

"She's going to be here for a few more days... maybe longer. She's here to look into the University of Washington, they have medical classes she is thinking about taking in the future," Peggy said.

"Yeah, I'm looking at medical classes. I want to be a doctor someday," I said.

"Oh, I didn't know that. I thought you wanted to be a marine biologist," Owen said.

"Ah... I did, ah...I'm trying to figure it out. Ah... I'm... I'm keeping my options open," I stuttered.

"Oh, that's a good idea," Owen said, "But why are you lying to me Selena? There's no reason to lie about it."

"Oh, am I turning red?" I asked. Then I knew... Owen knew Selena better than I thought he did.

"Well, of course you are. You always turn red when you lie," Owen said. "So why are the two of you lying to me?"

"Well, if you must know Owen, Selena is here because she ah... she rode the train with me. She has a friend who's in trouble and she's here to see if I can help her," Peggy said.

"Yeah, my friend's in a lot of trouble and I'm here to help her," I said.

"What kind of trouble?" Owen asked.

"I'd rather not say," I said.

"Well, maybe I can help."

"Thanks Owen, but Selena will help her," Peggy said.

"Okay, okay, but is it someone I know?"

"No, you don't know her," I said.

"You're lying again Selena." Owen pointed at my face.

"No, I'm not lying. You met her before but you don't know her," I said.

"I met her before but I don't know her? Hum." Owen looked at me, "Okay, I'm not going to pry. You let me know if I can help in anyway. I'll do whatever I can to help your friend. Selena, you know me. I won't let you down."

"Okay," I said.

We walked down the sidewalk, Jomba made his stops along the way. Then we kept walking.

"So, how's your family doing?" Owen asked.

"I don't know, I haven't talked to them since I left home," I said. "I'm sure they're fine."

"I know, but last time we talked you told me you and your mom weren't getting along I was just wondering if everything worked itself out by now."

I wasn't sure how to answer the question without Owen knowing I was lying again.

"Yes, they worked it all out," Peggy said.

"Oh, that's good to know," Owen said. "And what's going on with your brother?"

"What do you mean, what's going on with my brother?" I asked.

"You know Selena, I don't know what it is about you this time, I can't quite put my finger on it, but you're acting a little different than you usually do. I thought we were friends, you've always been able to tell me everything. Now you're a closed book. I don't get it." Owen glared at me and shook his head.

We walked down the sidewalk, turned around, and went the other direction. Owen didn't say another word the rest of the way and neither did we.

We crossed the street and railroad tracks and headed towards the house.

"Well, here's my house. It was nice to see you again Selena," Owen said, as he looked me in the eyes and nodded his head. "Bye."

"Bye Owen," I said.

Peggy and I kept walking.

We went in the garage and Peggy took the leash off Jomba.

"That was awful," I moaned.

"I know, how were you supposed to answer all those questions? You know nothing about Selena's life, and I didn't realize how close the two of them are." Peggy shook her head. "Oh... I forgot Selena was here for a whole month this summer," she groaned.

"I think he's in love with her. He knows her too well not to be," I said as I opened the door and went into the house.

175

"So, how did it go?" Rachel asked. She was sitting at the kitchen table looking out the window.

"It was a disaster, I don't think I'll be going on anymore walks around here." I shook my head.

"Why... what happened?" Rachel asked.

"Owen knows Selena way better than I thought he did. He caught me in a lie," I said.

"He caught you in more than one lie," Peggy said.

"Really... he knows her well enough to know when she's lying? Oh no, I'm not going on any more walks either." Rachel shook her head. "What happened?"

"He knew Selena wants to be a Marine Biologist, and he caught me in a lie about it. I told him I was keeping my options open and was checking out medical school. Then he starts asking me questions about Selena's family, and he knew Selena and her mom weren't getting along. She also told him something about her brother. I can't imagine what she told him about. But, he knows something isn't right with Selena. He said he couldn't put his finger on it but he knew I was acting different."

"He would probably fall over if he knew the truth," Peggy said.

"Danny didn't fall over," I smiled.

"Danny didn't, but we sure did." Rachel shook her head.

"I think we need a little stress release. How would you girls like to go swimming?"

"Swimming? I would love to," Rachel said.

"Me too," I said.

"There's a pool a few miles from here. So, as soon as we dry off, we'll head to the pool and get wet again," she laughed. "I think it'll be good to swim a few laps and get rid of some tension."

"Peggy, I don't have a swimming suit," I said.

"Neither do I," Rachel said.

"Don't worry girls, I have plenty of suits. I'm sure I have a couple that'll fit you. I'll go see what I can find," Peggy said as she headed upstairs.

"I'm not kidding you Rachel, the whole thing with Owen was awful."

"I guess the first day he was so excited to see her he didn't bother asking her any questions. Most of the time he just flirted and rambled on," Rachel laughed.

"I wish that's all he did. He's probably mad at Selena now. He said 'I thought we were friends.' From what he says, I guess she tells him everything. He said 'Now you're a closed book. I don't get it.' Then he shut up and didn't say another word." I shook my head.

"Yep, sounds like he's mad at her. Poor Selena, we really messed things up," Rachel sighed.

"Okay girls, here's a couple of suits. They should fit you." Peggy handed us each a swimming suit.

"Thanks Peggy," I said.

"Yeah, thanks Peggy," Rachel said.

"Here's a couple of towels for you too." Peggy handed us each a towel as we headed into the garage.

"Oh, I need to put Jomba in his kennel, hold on a second." Peggy went back into the house and returned a minute later with Jomba, put him in the kennel and unlocked the car doors for us.

She started the car and opened the garage door.

"One of you girls needs to duck, until we leave the neighborhood," she said.

"I'll do it," I said as I ducked in the backseat.

"Oh no, there he is," Rachel said.

"Who... Owen?" I asked.

"Yep, he's waving at me."

"Wave back. We don't want him to get more suspicious than he already is," Peggy said.

I peeked over the seat and could see Rachel raise her hand and wave at Owen as we drove by.

"I don't know, I might have to tell him Selena went back home. I don't want him coming over and knocking on my door all the time like he did last summer. It would not be good," Peggy said.

"He did?" Rachel asked.

"Yes he did."

"Oh, it would not be good," I said.

"Here we go again. Back to hiding," Rachel laughed.

"I don't see how you find it so funny Rachel," I said as I stretched out on the backseat.

"I just think it's funny how we can never quite get away from all this craziness. It just seems to be following us around wherever we go," she laughed. "We could probably move to the deepest jungles in Africa, and we'd still find someone who knows one of us girls. We'd still be hiding."

Everyone laughed.

"Yeah, I guess it's pretty funny," I said.

"You girls are great. Despite everything that's happened to you. You still manage to laugh," Peggy laughed. "Okay, you can sit up now Tara."

I sat up, looked out the window, and watched it rain.

"Well Peggy, if you can still manage to laugh with all this rain coming down day in, day out, day after day. We can too," I smiled.

"I love the rain girls. I've lived here all my life and I'm used to the rain. In fact, if I travel to a place where they don't have rain or clouds and I'm there for a long time, I start feeling sad and lost without them. I need my rain and my clouds, it's part of me," Peggy smiled.

"I never thought of it that way. You always hear how people get sad and depressed from the rain and clouds. But I guess if you grew up with rain and clouds and then it was taken away I could see how you would feel sad and lost without them," I said.

We pulled into the parking lot, parked and went into the building.

"The dressing rooms are this way," Peggy said. We followed her into the dressing room and changed. "Here girls, put your towels and clothes in this locker." Peggy opened a locker, and set her clothes, towel, and purse inside. Rachel and I put our towels and clothes on top of hers. Peggy locked the locker and pinned the key to her swimming suit.

"The pool's this way girls." We followed Peggy to the pool area where there was an Olympic size pool with a slide and diving board. I saw kids splashing one another in a smaller wading pool, next to a Jacuzzi stuffed full of people.

"I'm hitting the slide first," Rachel said.

"I'm with you," I said.

"I might as well," Peggy said.

We stood in line and waited our turns to go down the slide. When my turn came, I climbed the ladder, went down the slide, hit the water, and swam the distance of the pool. I popped out of the water just in time to see Peggy going down the slide for her second time.

I could see Rachel swimming under water. She grabbed my ankle for a second then shot out of the water laughing.

"I saw you," I laughed.

"Hey, let's see how long we can hold our breath under water," Rachel said.

"Okay," I said.

We swam to the shallow end of the pool.

"Are you ready?" Rachel asked.

"Yep, on the count of three...one, two, three," I said as I went under the water and started counting in my head, one thousand one, one thousand two, one thousand three...

When I couldn't hold it any longer, I came to the surface. Rachel popped up next to me.

"I counted to a hundred and twenty two," Rachel said.

"Me too," I said.

I looked over just in time to see Peggy dive off the high dive.

"Did you see that?" Rachel asked.

"Yeah, wow, she's a good diver."

Rachel and I hopped out of the pool and stood in line to dive off the high board. Then we swam back and forth across the pool several times.

Rachel stopped swimming in the middle of the pool and I bumped into her.

"Hey, Tara look!" Rachel pointed.

I saw Owen coming into the pool area.

"Oh no...what are we going to do if he sees us?"

"Let's make sure he doesn't." Rachel took a deep breath and went under the water.

I did the same. We swam underwater to the farthest corner away from Owen. We stuck our noses and mouths out of the water, took a breath, and went underneath again.

I motioned to her to poke her head out and see where Owen was. She nodded, stuck her head from the water, looked for a second, and then came underneath again. She motioned he was coming this way. We swam to the shallow end and went to a corner. We stuck our noses and mouths out of the water again and took a deep breath. I motioned to Rachel I would stick my head out and look for Owen this time.

My eyes scanned the pool area and I saw Owen talking to Peggy. They were standing in line waiting to use the slide at the opposite end of the pool. I went under and motioned to Rachel I was getting out of the pool. She nodded her head.

I looked once more. I could see Peggy and she could see me. She nodded and moved around to position herself so Owen wouldn't see me getting out of the water. I swam to the steps, climbed out of the pool, and ran into the dressing room.

"No running. Please walk," the lifeguard said over the loudspeaker.

I rinsed the smell of chlorine off in the shower and sat on the bench shivering. Peggy had the locker key and I couldn't grab my towel.

I waited for a long time and wondered why it was taking Rachel so long to leave the pool area.

I peeked around the corner and saw Rachel poking her head out of the water and going under again. Owen was still talking to Peggy. I could tell he was talking about swimming because he was facing the pool and making arm movements as if he were showing Peggy how he does it.

I could see why Rachel wasn't getting out of the pool. There was no way for her to leave without Owen seeing her.

After a couple of minutes, Peggy pointed to the diving board. I saw Owen nod his head yes. He followed Peggy to the line and continued talking to her.

When it was Peggy's turn she let Owen go in front of her.

Rachel poked her head out of the water just in time to see Owen climbing the ladder. She jumped out of the pool and ran into the dressing room.

"Bur... I'm cold," Rachel said as she hopped in the shower. "I thought he was never going to look away. He saw you leave the pool and come in here. There was no way I was going to let him see me too."

"What... he saw me?"

"Yeah, he yelled for Selena. Didn't you hear him?"

"No, I wasn't paying attention I just wanted to get out of there. He wasn't calling *my* name, so I didn't realize he was yelling for me."

"Poor guy, I really feel bad for him Tara." Rachel finished rinsing off and sat down beside me on the bench.

"Yeah, me too, but what can we do? We can't tell him. He'd freak out."

"I don't think he would. Paul didn't freak out, and neither did Danny or his brothers."

"You do have a point, but there are enough people's lives in danger because of us already. We don't want to add him to the list of possible victims do we Rachel?"

"No... I guess it's better if Peggy just tells him Selena went back home."

"Yeah, but we're never going to leave the house again. Rachel we'll be stuck inside until we're old, old, old women."

"I wouldn't mind if we grew old at Peggy's house. It's a very nice place to be stuck, and since it rains nonstop we might as well stay inside. I love the breathtaking view even in the rain. I wouldn't mind having that view for the rest of my life."

"I know... it's a breathtaking view, isn't it? Of course, we'll need jobs where we could work at home and never go out. We couldn't expect Peggy to take care of us for the rest of our lives."

"Tara, Peggy has her own business. I'm sure she could find a position for us where we could work right from her house. If she paid us... we could save our money and move to a house of our own someday."

"You girls sound like you're planning your lives," a woman said as she came into the dressing room.

"Yep, we're working on it," I smiled.

"Get a good education girls. Then you can be who you want to be, do what you want to do, and go where you want to go," the woman said.

"Thanks for the advice," Rachel smiled.

"I used to be the governor of this state," she whispered and put her finger to her mouth, "Shhh don't tell anyone," she smiled and winked at us.

"Really?" Rachel whispered.

"Wow," I whispered.

She grabbed her stuff out of her locker and headed out the door.

"Bye," Rachel and I said.

"Bye," She said.

"Wow, I can't wait to tell Peggy," I said.

"Tara, she just told us not to tell anyone," Rachel laughed.

"I'm sure she meant while she was here. She probably didn't want the press to hear about her swimming here. They would come, take her picture, and ruin her day. Then she would need to find another place to swim. I don't think she means we can't tell Peggy. I have to tell Peggy," I laughed.

"What was her name anyways?"

"She didn't tell us her name. I guess we will have to look her up on the Internet Rachel."

"Maybe she was joking. Maybe she was never the Governor. That's probably why she said not to tell anyone, Tara."

"Rachel, you are getting more suspicious of people all the time."

"Am I?" Rachel looked at me. "Oh no... I am."

"Well, after all we've been through, I don't blame you for being suspicious. I think I'm starting to be a little more guarded than I used to be."

Rachel and I sat on the bench for what seemed like forever. We took turns peeking out at the pool. Peggy was either swimming or diving every time we looked. Owen was in the pool talking to some kid the whole time.

"Tara, I wonder why Peggy is staying out there when she knows we're in here?"

"She probably doesn't want Owen to see her leave. He might decide it's time to leave too. Then how are we going to make it out to Peggy's car without him seeing us?"

"I see your point."

"She's probably working on a plan to sneak us out of here."

"I'm cold. I need my towel," Rachel shivered.

"Me too... I think I'm going to rinse off again, at least the water is warm."

"It's warm until you get out and sit in the breeze again," Rachel laughed.

"Oh yeah... I think I'll sit here and wait," I shivered.

We heard the announcement come over the loudspeaker saying the pool would be closing in fifteen minutes.

"Oh good, the pool is finally closing," I said.

Rachel peeked around the corner to see where Peggy and Owen were.

"Tara, I don't see either one of them anywhere. Where did they go?"

"I don't know." I went and looked out to see if I could see them. Peggy and Owen were nowhere in sight.

"She wouldn't just leave us here would she?"

"I don't think so Rachel. Peggy's purse is locked in the locker. I can't see her leaving her purse here. Besides, her car keys are probably in there."

People were getting out of the pool, coming into the dressing room, collecting their belongings and heading out the door. When the last girl was out of the dressing room Rachel and I sat quietly on the bench not saying a word.

We heard the announcement come over the loudspeaker. It said, *"The pool's closed now. Have a good evening."*

I peeked out the door and saw a few boys climbing out of the pool and heading for the dressing room, but no sign of Peggy or Owen.

"I don't know what to do Rachel. What do you think we should do?"

"I don't know either."

A few minutes later Peggy came in through the door leading out to the lobby.

"Oh, there you are. We were getting a little worried. You weren't out at the pool," Rachel said.

"I know, I was standing out front making sure Owen's mom picked him up." Peggy shook her head. "What a mess… let's hurry girls." She opened the locker and handed us our towels and clothes.

We dressed and headed for the parking lot.

"Let me look outside one more time just in case," Peggy said.

She opened the door looked both ways and motioned for us to follow her.

We jumped in the car in a hurry. Peggy started the engine, and we headed down the road.

"Girls, I don't know how you do it. I was totally stressed out the whole time Owen was there."

"What was he talking to you about?" I asked.

"He saw one of you when you were getting out of the pool and he yelled for Selena. He was upset because you didn't turn around when he yelled. I told him you probably didn't hear him because it was so loud in there. He asked me where you were going in such a hurry. I told him either you went to change your swimming suit or you were leaving with your friend. I told him you were planning to stay the night at your friend's house. So, when we get to the neighborhood you girls need to duck. I don't want him to see either one of you."

"That was quick thinking when you told him Selena went to change her swimming suit," Rachel said.

Well, I figured… if he saw Rachel leaving the pool in a different swimming suit he wouldn't think anything of it. I told him the elastic in Selena's favorite swimming suit was giving out. She wasn't sure if it was going to hold up in the pool, but she wanted to wear it anyways. I told him she didn't want to lose her bikini bottoms in the pool so she brought another suit just in case," Peggy laughed. "Running interference is hard work girls. I'm exhausted. I guess I should have stayed home and soaked in the tub."

"Thanks for taking us swimming Peggy," I said.

"Yeah, thanks Peggy," Rachel said.

"You're welcome. Sorry you didn't get to swim longer."

"We still had fun," Rachel, and I said at the same time.

"We're almost to the neighborhood girls," Peggy said as she turned the corner.

Rachel and I ducked in the seats and stayed hidden until Peggy parked the car in the garage and closed the door.

"Seriously girls, I don't know how you do it. I feel like a big ball of stress just from one day with you. And... it's not even you, it's Owen. That kid stresses me out," Peggy laughed. "Okay, I'm going to take Jomba for another walk and hopefully release a little of this stress, then I'll fix something for us to eat. So you girls go upstairs, take your showers and I'll be back shortly."

"Okay," we said.

Peggy took Jomba out of his kennel while we went upstairs to shower.

Rachel and I took our showers put our clothes on and went downstairs to the kitchen.

The doorbell rang.

"I wonder who's here," I said.

"I don't know. Let's go upstairs," Rachel said.

We went upstairs and sat on the bed in the dark.

"Tara... should I peek out the window and see who's here?"

"Sure go ahead Rachel."

Before Rachel was to the window, I heard a click sound of something hitting the window.

"Rachel, did you hear that noise?"

"I don't know it sounds like someone hitting the window with something little. I'm not going to look outside I'm scared whoever it is will see me."

"Selena, I know you're in there. I saw the light in the window a little while ago and I know it wasn't Peggy. I saw Peggy go by my house with Jomba. Come on Selena, why won't you talk to me? What's going on with you? Don't you love me anymore?"

"It's Owen. What are we going to do?" Rachel whispered in a panic.

"The guy is crazy over her. Listen to him, he's lovesick," I whispered. "Let's just sit here and hope he goes away."

We heard another click sound as something little hit the window.

"Do you think he's throwing little rocks at the window?"

"It sounds like it... what are we going to do?"

"I think we should go to the door, let him in, and tell him. He's obviously worried about her, Tara."

"Let's wait until Peggy comes home and talk to her about it, Rachel."

"He already stresses her out. She's not going to want to tell him. But, if we tell him, then she won't need to be stressed-out anymore."

"Yeah, that's true."

"Come on Selena, I just have to talk to you," Owen said. We heard something clink against the window.

"He's not going to stop. He thinks she's here," I said.

"Peggy should be home anytime now."

Just as Rachel said that, we heard another voice out in front of the house.

"That sounds like Peggy," Rachel said.

We listened but we couldn't make out what they were saying.

Then we heard the front door open and shut. We sat on the bed and didn't move. We heard footsteps coming up the stairs and didn't say a word.

"Girls, are you in here?" Peggy whispered.

"Yeah, we're here Peggy," I whispered.

"Owen was outside, he said he saw a light come on in the house while I was walking."

"Yeah, we came up and took our showers. We didn't think anything of it. Until Owen rang the doorbell," I said.

"I guess you'll need to keep the lights off from now on, at least, when I'm out with Jomba anyways."

"Yeah... uh, Peggy, we think we should just tell Owen," Rachel whispered.

"The way he's been talking outside the window we know he really cares about Selena. It doesn't sound like he's going to give up on her anytime soon. If we tell him... it will take the stress off you," I whispered.

"You girls really think we should?" Peggy whispered.

"Yeah, we think we should tell him. What did you tell him when he said the light went on," I asked.

"I told him Selena must have left the switch on and maybe the bulb was going out. I told him I would turn off the switch. I don't think he bought it."

"Is he still out front?" I asked as I peeked out the window.

"I don't know. I think he was going home," Peggy said.

"I don't see him."

"Can you see his house?"

"Yeah."

"Just wait a few minutes and see if the light goes on in his room. Selena told me it's the top window on the left. I'll turn on the light. If he sees you standing in the window I bet he'll run here as fast as he can, and beat on my door," Peggy laughed, "Are you sure we should tell him?"

"I think so," Rachel said.

"Yeah, I think so too," I said.

I stood and watched out the window waiting to sec if Owen would appear in one of the windows of his house.

After a few minutes, I saw Owen looking out the top left window of his house. He looked over in my direction and saw me standing in the window. He shook his head at me then disappeared from view. A few seconds later the light went out in the room.

"I'm not positive but I think he's on his way over here," I said.

"So girls, what are we going to do when he comes to the door?" Peggy asked.

"We're going to go downstairs and let him in," Rachel said.

"I'll let him in," Peggy said.

We headed downstairs and stood by the front door waiting for the bell to ring.

"We're going to stand over here by the counter Peggy. That way you have time to close the door before he sees us," Rachel said.

"Are you afraid he'll take one look at the two of you and run?" Peggy laughed.

"You never know. He's going to be in shock."

"I remember when we found out. Both of us were in shock, we couldn't stand up," Rachel said.

"Yeah, it was pretty bad for both of us," I said.

"I'm still in shock." Peggy shook her head.

The doorbell rang.

"Are you ready girls?"

Rachel and I nodded our heads. Peggy opened the door and let Owen inside.

"Where's Selena? I saw her standing in the bedroom window," he said, out of breath.

Peggy closed the door. Owen walked in the house and looked at Rachel and me. He stood there for a few minutes and didn't say a word. Then he passed out cold on the floor.

"Oh no!" Rachel screamed.

"Oh no! Wow, I didn't expect that," I screamed.

"Here girls, help me get him up," Peggy shouted.

We took Owen by the arms and lifted him to the sitting position. Peggy grabbed pillows off the couch and stacked them behind him

"Is this what you're supposed to do with someone who's passed out?" I asked.

"I don't know, but it sounds like a perfectly logical thing to do in my opinion. Of course, I could be completely wrong, but I think it's crash victims who aren't supposed to be moved," Peggy said. I could tell she was upset.

"Boy, this must've been a complete shock to his system. He just looked at us and went down instantly," Rachel said as she fanned him with her hand.

"I'm going to get a damp cloth," I said as I ran to the kitchen and looked through the drawers.

"Third drawer down," Peggy yelled.

I found a dishcloth, wetted it, ran over to Owen, and placed it on his face.

"He is breathing isn't he?" Peggy asked.

I removed the cloth and put my finger under his nose.

"Yeah, he's breathing all right," I said as I put the cloth back on his face.

We sat on the floor next to him, watching and waiting for some kind of response. After a few minutes, he started to move. Then he reached up and pulled the dishcloth off his face.

He looked at me for a minute and then looked at Rachel. His eyes rolled back in his head and he was out again.

"You girls seem to be causing him too much trauma. The poor boy's brain is confused." Peggy shook her head.

"I think I'll go in the dining room for a few minutes. Maybe only one of us needs to explain things to him," Rachel said.

"Okay, I'll sit here and wait for him to wake up again," I said as I put the cloth back on his face.

Owen was out for at least ten minutes. This time when he came to, I was the only one staring at him when he pulled the cloth off his face.

"Selena, I had the weirdest dream," he smiled. His speech was slurred.

"No Owen, you weren't dreaming, and my name is Tara. I'm not Selena."

"What?" He blinked his eyes several times as if he were having a hard time focusing.

"I'm not Selena, I'm Tara."

"What?" He blinked hard and then looked me in the eyes. "But you look like her."

"I look like her, but I'm not her."

"I didn't know she had a twin. She never told me she had a twin. How come she never told me she had a twin? How come I never met you before? Why don't I know you? I don't believe you. You're joking with me Selena." Owen was confused.

"I'm not her twin. I'm a clone. She's a clone too."

"No, that's not true. She's not a clone. You're Selena, aren't you? Why are you messing with me? I can't believe you're messing with me Selena." Owen stood up and looked at me. "Why are you messing with me?" He glared at me.

"She's not messing with you Owen," Rachel said as she came out from the dining room and stood next to me.

Owen's jaw dropped. He stared at both of us.

"I can't believe what I'm seeing here." He reached out with both hands, gently grabbed a curly lock from each of our heads, and ran his fingers down the whole length of our hair. "You feel real."

"We are real Owen. I'm Rachel. I'm a clone too."

"This is just crazy talk. I know there aren't any human clones. I studied all about clones. They banned human cloning in all fifty states. Ban, meaning it's against the law, illegal. You could go to jail for doing it. Now why would you tell me you're clones? Do you want to go to jail or something?"

"They wouldn't put us in jail Owen. You're not thinking right. I think you're still in shock," I said.

"Okay, maybe they wouldn't put *you* in jail, because you're the clones, so you're the product of someone's illegal activities. Someone needs to go to jail." He shook his head and sighed. "I think it's not a good thing when people mess with other peoples minds and get them all confused. I think I need to lie down for a while. Do you mind if I lie down over here? I don't think I feel so good right now," Owen said as he staggered towards the couch.

"No, I don't mind Owen. Just lie down until you feel better," Peggy said. "I'll get you a blanket." She grabbed a blanket out of a cabinet and covered Owen with it.

"Thanks Peggy. Maybe this will go away when my head stops spinning."

"I don't think we're going to go away," I whispered as I walked into the kitchen.

"Me either," Rachel whispered as she followed me.

"Well... that went well." Peggy shook her head. "All this before dinner... are you girls hungry?"

"A little," we both said.

"Okay, then I'll make dinner and relax," Peggy said calmly. "I do feel better now that he's asleep."

Peggy made spaghetti and meatballs, green salad and garlic bread, it was delicious. I ate everything on my plate and went back for seconds of spaghetti and garlic bread.

"This is great Peggy," I said.

"Yeah, this is great," Rachel said.

"We'll, thank you girls. I'm glad you like it," she smiled.

Owen came into the kitchen and looked at the three of us.

"So... I wasn't dreaming?" He shook his head.

"No Owen, you weren't dreaming. Tara and Rachel are real. Would you like some spaghetti?" Peggy asked.

"Sure," Owen said.

"Have a seat and I'll get you a plate." Peggy filled a plate for Owen and set it on the table in front of him while Owen stared at Rachel and me.

"Clones huh?" He mumbled as he took a bite of spaghetti.

"Yep." Rachel and I nodded.

"Does Selena know?"

Rachel and I looked at each other and shrugged our shoulders.

"Probably not," I said.

"Oh." Owen sat quietly eating his spaghetti and staring at us. When he finished he took his plate to the sink, rinsed it, and put it in the dishwasher. "I think I'll go home now. Thanks for dinner Peggy," he said.

"Let me walk you home Owen," Peggy said as she grabbed her coat.

"Okay."

Peggy and Owen headed out the door to Owens house.

"Well, that was fun," I laughed.

"Yeah, being stared at is always so enjoyable," Rachel laughed.

Rachel and I cleaned the kitchen and by the time we finished, Peggy was back.

"I think, I'm going to go upstairs and take a nice long bubble bath and go to bed early. I hope tomorrow will be a stress free day," Peggy said.

"Let's hope so," Rachel said.

"Owen's going to come by in the morning. I'm going to drive him to school so we can talk about things a little more. Goodnight girls," Peggy said as she went up the stairs.

"Goodnight Peggy," we said.

"Rachel, what do you want to do now?" I asked.

"I don't know but a bubble bath does sound good."

"It does...doesn't it. Okay, you go take a bubble bath and I'll hang out in the room till it's my turn," I said.

We went upstairs and Rachel went into the bathroom.

I sat on the bed thinking about Owen passing out cold. I hoped he didn't wake up in the morning thinking he had dreamed the whole thing.

I saw the backpack sitting next to the bed and picked it up from the floor. I remembered the pictures of us in Disneyland. I pulled them out and put one on each nightstand beside our bed.

I lay down on the bed and looked at the picture of Mickey Mouse, Rachel, Clare, Griffin, Parker, Eva, Houston, and Me. It was a great day with no stress or worry. Disneyland was truly the happiest place on earth. After the trouble with Owen, I was happy to remember a perfect day.

"Your turn," Rachel said as she came into the room wrapped in a towel.

"I can't wait," I said as I headed into the bathroom.

After I had my bubble bath, I came out and Rachel was sleeping with her picture in her arms. I took the picture, put it on the nightstand, and went to bed.

The next morning I took a shower.

Rachel woke up just as I was coming out of the bathroom.

"My turn," she said. "I wonder if Owen woke up this morning thinking he dreamed the whole thing last night."

"I don't know. I was wondering the same thing. It really hit him hard. I've never seen anything like it before," I said.

"I haven't either." Rachel shook her head.

"Things affect different people in different ways I guess."

"Yeah, I guess so."

I dressed and waited for Rachel. We went downstairs and into the living room.

Rachel and I walked into the dining room where Peggy was on the phone with Kate.

"Yes, bring your resume, driver's license, social security card, and proof of insurance just in case we decide to hire you. We'll want to get you started on the paperwork right away."

She paused, listening to Kate for a minute.

"Yes, well our address is fifty-three-eighty-three Franklin Boulevard Sacramento. We're in suite F."

Another pause

"Yes, that's right. Okay, I'll see you tomorrow afternoon at one-thirty pm."

Another pause

"Yes, thank you. Okay, see you then. Bye." Peggy hung up the phone. "Well, it looks like I'm going to be flying into Sacramento to interview Kate at my office at one-thirty tomorrow afternoon. She sounds like an intelligent woman. I'm sure I'll be able to put her to work."

"Isn't Sacramento a little far for her to drive from Windyn?" I asked.

"She said she has relocated several times and is willing to move again if the right job opportunity comes her way."

"I feel bad for her. She just moved to Windyn for the hospital job back in August. Billy and I helped her and Trevor move into the house she lives in now," I said. "Did she sound excited to get your call?" I asked.

"She said she has a couple other job interviews lined up, and she is going to take the best offer. She's working for a company called Foltex right now, but she says it's only part-time temporary. She lives in a small beach town, so I'm sure there are not a lot of good paying jobs there."

"Foltex? That's Danny's dad's company," I said.

"It sounds like he's helping Kate," Rachel said.

"That's really nice of him," I said.

"Do you girls have any questions you want me to ask Kate when I see her?" Peggy asked. "If you do, write them on a piece of paper and I'll take them with me. That way I won't forget any of them. If I don't have it in writing I tend to forget," Peggy laughed. "I don't think they're going to have anyone follow her to a job interview. I think it will go fine."

Rachel and I looked at each other. Rachel could tell what I was thinking before I said anything.

"I want to know how Danny's doing," I said.

"Well, here's a piece of paper Tara. Write it down so I don't forget it. I have a million questions for her I need to write down. I don't want to forget anything I need to ask. Is there anything else you want me to ask her?"

"No, I can't think of anything right now. I just want to know about Danny, that's all."

"Well, I'm going to get as much information from her as I possibly can about her niece Isabella," Peggy said.

"So Peggy, what are you going to tell Kate?" Rachel asked.

"I'm going to tell Kate the two of you are at my house staying with me and you're both fine. I'm also going to tell her about my niece Selena. Do you think Kate knows you girls are clones?"

"I don't know," I said. "I know Mr. Parker knows, but I don't know if he told Kate or not."

"Mr. Parker? Who's Mr. Parker?" Peggy asked.

"Oh, didn't we tell you Mr. Parker is Danny's dad?"

"No. You must've left that part out. Do you know what his first name is?"

"Yes, his name is Peter Parker, not to be confused with Spiderman," Rachel smiled.

"Of course, I'll try not to confuse him with Spidey," Peggy laughed. "But, if he were Spidey we could use his help right now," she smiled.

"Mr. Parker is a very nice man. He's helped us a lot. I don't know where we'd be if he hadn't helped us get out of Windyn when we did," Rachel said.

"We'd probably be dead already," I said.

"Well, that's an awful thought." Peggy shook her head. "You know girls since the swimming didn't work out so well, because of Owen. I was thinking I want to take you somewhere fun," Peggy said. "I need to go to the office and take care of a few things. I think I'll just take you with me. Would you like to walk around the city today?"

"That would be fun," I said.

"We went by the city when we were on the motorcycle, but we never stopped," Rachel said.

"What I'll do is I'll take you to the office with me and then you two can go walk around town and I'll meet you for lunch. We'll have lunch and then you can walk around a little more until I'm done working and then we'll head home. How does that sound?"

"Yeah, that sounds like fun. Do they have lots of things to do in Tacoma?" I asked.

"I think we can find lots of things for you to do. Let's see what I can find on the computer." Peggy turned on her laptop and went on the Internet. "Let's see... what is there for teenage kids to do?" She typed on the computer and waited. "You girls can go to the museum of glass and look around, how's that?"

"The Museum of Glass?" Rachel and I said.

"Yes, the Museum of Glass," Peggy smiled

She could see this didn't excite us by the tone of our voices.

"Okay, there's also an old car museum. You could go look at old cars."

"Old cars? Huh," Rachel said.

"Okay, looking at old cars could be fun. Don't you think so?" Peggy nodded.

Rachel and I looked at each other.

"Yeah," I nodded.

"Yeah, looking at old cars could be fun," Rachel said.

"Sure, we could go look at old cars," I said.

Peggy wasn't convinced it was something we wanted to do.

"Okay, well, how about there's the Maritime Museum down on the waterfront. Do you want to go to the Maritime Museum?"

"Maritime Museum? We walked right by one in San Diego. It had a whole bunch of old boats there," Rachel said.

"You girls want to do that? Does that sound like fun?"

"Um yeah, that could be fun," I said.

"Okay, girls you need to help me out a little. I don't feel I'm getting anywhere with you two. You don't sound that enthusiastic about any of the choices so far," Peggy laughed. "What would you girls like to do?"

"Well, it's raining. Can we go someplace we don't have to walk in the rain?" I asked.

"Like what girls? What do you have in mind?"

"Do you have a skating rink in town?" Rachel asked.

"Yes, as a matter of fact there's one about fifteen minutes from here. Now, that sounds like fun. Why didn't I think of it?" Peggy smiled. "I guess I forgot what it was like to be a kid. That's it then, I'm going to take you to the skating rink and you girls can skate. Oh, that sounds like so much fun. I haven't been skating in a long time." Peggy pulled up the website for the skating rink. "Let's see it doesn't open until one o'clock. You can hang around here, I'll come home at noon, we'll have lunch, and I'll drop you off at the skating rink on my way back to the office. Then I'll come back and pick you up around four o'clock, that's when they close. How's that sound?"

"Thanks Peggy that would be great," I smiled.

"Yeah, I can't wait," Rachel said.

I heard a knock at the door.

"It's probably Owen," Peggy said as she headed to the door. She looked out the peephole. "Yep, it's Owen." She opened the door and let him inside.

"Hi Peggy, I'm ready for school. You did say you would take me... didn't you... or was I dreaming?"

"No, you weren't dreaming. I did say I would take you," she said.

Owen came inside and Peggy closed the door. Owen looked at Rachel and me.

"This is so weird." He shook his head and rubbed his face. "Where's Selena and why are you two girls here and not her?"

"We're not sure where Selena is right now," Peggy said. "I just came back from her house and she was gone the whole week I was there."

"Where was she?"

"My sister said she was camping with her friends."

"Camping with her friends for a week? She should've been in school don't you think?"

"You know... that thought never occurred to me. You're right. She should have been in school."

"Well, what if something bad happened to her?" Owen shook his head. "So, why are you two girls here at Peggy's house?"

"They met me on the train. I'll explain it to you on the way to school," Peggy said.

"Okay, because I'm still in shock and a little confused about this whole thing. So, who have I been talking to the last couple of times we were walking Jomba?"

"The first time you were talking to me, I'm Rachel."

"The second time you were talking to me, I'm Tara. I'm so sorry."

"No wonder you were acting strange when I'd ask you a question."

"Yeah... I know nothing about Selena. You know way more about her than I do," I smiled.

"Yeah, I really like her," Owen smiled.

"Come on Owen, I'll take you to school. You girls get something to eat and I'll be back shortly," Peggy said as she went out the door.

"Bye girls, will I be seeing you again?"

"Probably," Rachel and I said.

"Oh, and I'm not going to tell a living soul, they won't believe me anyways," Owen said as he went out the door.

CHAPTER 8

Read the Contract

Rachel and I made cereal for breakfast, finished it, went downstairs, turned the TV on, found the station with the cartoons, and sat down to watch.

"Rachel, I want to go to school. I miss it," I said.

"I know, I feel like we're getting farther and farther behind. We've already missed a month and a half. Can you imagine how hard it's going to be to catch up on homework?" Rachel shook her head.

"I know, I've always been a straight A student. But, I know it's going to take a lot of brainpower to catch up in class."

"Maybe we should find something on TV a little more educational to watch instead of watching cartoons. Our brains are going to turn to mush if we spend all of our free time watching stuff like this."

"Why don't you see if you can find a channel we can learn something new from Rachel? I don't want to become a big mush brain," I laughed.

Rachel surfed the channels.

"What should we learn today?" she asked.

"Let's find a science or health show. If we're going to be doctors one day, we need science," I said.

"Okay, science, or health, let's see what I can find." Rachel surfed until she found a show. "Mystery ER."

"Okay, let's watch it."

Rachel and I watched one medical show after another. There were lots of interesting cases with all sorts of weird diseases we had never heard of before we started watching.

"Hey girls, I'm home," Peggy yelled when she came into the house.

"We're in the TV room. We'll be right up," I yelled.

Rachel turned off the TV and we went upstairs.

"Hey girls, are you having a good day?" Peggy asked as she opened the refrigerator door.

"Yeah, we've been watching doctor shows learning medical stuff. We figured since we can't go to school right now we might as well learn something new on TV," I said.

"Well, that's a really good idea girls," Peggy said as she pulled the mayonnaise out and set the jar on the counter. "Do you want sandwiches for lunch?"

"That would be great," Rachel said.

"Yeah," I said. "So how'd it go with Owen?"

"Owen said he's not going to say a word to anyone, and if we need his help with anything he'll do what he can," Peggy said.

"He seems to be a very nice boy," Rachel said.

"He's all right. I thought he was going to go off the deep end for a few minutes," Peggy laughed. "I think he seems to be handling it fine right now. It just took a while for things to sink in, but I don't blame him. It still hasn't sunk all the way into my brain."

Peggy finished making sandwiches and we sat at the kitchen table and ate.

"Well after watching a bunch of medical shows and seeing how many weird things happen to people, we're feeling pretty good about ourselves," Rachel said.

"Yeah, we watched a sixteen year old boy who caught a virus and almost died. His mom said 'Going through something like this makes you appreciate life itself. It makes you aware of how fragile life is, and it truly is a gift.' Rachel and I have it pretty good despite everything," I said.

"You're right. Life could be a whole lot worse, we need to count our blessings don't we," Peggy said.

"Yep, we do need to count our blessings and Peggy you are one of ours," Rachel said.

"Wow, first an angel, now a blessing. I'm doing good," she smiled.

Everyone laughed.

We finished our lunch and headed out the door. Peggy drove us to the two-five-three roller skating rink.

I'll be back to pick you up at four o'clock. You girls have fun," she said as Rachel and I climbed out of the car.

"Okay," we said.

Rachel and I went in the building and paid for the skate session.

"Here's your tickets for your skate rental," the girl behind the counter said. "Do you think it's fun being twins?" she asked.

"Sometimes," Rachel and I said at the same time.

"You girls have that twin thing going on. That's weird," she laughed.

We laughed.

"The skate rental's through the door to your left on the other side of the snack bar, you'll see the skates painted on the wall."

"Okay, thank you," I said.

"Yeah thanks," Rachel said.

Rachel and I took our tickets, exchanged our shoes for skates, sat at a round bench, and put on our skates.

"It's been a long time since I've skated Rachel, this is going to be fun. This rink is huge, look Rachel. The rink back home is half this size."

"The roller dome by my house is small too. I haven't skated in a long time either. I hope I'm not too rusty," Rachel laughed.

Rachel had her skates on and headed for the floor before I had my skates laced. I hurried, tied the strings, and headed for the rink. Rachel was on her second lap when I skated onto the rink.

The music played hip-hop, and kids were moving to the beat as they rolled around the rink. Rachel whizzed by me at a high-speed.

"You were worried about being rusty?" I shouted as she skated by me.

She laughed.

I sped up to catch her, but couldn't. She was too far ahead of me. I waited for her to come around the rink and skated as fast as I could. We kept pace with each other as we rolled around the rink. Rachel grabbed my hand, and we pulled each other around the rink.

A good song came over the loudspeaker and we sang to the music. We were having a great time skating.

"This is a lot of fun! I'm glad Peggy brought us here," Rachel said.

"Yeah, me too," I said.

Rachel and I were talking to each other, not paying attention, when a little kid came from nowhere and skated right in front of us.

"Rachel, watch out!" I yelled as I watched her trip over the little girl. Rachel still had ahold of my hand so I went down too.

Rachel, me, and the little girl landed on our butts in the middle of the rink.

"Ouch," the little girl cried. "I'm okay."

"Hey, are you sure?" I asked as I stood up, grabbed her hand, and lifted her to her feet. Our green eyes met, and I knew I looked like her when I was little. I smiled at her.

"Hey look," Rachel said as she stood up and pointed at the little girl who she was seeing for the first time.

"Hey look," the little girl smiled. "You have curly red hair, like mine." She put her finger in one of my ringlets and pulled it gently.

"And you have big green eyes like mine," I laughed. "Are you okay?" I asked.

"I'm fine I think. Momma says shake it off." The little girl shook her arms, legs and head. "Yep, I'm okay. Everything works," she laughed "Hey, you look like her," she pointed at Rachel.

"Yep, I do," I smiled.

"You be careful out here," Rachel scolded.

"Okay, I will." The little girl skated off slowly.

"Tara, she looks just like me when I was little," Rachel whispered.

"I know she looks like me too. I can't believe my eyes," I whispered. "I think we need to take a second look just to be sure."

"Okay, I'll skate around," Rachel took off like a rocket. She skated by the little girl, turned around, and skated backwards in front of her. She waved at her and the little girl waved back. Rachel turned around and skated around the rink until she caught up to me.

"Tara, that little girl is definitely one of us," Rachel whispered.

"You really think so?"

"Yep, I'm pretty sure she's one of us."

"That's what I thought too. I just wanted to make sure."

We skated alongside each other and watched the little girl as she went around the rink slowly.

"Let's catch up and pass her," Rachel said.

"Okay," I said as we took off around the rink. We came up behind her and went by her on both sides.

"Hi," I said.

"Hi," Rachel said.

"Hi," the little girl said.

Rachel and I smiled and waved. The little girl smiled and waved back.

"She is definitely one of us. I can't believe this!" I was very surprised.

"Come on," Rachel said. I followed her off the floor. We stood on the side by the buffer wall and watched the little girl go around and around the rink.

"We should talk to her," Rachel said.

"Yeah, we should, but what are we going to say?" I questioned.

"I don't know. Let's just talk to her."

"Okay well, let's wait until she gets off the rink."

"Okay."

The little girl went around the rink repeatedly.

"Looks like she's going to be skating longer," Rachel said.

"Let's skate," I took off and skated onto the floor.

Rachel zoomed by me.

We skated and kept our eyes on the little girl, waiting for her to take a break and leave the floor. Just when I was beginning to wonder if she was ever going to take a break, I watched as she made her way off the rink.

Rachel and I nodded our heads, skated around one more time and headed off the floor. Rachel was in front of me so I followed her to where the little girl was.

"Hi," Rachel said.

"Hi," the little girl said.

"Hi," I said.

I bent down to talk to her.

"You sure are a pretty little girl," I said.

"You're pretty too," she said.

"What's your name?"

"Avery."

"Avery. That's a pretty name."

"A pretty name for a pretty girl," Rachel said.

"What's your name?" Avery asked.

"My name is Tara, and my sister's name is Rachel. How old are you?"

"I'm this many." Avery held up four fingers. "Are you twins?"

"Yes we are," I said. "So do you like skating?"

Avery nodded her head yes.

"Where's your mommy at?" Rachel asked.

Avery looked around, she pointed at a woman who was sitting by a little girl in a wheelchair.

"That's your mommy?" I asked.

"Uh huh, and that's my big sister," Avery pointed.

Her mom looked over at us.

She waved to Avery.

I could see Avery's mom had a strange look on her face. She said something to a woman who was sitting next to her. Then Avery's mom stood up and walked towards us.

"Rachel, she's coming over here," I said. I was feeling very uncomfortable.

"What are we going to do?" Rachel's voice was trembling. I could tell she was just as uncomfortable as I was.

"I don't know."

We stood there trembling as we watched Avery's mom get closer to us.

"Mommy, can I get some pop?" Avery asked.

"In a minute Sweetie," she said. "Can I help you girls?"

"Who us?" Rachel asked.

"Yeah, is there a reason you're hanging around my little girl?"

"Yeah, we wanted to make sure she was all right, after we tripped over her out on the floor," I said.

"Oh, I didn't see that," she said. "You know you girls look familiar. Do I know you from somewhere?"

"I don't think so," Rachel said.

Rachel and I looked at each other.

"Mommy, can I have some pop please," Avery asked.

"In a minute Sweetie," she said. "You know... I think I've seen one of you girls somewhere but I just can't put my finger on it. You wouldn't happen to go to school in the Orting school district do you?"

"No," Rachel said.

I shook my head.

"I'm Jessica," She said.

"I'm Martha and this is my sister Rita." Rachel turned a little red, but it was hot so it wasn't too noticeable.

"Nice to meet you. You girls enjoy your skate."

"Nice to meet you too Jessica," I said.

Rachel and I went out on the floor and skated.

"This is just weird," I said.

"I know, I wanted to tell her we look familiar to her because she sees us in Avery's face every day, but I couldn't."

"I was thinking the same thing Rachel. Yeah, and I was afraid she was going to tell us she knew we were the missing clones, and she was going to turn us in for a reward or something. I don't think she knows we're clones or she would have said something to us."

"Yeah, that's what I thought too. She must not know we're clones. Tara, what are we going to do.

We can't let Avery leave. We need to find out more about her."

"I wonder if they live in the Orting school district. She asked us if we went to school there."

"I don't know. I think we need to ask Avery her last name when she comes out on the floor again."

"She's so little and cute," I said.

"I know we look just like her when we were little."

"This is so weird seeing her."

We looked over at the three of them as we skated around the rink. Jessica was wiping the chin of the little girl sitting in the wheelchair.

"I wonder what's wrong with her," I said.

"I don't know. She looks a few years older than Avery."

"Avery said she's her sister right?"

"Yeah, that's what she said."

"Rachel, do you think it's a little odd all the girls we've met so far have had a brother or sister who has something wrong with them?"

"I never thought of it. Let's see, my brother has cancer, your brother has allergies, Amanda's brother has epilepsy, Nichole had a brother who died before she was born, and Avery's sister is in a wheelchair."

"Oh no, Rachel, I just had a horrible thought. What if we're the ones causing our brothers to be sick? What if we have weird radioactive stuff in our bodies making our brothers sick?"

"Oh no, that would be awful! But I don't think we do or our parents would be sick too."

"Oh yeah, I guess you're right. Oh, I was scaring myself for a minute." I shook my head and sighed.

"No, I don't think we're the cause of their health problems, but it makes me wonder why they're sick."

"Maybe it's just a coincidence," I said.

"Yeah maybe," Rachel said, "Hey look, here comes Avery."

"Let's go ask her what her last name is."

Rachel and I skated around the rink a few time so we wouldn't draw attention from Avery's mom. We didn't want it to appear as if we went on the floor just to talk to Avery.

We rolled around the rink again and waved at Avery.

She smiled and waved back at us.

The next time around, we slowed to Avery's speed and skated beside her.

"Hi Avery."

"Hi Tara, and Rachel."

"So, Avery do you know what your last name is?" Rachel asked.

"Yep, it's Jenkins," she nodded.

"Well, that's a pretty name Avery Jenkins," I said.

"So, do you live in Orting?" Rachel asked.

"How did you know that?" Avery laughed.

"Your mommy told us," Rachel said.

"Yep, and I go to preschool too. My mommy works at the big kid school."

"The big kid school?" I asked.

"Yeah, the one with the big kids like you."

215

"Oh I see," I laughed.

"Is that what you call it, the big kid school?" Rachel laughed.

"Yep," she nodded.

"Avery, why is your sister in a wheelchair?" Rachel asked.

"Because she doesn't feel good." Avery shook her head.

"She doesn't feel good?"

"Yeah, she's sick. We took her to the doctor today and that's why I get to go skating. Mommy said I was a good girl," she smiled.

"Oh, I see. You are a very good girl." Rachel looked at me with a puzzled look on her face. She shrugged her shoulders and shook her head.

I shook my head and shrugged my shoulders back at her. I figured Avery was too young to understand why her sister was in the wheelchair.

"What's your sister's name Avery?" Rachel asked.

"My sister's name is Ashlyn. She's my cutie pie. She likes to watch me skate." Avery waved as we skated by her mom and sister who were on the other side of the short wall.

"Okay, you have fun skating, we're going to skate fast now, bye. We'll see you in a little while," Rachel said.

Rachel and I took off around the rink. We skated slower as soon as we were on the opposite side of the rink from Avery.

"Tara, what are we going to do?"

"I think we should wait until Peggy gets here. She'll know what to do."

"Well, at least we have Avery's last name and we know she lives in a town called Orting."

"And we know her mom works at the high school too Rachel."

"I'd like to talk to Jessica and find out what she knows."

"I'm sure she only knows what she's been told just like Malory and the rest of our parents. Maybe it's just like Peggy said...they probably told her she is one of a select few."

"Yeah, that's a good one Tara," Rachel laughed.

"I know, especially since the list has grown by two in the last few days," I laughed.

We skated around the rink. Rachel and I waved at Avery every time we skated by her. Avery waved back, laughed, and smiled at us.

The announcement came over the speaker telling everyone the skating session was ending and to please slow down and clear the floor.

Rachel and I waited in line to return our skates and pick up our shoes. As soon as we had our shoes on, we headed for the door to find Peggy.

Peggy was already standing inside the lobby waiting for us.

"Did you have fun girls?" Peggy asked.

Avery walked by us on her way to the door.

"Bye Rachel, bye Tara," she said.

"Hey! You girls told me your names were Martha and Rita. What's going on here?" Jessica questioned as she pushed her daughter Ashlyn in the wheelchair and stopped next to us. "Why'd you lie to us?" Jessica demanded to know.

"What's going on girls?" Peggy asked.

217

"Yes, what's going on girls?" Jessica asked.

"I'm sorry Ma'am, what did the girls do?"

"They told me their names were Martha and Rita and I just heard my daughter Avery call them Rachel and Tara. I just want to know why they're lying. That's all."

Peggy looked at Rachel and me.

Rachel and I pointed at Avery who was standing by the door waiting for her mom and sister.

Peggy looked at Avery and her mouth flew open.

"Oh my." Peggy stood looking at Avery. She didn't know what else to say.

"Are these your daughters?" Jessica asked Peggy.

"I don't believe I caught your name," Peggy said.

"Her name is Jessica," Rachel, and I said.

"Well, Jessica, I think we should sit down and talk," Peggy said.

"Sit down and talk?" Jessica was confused. "Look lady, I just wanted to know why your kids are lying to either me or my daughter, that's all. That's all I want to know. I don't have time to sit down and talk. Never mind." Jessica pushed the wheelchair towards the door. Avery pushed the door open so her mom could get the chair out the door.

We followed them out into the parking lot, and watched as Jessica put Ashlyn into the car, buckled her in, and shut the door. Then she popped the trunk, put the wheelchair in, and slammed it shut. Avery climbed into the car by herself and buckled up her car seat.

"Jessica, I really think we need to talk," Peggy said.

"Look lady, what was your name? And could you give me your real name. Not a fake name like your daughters gave. Anyway I need to get home." Jessica shook her head and climbed in the driver's seat.

Peggy leaned in the car door.

"My name is Peggy and the girl's names are Tara and Rachel. They're clones like your daughter Avery," Peggy whispered to Jessica.

Jessica looked at me and Rachel and her mouth dropped. She sat staring at us shaking her head and didn't say a word for a couple of minutes.

After the shock wore off, she blinked her eyes, took a deep breath, and looked at the three of us who were still standing in the rain waiting for a response.

"I think we should talk," she said.

"Okay, why don't you follow me to my house," Peggy said.

"Oh, I can't. I need to get Ashlyn home. Come to our house," Jessica insisted.

"Okay, I'll follow you," Peggy said.

Rachel and I followed Peggy to her car, which was on the other side of the parking lot.

"Boy, I wasn't expecting this," she said as she unlocked the doors.

"I know, who would have thought," I said as I climbed in the backseat.

"It's funny, I've gone my whole life without thinking about clones and now you girls are everywhere," Peggy laughed.

"Apparently we're a popular series just like Barbie Dolls," Rachel laughed.

"I'm still looking for the manufacturers stamp on my butt. I haven't found it yet," I laughed.

We followed Jessica's car out of the parking lot and down the road. It was a dark rainy afternoon and traffic was slow. It seemed to take forever to drive from Tacoma to the little town of Orting were Jessica lived.

"I wonder why she would drive so far to go to the skating rink. You would think there would be a rink closer to her house," Rachel said as we pulled up in Jessica's driveway behind her.

We climbed out from Peggy's car and helped Jessica carry the girls into her house.

"My husband is out of town on business. We can talk in the living room. Please, go in the living room and have a seat," Jessica said. "I'll be right with you as soon as I get Ashlyn settled in and give her, her meds. Avery... Sweetie... why, don't you show your friends where the living room is... for mommy."

"Okay, come on Rachel and Tara I'll show you." Avery grabbed our hands and led us to the living room. Peggy was not far behind us.

"Here's the living room," Avery said. "You can sit on the couch," she let go of our hands and patted the cushions where she wanted us to sit.

"Why, thank you Avery," Peggy smiled and sat on the couch.

"Do you want to see my dolls?" Avery asked.

"Sure, we'd love to see them," I smiled.

"Okay, you stay here. I'll be right back," she said excitedly and ran out of the living room.

They had pictures of Ashlyn and Avery on every wall of the living room. The girls looked nothing alike.

220

I thought of how I always felt. I didn't look like my family. My mom would always reassure me I looked like one of my great-grandmothers. She would never say which and she'd never show me a picture. She would always tell me they were old, and they didn't take many pictures back in the olden days.

"I don't look like my brother either," Rachel whispered.

"Well, of course we don't," I said. "Hey Peggy, does Selena have a brother or sister?"

"Yes, my nephew is a few years older than her."

"Does he have anything wrong with him?"

"Why?" Peggy questioned.

"Well, it's strange all of us girls have a brother or sister who has health problems," I said.

"What do you mean? Lots of people have health problems."

"Yeah, maybe it's a coincidence," Rachel said.

"Well, what kind of health problems are you talking about?" Peggy asked.

"Well, my brother has allergies, Rachel's brother has cancer, Amanda's brother has epilepsy, Nichole's brother died before she was born, and Avery's sister has health problems too."

"Come to think of it, my nephew came close to dying when he was a baby. He had some rare form of kidney disease. That's a little strange." Peggy shook her head. "Maybe they're clones," she whispered.

Rachel and I looked at her.

"Who knows?" We looked at each other, shrugged our shoulders and shook our heads.

"Look Rachel!" I pointed at the picture of Avery on the small wooden pony.

"She has one too." Rachel stood up to take a closer look.

"One what?" Peggy asked.

"The wooden pony Avery's sitting on, in the picture. We each have one," I said.

"That's odd," Peggy said, "I wonder if Selena has one too?"

"She probably does," Rachel nodded. "Amanda has one too."

"I wonder what the significance of the pony is," Peggy said.

Avery came into the room carrying her dolls under her arm.

"Do you want to play dolls with me?" Avery handed us each a doll.

"Sure," Peggy said.

"Okay, I'm going to go get my tea set and we can have a tea party." Avery smiled, set the rest of her dolls on the couch next to Peggy, and headed out of the room again.

A few minutes later Jessica came into the room.

"So, you girls are just like Avery?" she asked.

Rachel and I nodded yes.

"I didn't know they had older girls. I thought they were all around Avery's age. They told me I was one of a very small group of woman who were selected to participate in the clone program."

"It sounds like they told more than one of you that," Peggy said.

"How many?"

"There are seven we know of. That includes Avery," Peggy said.

"Seven? So, you know Cassidy, Rory, and Tilly. Who's the seventh one?"

"Cassidy, Rory, and Tilly are those names of the clone girls in your small group?" Peggy shook her head and sighed. "That's three more we'll have to add to the list."

Rachel and I looked at each other, shook our heads, and sighed.

"You mean you weren't talking about them?" Jessica looked shocked. "Wow! We thought our four girls were the first and only clones," Jessica shook her head. "So... you're saying there's ten. Do you know the other clones and how old they are?"

"Well, Selena is fourteen," Peggy said.

"There's Amanda and Nichole. They're both fourteen. And Isabella is nine," I said.

"Our birthdays fall on the eleventh. Is Avery's birthday on the eleventh?" Rachel asked.

"Yes, her birthday is February eleventh. The other clone's mothers gave birth to them on the eleventh too. Cassidy's is January eleventh, Rory's is March eleventh, and Tilly's is April eleventh," Jessica nodded.

"So, did they schedule the delivery on the eleventh?" Peggy asked.

"No, I went into labor and had her on the eleventh. The women in my group had the girls naturally, the date was never set."

"Really, I wonder what day the original was born. I bet it was the eleventh," Rachel said.

"Original?" Jessica asked.

"I'm talking about the girl we were cloned from," Rachel laughed.

"Oh, yeah they told us the donor's birthday was on the eleventh. They never told us which month," Jessica smiled.

"So, pardon me for asking, but what's wrong with Ashlyn?" Peggy asked.

"She has leukemia. They diagnosed her when she was a baby and they didn't think she would live to see her first birthday. She's six now and by the grace of God she's still holding on. We were at the doctor's today and he told me he'll be surprised if she makes it to her next birthday." Jessica shook her head and sighed, "It's been tough."

"I can see it has been, I'm so sorry," Peggy said.

"Jessica, don't let the doctors tell you that stuff and make you feel bad. My brother has been fighting cancer all his life, and he's a teenager now," Rachel said. "You keep fighting for her."

"Thank you. What was your name?" Jessica asked.

"I'm Rachel."

"So girls, why did you give me fake names?" Jessica asked.

"We're on the run. We've been running for months now," Rachel said.

"Why are you running?"

"The government agency that started the clone program wants me dead," I said.

"Yeah, they probably want me dead too. But we're not sure if they know we're together," Rachel said.

"Hold on girls. Why would the government agency want you dead?"

"It's in your contract," Peggy said, "Do you have a copy of the contract you made with them when you signed up for the clone program?"

"Yes, I have it," Jessica said.

"Did you read the fine print?"

"No I didn't."

"Most people don't read the fine print on contracts, but they should." Peggy shook her head. "Can I see the contract?"

"Sure let me go get it." Jessica left the room.

Avery came into the room carrying a little bag, which she set on the floor. She took a small blanket from the bag and placed it neatly on the floor. She pulled a tea set from the bag, and placed the teapot in the middle of the blanket.

"Are you ready for tea?" she asked as she went over to the couch, picked up her dolls, moved them onto the floor, and sat next to them on the blanket.

"We are," I said as I took a seat on the floor with the little doll in my hand.

Rachel and Peggy moved from the couch to the floor with their baby dolls.

Avery pretended to pour us each a cup of tea and set the cup in front of us on the blanket.

"Here you go," she said.

"Thank you Avery." I picked up my teacup and pretended to drink.

"Mmm, that's good," I said.

"Yes, it's delicious," Peggy said.

"Simply fabulous," Rachel said.

Avery laughed and pretended to drink her tea.

"Would you like a crumpet?" she asked.

"Yes, I would love one," Peggy said.

"I'll take two crumpets Darling," I said.

"Yes, Yes. Two crumpets for me too," Rachel said.

Avery pretended to put crumpets on the small plates and put them in front of us.

We pretended to eat the crumpets.

"Here's the contract," Jessica said when she came into the living room. "Oh, I didn't see you're having tea and crumpets. May I join you Sweetie?" she asked Avery.

"Yes," Avery laughed. She pretended to pour Jessica tea and handed her a plate with imaginary crumpets. Jessica pretended to drink the tea and eat the crumpets.

"Your cooking is wonderful my dear Sweetie Pie."

"Thank you my dear Sweetie Pie Mommy," Avery smiled.

"Here's the contract Peggy." Jessica handed Peggy the contract and continued to drink the make-believe tea.

Peggy read the contract while sipping on her imaginary tea.

"Here it is, here it is." Peggy read the contract aloud, *"If for any reason this experiment does not fulfill government expectations the human clone specimens will be terminated."*

"What?" Jessica shrieked. "It doesn't say that, does it? They went over the contract with us. I don't remember anyone reading that part to me. I think I'd remember."

"Well, maybe they just skipped through that part," I said.

"I think that's a pretty important part for them to be skipping though don't you think?" Jessica was angry. "You know the only reason we decided to join the program was because they came to us. They knew we had one sick child, and they knew I wasn't able to have any more children. They came to us because we fit the criteria they were looking for."

"What? You mean they were looking for people who had a sick child at home and couldn't have more children?" Peggy asked.

"Yes, and we had to live in a small town with no desire to move to a big city."

"Was there anything else?"

"Just the usual, you have to pass a criminal background check and be a law-abiding citizen, that's all."

"I wonder why they want you to live in a small town," Rachel said.

"Probably so they wouldn't have this problem...you know... clones bumping into each other and experiencing the shock of their lives. I can't imagine what it's like running into someone who looks exactly like you?" Peggy said.

"It's a shock all right," Rachel said.

"Yeah, and Avery is the biggest shock so far," I said.

"It says *"If there are any reoccurring illnesses or injuries they have the right to revoke your parental rights*," Peggy said as she read the contract.

"Yes, I remember going over all of that," Jessica said. "They said they were looking out for the best interest of the child," Jessica nodded.

"It says, *you must have the specimen brought to the testing facility bi-annually for a one-week testing*

227

period, which may be more frequent if deemed necessary to the health and well-being of the specimen."

"Yes, it's a lot more frequent than bi-annually and it's never just a week. They call us sometimes three to four times a year and tell us they want to make sure she remains healthy. They have us give her sleeping meds in her water. They put her in a plastic sleep chamber, pick her up in a van, put her on a plane and sometimes we don't see her for weeks at a time."

"You just let them take her?" I asked.

"Well, I already have one very sick child at home. I really want Avery to be as healthy as she can possibly be," Jessica nodded.

"It also says...*if the specimen lives to the age of eighteen and when the specimen becomes an adult. The specimen is no longer subject to the guidance of the parental guardians. The specimen will be placed into custody of this government agency for further scientific studies and experiments for the betterment of mankind.*"

"What?" everyone gasped.

"They didn't go over that with me either." Jessica picked Avery up off the blanket, set her in her lap, and held her tight. "Oh baby, what are we going to do? What has mommy gotten you into?"

"Peggy, if you're not Tara or Rachel's mom, how are you involved in this?"

"Jessica, has the clone agency contacted you lately?" Peggy asked.

"Yeah, they contacted me a few weeks ago. They said they would be contacting me with a date and time for me to have Avery ready to go to the island for testing. She went through a month of testing in April. They told me they need to retest her because they were having some kind of problems with the testing equipment. It's been fixed now so they want to bring her back for more accurate test results."

"No, they want her to come in because they're getting ready to shut down the entire operation I bet," Peggy said.

"They are going to terminate her along with the rest of us," Rachel said.

"They wouldn't do that, would they?" Jessica screeched.

"Our friend Jess, who is a police officer, told us cloning humans is against the law in all fifty states. He said it sounds like one government agency is responsible for making us and if they are caught doing illegal activities they will get themselves into a lot of hot water. They could be fired from their government jobs and they could go to jail for breaking the law. That's why they want us back and they want us all dead. They are trying to clean up the mess they made before it causes a big scandal. If the president finds out, heads will roll," I said.

"Why haven't you gone to the police?" Jessica asked.

"We don't know which police agency to trust," I said.

"Yeah, if we told the police this story they would laugh us out of the police station. They would try to send us back home to our parents, but our parents have moved and we don't know where they are. So, they would end up putting us in foster care, and the next thing we know the agency would find out where we were and take us to the island for termination," Rachel said.

"Peggy if you're not their mom, how are you involved in all of this?"

"I was coming home from my sister's house and I met the girls on the train, they both look like my niece Selena. I was shocked when they told me the whole story. After talking to Tara and Rachel, I realize just how much danger my niece is in. I had no idea she was a clone. I'm trying to help the girls and my niece."

"How is your niece doing?" Jessica asked.

"I don't know, she wasn't at my sister's house when I was there. My sister said Selena was camping with her friends for the week. I didn't question her. I don't have kids, so I don't pay attention to when kids are supposed to be in school. Selena's friend Owen and the girls brought it to my attention. I don't know why my sister would let Selena go camping when she should've been in school. It makes me wonder if she was taken to the island and is in real danger."

"I don't know what to do. Should I pack the kids up and go into hiding? I don't want to lose my Avery." Jessica kissed her on the cheek and sat her on the blanket. Avery went back to playing with her tea set and dolls.

"I don't know what to do either." Peggy shook her head.

"I guess we'll have to put our heads together and come up with something," Jessica said.

"Yes, we need to come up with something. Well, we better get going it's getting late. Here's my phone number. You can text me or call me anytime. I'm going to be in Sacramento tomorrow meeting with a friend of Tara and Rachel's who may be able to help us," Peggy said as she handed Jessica her business card, stood up, and put the baby doll on the couch.

"Let me give you my number too." Jessica left the room, came back with her number written on a piece of paper and handed it to Peggy. "If you find out anything at all, please call me."

"I will Jessica. Just hold on and don't do anything out of the ordinary, I'll keep you posted."

"Bye Avery, can I get a hug?" I reached out my arms to her. Avery set her dolls on the floor, came over, and wrapped her arms around my neck.

"Bye Tara, maybe you can go skating with me again."

"Maybe I can," I said as I squeezed her tight.

"I want a hug too please." Rachel put her arms out for a hug.

Avery wrapped her arms around Rachel's neck.

"I like you two, you're nice," Avery said.

"We like you too," Rachel smiled.

"Okay girls let's go." Peggy headed for the door. Rachel and I stood up, put the dolls on the couch, and headed out the door.

"Bye," we said.

We pulled out of the driveway. Jessica and Avery were standing at the window waving at us.

"Well, I wouldn't have believed it if I wouldn't have seen it with my own eyes." Peggy shook her head.

"Believed what?" I asked.

"Yeah, believed what?" Rachel asked.

"The line which read... *If for any reason this experiment does not fulfill government expectations, the human clone specimens will be terminated.*" Why would they give people hope and take it away like that."

"Give them hope?" I asked.

"Yes, they gave all the parents who are involved hope. They let them think they're going to get a special child to love, since they can't have a child on their own. Instead the parents get to worry if the government's going to take their children and terminate them as if the children were never real people. The child's just a specimen for the sole purpose of the government to use to conduct experiments. This whole thing makes me angry."

"I know, my life was just fine before this happened. I could've spent the rest of my life never knowing. I would've been happy if I never found out. Except... if I would've never found out, I would've never met Rachel, or you or all the rest of the nice people I know now."

"I feel the same way," Rachel said.

"Hey Peggy, if the government picked people who couldn't have kids then I think the Stevens must have adopted Billy," I said.

"Why do you think that?" Peggy asked.

"Because... Billy is Amanda's younger brother."

"Well, maybe they did or sometimes after adopting a child people who couldn't have a baby end up pregnant. It happens all the time." Peggy shook her head.

"Oh," I said. It made me wonder about Billy and if he was safe.

I watched out the window at the pouring rain.

"You girls want to listen to the radio?" Peggy asked.

"Sure," Rachel and I said.

Peggy turned the channel to top-forty music, and we listened to the radio on the drive home.

"Are you girls getting hungry?" Peggy asked.

"A little," I said.

"I am," Rachel said.

"I'm going to stop at Burger Jo's and go through the drive through. Do you like Burger Jo's?"

"Oh yeah, Burger Jo's is my favorite," Rachel said.

"Mine too," I said.

"Good, what would you like to eat?"

"The chicken and mashed potato meal please," Rachel, and I said at the same time.

"Okay, I guess we're all having the Chicken meals tonight," Peggy said as she pulled into Burger Jo's and went through the drive-thru.

The chicken meal was a nice treat for the drive home.

K J Scott

CHAPTER 9

Good Days and Bad Days

Peggy pulled the car into the garage, we climbed out, and headed into the house. She let Jomba out of the kennel and brought him in the house with us.

"Okay girls, are you ready for some ice cream?"

"Ice cream, I'd love some," Rachel and I said.

Peggy opened the freezer and looked inside.

"I have rocky road, chocolate chip mint, peach pie, and white chocolate raspberry truffle, which kind do you want?"

"I'll have the chocolate chip mint," I said.

"Me too," Rachel said.

"Me too." Peggy grabbed the bowls from the cupboard and scooped the ice cream into them. She pulled spoons out of the drawer and set them on the counter. "Dig in girls."

We each grabbed a bowl of ice cream and a spoon and sat at the kitchen table. We ate our ice cream and watched out the window at the pouring rain.

"Peggy, does it always rain like this here?"

"Always," Peggy smiled. "We get a large amount of rain here. That's why it's always green outside. I think this is the most beautiful state in North America. Of course, I was born and raised here. Most people from other states can't stand our rain. They come for a year, maybe longer and then when they've had enough rain they pack up their

235

belongings and move back to whatever dry state they came from. To me, the rain is very soothing."

"Soothing? How do you mean?" Rachel asked.

"There's always a nice rhythm to the raindrops. It makes white noise which drowns out other sounds. It makes me feel very comfortable."

"White noise?"

"Yes, white noise. Haven't you ever heard of white noise?"

"I've heard of it, but I'm not sure if I remember what white noise is exactly," I said.

"You can think of white noise as twenty-thousand tones all playing at the same time," Peggy said.

"Twenty-thousand tones?" Rachel and I looked at each other.

"Here's one way you can think of it. Let's say two people are talking at the same time. Your brain can usually 'pick out' one of two voices, and actually, listen to it, and understand it. If three people are talking simultaneously, your brain can probably still pick out one voice. However, if a thousand people are talking at once, there's no way your brain can pick out one voice. It turns out a thousand people talking together sounds a lot like white noise. So... when the rain is pouring down it creates white noise, it's essentially creating a source of one-thousand voices. The dog barking next door makes it one-thousand-one voices, and your brain can't pick it out anymore. It works the same as having a fan going continuously," Peggy said. "I like my rain better than a fan."

"Wow, you are very smart Peggy," I said.

"Well, thank you," Peggy smiled. She took a bite of her ice cream and put her bowl in the freezer. "I'll have to eat the rest later. I'm going to take a shower and head to bed girls. It's been a long day and I'm very tired. Good night girls," she said as she headed up the stairs.

"Night," Rachel and I said.

Rachel and I sat quietly, ate our ice cream, and stared out the window at the rain.

"White noise," Rachel said. "That's a beautiful sound."

"Yeah, it's very soothing now that Peggy pointed it out to me."

"I know, just sitting here listening to the rain coming down makes me feel all warm and fuzzy inside."

"Yeah, warm and fuzzy," I said as I stared out the window in almost a trance-like state of mind.

"Tara? Are you okay?"

"Yeah, I'm fine. I was just sitting here thinking about things. About the white noise, I guess. What Peggy said made a lot of sense to me. White noise drowns out the sounds. I don't know, I just have this feeling I've been someplace where there was a lot of white noise," I said.

We sat watching the rain pour out of the sky and I felt at peace. Rachel asked me a question, but I was thinking about white noise and didn't hear her.

"I didn't hear you Rachel... what did you say?"

"What do you want to do Tara?" she asked. "Do you want to play a game of cards?"

"Yeah, let's play cards."

I went around, grabbed the cards out of the cabinet, and handed them to her.

"Here you can shuffle."

After Rachel shuffled, I dealt the cards. We played Old Maid for a while, then a long game of War. After that, we were tired of card games.

"What time is it now?" Rachel asked.

I looked over at the clock.

"It's ten-fifty-two," I said.

"I'm tired. I think I'll go to bed," Rachel said.

"Yeah me too."

I put the cards away and followed Rachel upstairs.

We put our pajamas on and climbed in bed.

"Rachel I can remember when I was a little girl like Avery. I played with my dolls and had tea parties with my friends just like she does. I remember when I was missing *time...* and my mom would tell me... she didn't know what I was talking about. Here... all this time she knew exactly what I was talking about. I suppose Jessica probably does the same thing to Avery. I guess it can't be helped."

"I wonder what they do to us in the testing facility. I wonder why I can't remember any of it," Rachel whispered.

"Maybe it's a good thing we don't remember. They probably poke us with needles, take our blood, and examine it under a microscope. Yeah, I think it's best we don't remember any of it Rachel."

"You're probably right. If we remembered it, we'd probably never let them take us there. We'd be kicking, screaming, and running away. It would be just like going to the dentist, I'm sure."

"Rachel, you don't like going to the dentist either?"

"No, but who does. The last time I went to the dentist, he stuck his fingers in my mouth, and I bit him," Rachel laughed.

"You bit the dentist?" I laughed.

"Well, I didn't mean to, he just had big fat fingers and I had a small mouth. It was an accident... really... it was. He made me say I was sorry," Rachel laughed.

"Were you sorry?"

"I told you... it was an accident. But, no I wasn't sorry," Rachel said.

"I didn't think so," I laughed. "Goodnight Rachel."

"Goodnight Tara."

I listened to the sound of the rain hitting the window. The white noise was soothing like Peggy said. I fell asleep in a matter of minutes.

I woke up the next morning feeling great. The rain was still hitting the window, but now I looked at the rain differently. It made me smile.

Rachel wasn't in the room. I climbed out of bed, and headed to the bathroom to take a shower. I tripped over Jomba who lay at the foot of the bed.

"Jomba... why are you lying right in the middle of the floor?" I yelled as I picked myself up off the floor. I shook my head, went into the bathroom, and took a shower.

I opened the bathroom door and tripped over Jomba who was lying in front of the doorway.

"Jomba, what are you doing here?" I yelled as I picked myself up from the floor. "Darn dog."

I dressed and went downstairs.

Rachel was sitting at the kitchen table eating a bowl of cereal and staring out the window at the pouring rain.

"Hey Rachel, do you know why Jomba is in our room?"

"Oh Peggy took him for a walk earlier this morning and let him in the house. She left for the office already. She wants to get a bunch of paperwork done before she flies to Sacramento for her one o'clock interview with Kate. She said she'll be back later this evening," Rachel said.

"She said she'll be back this evening?"

"Yep."

"So she's flying to Sacramento and back, in one day?" I questioned.

"I asked her the same thing. She has her own plane."

"She does?"

"Yep."

"What time did she leave?"

"Six-thirty."

"You've been up since six-thirty Rachel?"

"I've only been up for an hour it's seven-thirty now and I woke up feeling great."

"Me too."

I grabbed a box of cereal and poured it into a bowl. I turned around just in time to see Jomba sprawled on the kitchen floor in front of me with his large body taking up my walking space. I stepped over him and put the box away.

"I'm beginning to wonder if Jomba's trying to kill me," I said.

"What? Why would you say that?" Rachel laughed.

"Maybe the government hired Jomba to trip me to death. Maybe this is part of the termination process. I swear he's trying to kill me. If I trip over him again I'm going to fall and hurt myself. I won't be able to pull my poor body up off the floor," I laughed.

"You tripped over Jomba?"

"Twice already."

"Twice?"

"Yeah, he was lying at the end of the bed and I didn't see him. I fell right over him. Then I was coming out of the bathroom and he was right in front of the bathroom door waiting to trip me. Now he's in the kitchen trying to kill me. If I wasn't paying attention I bet he would have lay down, right in front of me and I would have tripped over him again."

"It sounds like he's following you around. He was following me earlier. I think he's trying to protect us."

"I wish he'd stay in one spot for a while."

"I'm sure he will. He's probably trying to decide which one of us is the real Selena and which ones the fake," Rachel laughed.

"I wonder if Selena's on the island," I said as I grabbed the milk and poured it on my cereal.

"I was wondering the same thing. Well, it sounds like they're going to take Avery there soon. I wonder what Jessica's going to do."

"Who knows, I can't believe she didn't read the contract."

"It doesn't sound like our parents read the whole thing either Tara."

"I know, from what Jessica said it sounds like they had someone go over the contract with her, but the person who was going over it skipped all the important parts. I don't think Jessica or our parents would've signed it if they knew it said all the stuff about terminating specimens."

"Malory Beck signed it and she knew what it said. She's the one who told Amanda what it said." Rachel took her bowl to the sink, rinsed it, put it in the dishwasher, and sat on the floor next to Jomba.

"Yeah, but she probably didn't read it before she signed it. She probably read it sometime after that and that's why she went crazy when Nichole was in the car accident. Remember the contract said *"If there are any reoccurring illnesses or injuries, they have the right to revoke parental rights."* I'm surprised your mom let you anywhere near a motorcycle. One broken leg and you would have been taken away for good." I shook my head.

"Oh no, I bet my mom never read the contract," Rachel gasped. She thought for a moment. "Oh well, I'm really glad she didn't. I really like motocross. I have my best memories of my mom, dad and my brother Robert at motocross events. I don't know how the government agency can be so cruel. I mean really, revoking parental rights. Who do they think they are?"

"They're the government, that's who they think they are." I shook my head.

"Tara, this is so crazy."

I finished my cereal, rinsed the bowl, and put it in the dishwasher.

"Crazy for sure and odd, very odd." I shook my head.

"Yeah it is... hey, Tara do you want to play a game of cards?"

"No, not right now, the game of War we played last night was enough for me for a while, it took forever for you to win."

"I know, you just wouldn't lose," Rachel laughed.

"Believe me, I tried more than once to give my cards to you. You just wouldn't take them," I laughed.

"Let's go watch Mystery ER on TV," Rachel said.

"Okay."

We went downstairs and sat on the couch. Rachel turned on the TV.

"Mystery ER isn't on right now," she said.

"Well, let's find another doctor show," I said.

"Okay."

Rachel surfed through the channels looking for a good doctor show so we could learn something new today.

"I wonder what Kate's going to say when Peggy tells her we're here," Rachel said.

"I don't know, Kate's probably going to be surprised. The last time she saw us we we're leaving her house to get on the boat. She's probably going to freak out, because we're all the way in Washington now."

"Yeah, she will freak out, especially if she's been watching the news and heard about what happened to Danny and Drake in San Diego. She's probably been wondering what happened to us, since they don't ever say anything about us on the news."

"Hey, I need to watch the news and see if they say anything about Danny and Drake. I'd like to know how they're doing. I wonder if they're still in the ICU," I said.

"Okay, I'll see if I can find anything on the news about them. They're probably at home by now Tara. We didn't see anything about them on the news yesterday and we probably won't see anything today either. You know the news stations only report bad news," Rachel said as she surfed the channels looking for a news station. She stopped on the fox news channel.

"I know, if it's good news, they never say anything about anything. You never hear about the boy scout who helped the little old lady cross the street." I shook my head.

"Tara, the only time you hear about stuff like that is if the little old lady were hit by a bus... then they'd put it on the news," Rachel laughed.

"You are so right," I laughed.

"You know I can picture Peggy and Kate sitting in a room together. I can picture the look on Kate's face when Peggy explains to her we are at her house safe and warm," Rachel said.

"Me too, I can picture Kate smiling and hugging Peggy," I said.

"I wonder what she's going to do when she hears her niece is probably a clone," I said.

"She's going to freak out. Especially if she doesn't already know, you and I are clones," Rachel said.

"Drake and Danny Parker, sons of Peter Parker the CEO of Foltex, died last night, due to complications from their near drowning. The two teens were admitted to Scripps Mercy Hospital after a boating accident, which occurred over a week ago. The teens remained in the ICU until the family reached the decision to take them off life support.

The bodies of the two boys will be flown to their hometown, Windyn California. Their funerals will be held Thursday. Peter Parker has stated 'The family has suffered an insurmountable loss this year with the passing of their oldest son Dillon less than a month ago. The family is asking for complete privacy while they deal with the loss of their children."

I was numb. I couldn't believe what I heard.

"Oh no... Tara, what did they say? I don't think I heard it right. Did they say Danny and Drake died? Tara... did you hear it? Tara... did you hear it?" Rachel cried.

I sat motionless not saying a word. I couldn't believe what I just heard.

"Tara...Drake...Tara..." Rachel cried.

"What did you say?" I asked. Nothing was sinking into my head.

"Tara...Danny, and Drake died. They died Tara," Rachel screamed at me.

I didn't move. I sat motionless staring at the TV screen. Rachel was bawling.

"Tara, are you okay," Rachel asked.

I was feeling numb.

"It can't be true!" I started to shake. "It can't be true... can it, Rachel? Rachel, it can't be true... can it?" I burst into tears. Rachel grabbed me and hugged me.

We both bawled.

"He can't be gone Rachel... He can't," I sobbed. "I can't take it Rachel... I just can't take it."

Rachel held on tight and didn't let go.

"Tara, Drake saved my life," Rachel sobbed.

245

"I know... Danny saved mine," I cried. "Rachel... am I really here or is this just a bad dream?"

"It's a bad dream Tara," Rachel cried. "It's a bad dream."

"I want to wake up...Rachel I want to wake up," I screamed. "I don't want to feel this way anymore," I cried. I let go of Rachel. "I think I... need to lie down for a while."

Rachel wiped the tears from her eyes, reached over, and wiped the tears from mine too.

She grabbed my hand, helped me to my feet and led me up the stairs to the bedroom.

I lay down on the bed and Rachel covered me with a blanket. She kissed me on the forehead went around to the other side of the bed and lay down facing me.

"I think I need to lie down too. Drake saved my life and now he's gone." She covered herself with a blanket and cried.

Rachel wrapped her arms around me and I held on to her and cried.

I closed my eyes and listened to the sound of the rain hitting fiercely against the window.

"You know... Peggy is right about the rain. You can't hear anything but the rain. It's a very soothing feeling when it's raining. It is a white noise just like she said it was. It's drowning out the thoughts in my head... but it's not drowning out the pain in my heart," I whispered. The tears continued to stream down my face as I held onto Rachel. "I don't want to be here Rachel."

I closed my eyes.

I woke up screaming.

"Tara, are you all right?" Rachel asked.

"I dreamed they said on the news Danny and Drake died," I cried.

"Tara, that wasn't a dream," Rachel cried.

"No! Danny can't be dead. He just can't be... I just saw him. He was alive... he was talking to me. He can't be dead... I don't want him to be dead. I cried. "Someone must have killed him. If I could go in and see him that easily, someone else could do the same thing," I sobbed.

"Tara...do you think someone killed them?" Rachel cried. "It's our fault they're gone."

"I know Rachel," I cried. I sat up and looked around the room. "I need to leave this place and go far away." I went downstairs to the kitchen.

"Tara, we can't leave the house. Peggy doesn't want the neighbors to know we're here," Rachel said as she followed me into the kitchen.

"You know what Rachel... I don't really care anymore."

"What do you mean you don't care anymore?" Rachel asked.

"I mean I don't care anymore. These government people, who are after us, can do whatever they want to me. I just don't care anymore."

"You don't mean that Tara."

"Yeah, I do... If they're going to take away all the people I love. Then what's the point of living? I don't want them to kill everyone I know just to find me." I shook my head, "I think the Parker family alone, has suffered enough... don't you think?"

"Yeah, they've suffered a lot."

"Don't forget the other people who have suffered? My parents, your parents, our brothers, Billy and Billy's parents I'm sure that's just the beginning of the list. I wonder what they're doing to

Peggy's niece Selena right now. Boy, hurricane Malory left a huge mess for everyone." I shook my head. "I really have to figure things out Rachel."

"Tara, you're scaring me! I don't want you to get yourself too worked up. You know where it leads."

"Yeah, I know where it leads. Right back to crying," I nodded. I sat down at the table.

"Rachel, I need to go there. I need to say good-bye to Danny."

"How are we going to do that Tara? They're looking for us."

"I don't care Rachel. I told you, they can do whatever they want to me. They can kill me if they want. It doesn't matter anymore."

"You say it... but you don't mean it Tara. You're just hurting inside that's all. Let's get our minds off things. Do you want to play a game of cards?"

"No, I really don't feel like it Rachel. I think I need to lie down. I don't feel good." The tears swelled in my eyes.

"Oh Tara!" Rachel hugged me. "We're going to get through this together."

"Right now I can't see how," I said as a tear rolled down my face.

"I know it's hitting too close to your heart right now, but we'll make it through you'll see."

"Hitting close to my heart is an understatement. My heart has been ripped completely out of my chest and shattered into a million pieces," I cried.

"Tara, let's try not to get all worked up again...okay," Rachel bawled.

"Yeah, you're right Rachel," I cried. "I shouldn't get all worked up about my boyfriend dying. I loved him Rachel, now he's gone and there's no reason to get worked up about that!" I was angry.

"Do you want to hit something Tara?"

"I do. I want to hit something hard. I want to hurt it. I want to hurt it until I stop hurting."

"Me too, Tara, me too." Rachel held on to me. "I can't make it go away for you. I wish I could, but I can't."

We went upstairs and lay down again. All the pain I was feeling was exhausting to me.

I dozed off and woke in a panic.

"Rachel, where's Peggy? What time is it? Isn't she supposed to be home by now? I don't want anything to happen to her too."

"I don't know Tara. She didn't say what time she would be back. I hope nothing's happened to her."

"Yeah, me too Rachel, and at this point I couldn't take something else happening to someone I care about," I cried. "Rachel, this stuff doesn't seem to want to go away."

"You mean the pain. I'm sorry Tara, I'm so sorry."

I lay on the bed, looked at the ceiling, and listened to the sound of the rain hitting the window.

"Tara, do you want something to eat?" Rachel asked.

"I'm not hungry." I shook my head.

"But Tara, you need to eat something. We haven't eaten since breakfast. How would you like it if I fixed you a bowl of ice cream? You know, Peggy has Chocolate Chip Mint and a few other flavors in the freezer."

"Well, maybe a little," I sniffed.

249

"Okay, let's go downstairs and get a bowl. I think it will help you to feel a little better. Ice cream always makes us feel better."

"Yeah, I guess you're right," I nodded as I drug myself off the bed and moped down the stairs.

"What kind do you want? There's rocky road, chocolate chip mint, peach pie, and white chocolate raspberry truffle."

"I'll have the white chocolate raspberry truffle," I said.

"Me too."

Rachel took two bowls out of the cupboard and filled them full of ice cream. We sat at the kitchen table and watched out the window at the rain as we ate.

"You know Tara, even though Danny was only in your life for a short time, he made a huge lasting impression on you. He sure knew how to make you smile," Rachel said as she took a bite of ice cream.

"Yeah, he did," I nodded my head and smiled as I remembered the first time we kissed.

"It's good to see a smile on your face Tara. I know it's hard for you."

We sat, ate ice cream, and didn't say another word as we stared out the window at the rain. I didn't feel like talking, I could tell Rachel knew this. Hours went by and we never moved from where we sat.

I heard the sound of the door opening.

"Hi girls, I'm home," Peggy said as she walked in the door with a pizza in her hands.

She handed it to Rachel. Rachel put it on the table and grabbed plates from the cupboard.

"Does anyone want something to drink?" Rachel asked.

"I'll have a water," Peggy said as she headed up the stairs to her room.

"I'll have a water too, please," I said.

Rachel filled the glasses with water from the refrigerator door, and set them on the table.

She opened the box of pizza and handed me a slice. I set it on my plate and waited for Peggy to come downstairs.

"I'll be down in a minute girls, go ahead and start without me," Peggy shouted from upstairs.

Rachel and I waited anyway.

Peggy was down a few minutes later.

"What's with the glum faces girls?" she asked.

"We heard some bad news today," Rachel said.

"Oh you did?" Peggy asked as she took a bite of her pizza. "What bad news?"

"Tara's boyfriend Danny and his brother Drake passed away sometime last night."

"What?" Peggy choked on her pizza. "You mean the two boys you said were in the hospital since last week. Tara, your boyfriend who was talking to you and told you he loved you?"

"Yeah," I said.

"Oh, I'm so sorry to hear that Tara." Peggy reached over and gave me a hug. "This must feel like the worse day ever for you, Tara. I feel so bad for you. A young girl like you shouldn't have to go through something tragic like this. I'm sorry honey, I'm so sorry."

The more Peggy talked the worse I felt. Tears welled up in my eyes and they streamed down my face. I was a mess. I couldn't eat.

"I need to go to bed now," was all I could say. I excused myself from the kitchen table and headed upstairs to bed.

The next morning I woke up, and I was still feeling the pain of losing Danny. I knew the heartache would never go away. I wondered how long it would take before they caught up to me and killed me so I could be with him again. What I had told Rachel about not caring if the government people took my life was still the way I was feeling. I had lost all hope.

I rolled out of bed and skipped the shower. I wasn't feeling the need to be clean. I didn't bother brushing my hair or my teeth. I didn't care.

I went downstairs. Rachel and Peggy were sitting at the kitchen table.

"Hi Tara, how are you feeling today?" Peggy asked.

"I'm okay," I lied.

"Are you sure you're okay? You don't look okay Tara," Rachel said.

"I'm not okay, I just feel like I could die," I nodded my head.

"I understand Tara." Peggy grabbed ahold of my hand. "You've suffered a huge loss."

"Peggy, I need to go to Danny's funeral, is there any way you can make it happen for me? They said it would be held on Thursday in Windyn."

"Tara I don't think it's a good idea." Peggy shook her head.

"Peggy, Danny was my boyfriend. I need to say good-bye to him," I begged.

"I know, I know. I just don't want anything to happen to you Tara."

"The worst has already happened to me Peggy. I don't think they can do anything to me that would be worse than what they've already done," I sobbed. "Look Peggy...Rachel, and I went to Danny's brother Dillon's funeral, and no one knew we were there."

"Yeah, we did," Rachel nodded. "Kate let us borrow a couple of her dresses and hats. No one recognized us all dressed up like that. Even Danny didn't recognize us.

"Really? No one recognized you with all that beautiful red hair?"

"Nope, we wore wigs," Rachel said.

"Okay, okay, I know you are dying inside right now and it would probably be good for you to say good-bye to him. So, let me see what I can do for you." Peggy rubbed my hand and squeezed my fingers gently. "Come. Sit down by me." She patted the chair next to her.

I sat down and looked out the window. It was still raining.

"Why is it always so gloomy out here?" I asked.

"Gloomy? It's not gloomy. Look over there," Peggy pointed. "See the sun peeking through the clouds. There's a rainbow right over there. What's gloomy about a rainbow?"

The rainbow was beautiful, but the way I was feeling I didn't care.

"I guess it's just me," I said.

"Kate said to thank you two girls for thinking of her and she is excited for the new job opportunity. She is going to be in Sacramento looking for a place close to the office for her and Trevor before she starts work next Monday. She told me to tell you

253

she misses the two of you and she isn't going to tell Trevor because she's afraid he'll be so excited he'll tell everyone. She'll wait until they move before she tells him. She must not have heard about Danny and Drake before she left Windyn because she never said a word to me about it."

"She probably didn't find out until she went home last night," Rachel said.

"I'm sure Mr. Parker called her and told her," I said.

"No, Kate says they don't talk at all. They don't want to draw any attention to the fact they know each other. They don't want anyone to know they're working together to find out what's going on at the island. Mr. Parker knows they are bugging his house, and his office in San Diego. No one ever knew the two of you girls stayed at Kate's house so no one has ever bothered her. She says Mr. Parker communicates with her through a third party. She calls him the *mystery man.* If anyone ever asks her she tells them he's a friend from out of town," Peggy smiled. "He brings her papers from Mr. Parker in candy boxes, and she sends papers back to Mr. Parker through him. She says she was able to get into the office where she used to work scanning hospital documents. She was able to email all the scanned documents from the memory on the scanner to her personal email address. She has every name of every patient admitted to the El Amor De Mi Vida hospital in the last year. She put a list together, and she was shocked at the names she saw on it. Both of you girls, Amanda Stevens, and her niece were on the list."

"Is your niece on the list?" Rachel asked.

"Kate didn't know. She is going to check for me. She is going to call me today and let me know if Selena's name was on the list. I'm sure she is."

"So what else did Kate tell you?" I asked.

"She told me they still don't know what government agency runs the clone operation, it's a big mystery. She says she knows they are looking for you and Rachel but they don't know the two of you are together. Tara they think you're with Nichole because you were in San Diego and she's missing too," Peggy said.

"So Amanda's missing again?" Rachel asked.

"Apparently, Kate heard it on the news yesterday. Kate said there was a story about Nichole Beck, an heir to an oil tycoon, who was missing from San Diego. Kate said the news story said they believed she ran away from home and was last seen getting on a train. Kate said the story said her mother Malory Beck, thinks she is headed to Windyn, where she had met Danny Parker while vacationing with her mom and grandparents during the summer," Peggy said.

"Really? Did they show a picture of her on the news?"

"Kate didn't say. She thought it sounded like they had Nichole mixed up with you Tara."

"Did you tell Kate what really happened? Did you tell her Amanda was alive and pretending to be Nichole?" Rachel asked.

"Yes. She had no idea," Peggy said.

"So, Mr. Parker didn't tell her everything," Rachel said.

"Does Mr. Parker know?" Peggy asked.

"Well, I would think one of the boys would have told him. Derek, Damian, and Devin all knew. They were there on the boat with us when we found Amanda and she told us all about Nichole," Rachel said.

"Well, she didn't know. When was it you girls found out Amanda was trying to pass herself off as Nichole?"

"It was a little over a week ago I think. We were just getting into San Diego on the boat."

"I wonder why the story's on the news," Peggy said. "It doesn't make any sense. If they were asking for help to find a missing girl they would post a picture of her on the news."

"But, they can't post a picture of her. If they did, there would be people calling in saying, "I know that girl and her name's not Nichole Beck her name's Rachel Everhart or Tara Magee or Amanda Stevens..." Rachel said.

"... Or Selena Anderson. I get that, so why was it on the news?" Peggy questioned.

"I'll tell you what I think... I think Malory called the news station and put it on the news to keep herself from getting into trouble with the government agency. I wonder if she is hiding Amanda somewhere and told the agency Nichole ran off just so she could keep Amanda to herself?"

"You know Tara, you sound like a detective," Peggy smiled.

"It's all those detective shows she used to watch," Rachel laughed.

CHAPTER 10

Pack a Bag

Peggy's cell phone rang.

"Consolidated Finance, this is Peggy," she said. She listened for a couple of minutes then looked at her watch. "Okay, yes, today at one o'clock, yes that'll work," she listened. "Uh huh, Yes, I can do that." There was a pause. "Yes that'll work, see you there. Bye." Peggy hung up the phone. "That was Kate...something's up... she wanted to know if I could bring the two of you to Sacramento. She said she was able to get a babysitter, and she wanted to meet me at the office at one o'clock."

"Did she say why?" Rachel asked.

"No, she just said it was important. Tara, Windyn is only four hours from there. Then you'd be close to Windyn and you could go to Danny and Drake's funeral tomorrow. What do you think? Are you feeling up to a plane ride?" Peggy asked.

I hugged Peggy and started to cry.

"Thanks Peggy," I said.

"You're going to make it through this Tara." Peggy hugged me and wiped the tear from my cheek. "Okay girls, go upstairs and pack your bag. We're going to take my plane and go to Sacramento."

"I've never been on a plane before," Rachel said as she headed upstairs.

"Neither have I," I said as I followed her.

"Wow, I get to take you on your first plane flight. You're going to love it. I'm excited for you both."

Rachel and I put enough clothes in our backpack to last us two days. We weren't sure how long we would be there, and we wanted extras just in case.

We came out of the room and saw Peggy waiting at the bottom of the stairs with her small overnight bag.

"Are you ready to get going?" she asked.

"Yeah," Rachel said.

"How are you feeling Tara?" Peggy asked.

"I'm not feeling very good right now, but I'm really glad I'm getting out of the house for a couple of days. I was beginning to feel like I was going to suffocate in here," I said.

"This trip will be good for you." Peggy put her arm around me and kissed me on the head. "You're going to be okay. You'll see."

We went into the garage.

"I'm going to run Jomba over to the neighbor's house, I'll be right back," Peggy said as she took Jomba out the side door.

"Bye Jomba. See you later," I said as I hopped in the front seat of the car.

"Bye Jomba," Rachel said as she hopped in the backseat.

It only took Peggy a few minutes before she was back in the garage hopping in the car with us.

"Okay girls, I'm going to need you to lie down until we get out of the neighborhood."

Rachel and I lay down before Peggy opened the garage door.

Peggy backed out and stopped. I heard her roll down the electric window.

"It's Owen," she whispered. "Hi, Owen," she said.

"Hi Peggy, is it all right if I go in and say hi to the girls before I go to school?" he whispered as he stuck his head in the car. "Oh, they're here? Hi girls."

"Hi Owen," Rachel and I whispered.

"Where are you going?" he asked.

"We're going to Sacramento, we'll be back tomorrow night. You can come visit then, okay?"

"Okay, have a safe flight. Bye," Owen said.

"Bye," Rachel and I said.

"Bye," Peggy said as she rolled up her window and took off down the road. "Okay, we're out of the neighborhood girls, you can sit up now."

Peggy drove up one street, turned and went up another then she merged onto a highway. A few minutes later, we were crossing a huge bridge.

"Peggy, this is beautiful here," I said as I looked around at the water and the green trees.

"It sure is, even in the pouring down rain. This is the Tacoma Narrows Bridge."

"Look at the water," Rachel said. "It's way down there."

We crossed the bridge, took an exit, and drove a ways until we came to a little airport. Peggy parked, and we hopped out of the car.

"The plane's over here girls," Peggy said.

We followed her to a hangar with several small planes lined up in a row.

"Wow! Look at all these planes," Rachel said.

"Mine's right here," Peggy pointed.

"Wow! This is your plane?" I asked.

"Yes, it's a small business jet. It seats six including the pilot. Tara, would you like to sit in the copilot's seat?" Peggy asked.

"Yeah, I think I'd like that," I smiled.

"Rachel, you can sit in the copilot seat on the way home. Okay?"

"Sure," Rachel smiled.

Peggy grabbed the blocks from under the plane's tires and set them off to the side. She pushed a button on the side of the plane, pulled a handle, and opened the door. I watched as steps appeared on the other side of the door as she pulled it open.

"Okay girls, wait here I'm going to get my clipboard and check the plane before we take off," Peggy said as she went up the steps and into the plane. "It's only going to take me a few minutes," she shouted.

Rachel and I stood looking at the planes lined up neatly in a row. A few minutes later Peggy came down the steps with a clipboard and pen. She walked around the plane looking it over thoroughly, marking things on her list.

"Okay girls, let's get going." She motioned us to follow her up the steps. "Rachel, pick a seat and buckle up, please. Tara, you can sit right there," she pointed then she closed the plane door.

I sat in the seat next to Peggy and watched while she checked the instruments, turned a few knobs and checked things off her list. Once she was done, she put the clipboard away.

"Okay, are you girls ready?" she asked.

I looked back at Rachel and she was nodding her head. I nodded yes to Peggy.

"Okay, here's a headset. Plug it in so we can talk to each other and we're ready to go," she said as she handed me a headsets and then started the engine.

Peggy drove the little jet to the runway while talking to someone on the radio. Once they cleared her for takeoff, we headed down the runway.

I watched from the window as the rain poured from the sky. I could feel as the plane was gaining speed. It shook as we sped down the runway faster and faster. I could feel the vibration stop as the wheels of the plane left the ground. The plane shook as we gained altitude.

I looked out the window and could see we were getting farther away from the ground.

Next, we flew through what appeared to be fog and soon we were above the clouds looking down on them. I saw blue sky and the sun shining brightly from this side of the clouds.

"This is beautiful," I said.

"Yeah, beautiful," Peggy said. "The clouds look like fluffy cotton pillows."

I liked the view from the sky better than the view from the train.

"Okay, it looks like clear skies ahead." Peggy said.

"Peggy, how long does it take to go from Washington to Sacramento?" I asked.

"Speak into the mic Tara, I can hardly hear you," Peggy said.

"Oh, sorry," I said as I adjusted the mic closer to my mouth. "So tell me, how long is the flight?"

"It's an hour and a half, that's all."

"Really?" I said. "That's faster than the train."

"It sure is," Peggy laughed.

I saw the ocean and mountains at the same time. I watched as the big jets flew above us and small planes, flew below us.

"Okay girls, we're going to be landing soon," Peggy said. Then she talked to someone and asked if she was clear for landing. Once they said yes she headed down towards the small airport runway and landed the plane softly.

"Peggy, why were you taking the train anyways? Flying is so much faster," Rachel said.

"I like the train. I don't take it very often, but when I do, I seem to get a lot of work done and no one bothers me. Besides it's very relaxing to me, because I don't have to drive."

"I like the train, but I like the airplane better," Rachel said.

"Me too," I said.

"I took flight training while I was in college just for fun. I think it was the best thing I have ever done. It keeps me out of airports," Peggy laughed.

Peggy parked near the hangars, grabbed her clipboard and made some notes. When she finished she opened the cabin door.

"Watch your step," she said as we followed her off the plane. Once she had the door closed, we followed her to the parking lot. "My car's right over here girls," she pointed.

"You have two cars Peggy?" I asked.

"Yes, I'm back and forth a lot," Peggy said. "Hop in girls."

Peggy unlocked the doors with her key fob. I took the backseat and let Rachel sit up front.

When we arrived at Peggy's office, she unlocked the back door and led us down the hall to a large room with a big oblong table and lots of chairs.

"Okay, you girls sit in here. It's only nine-thirty. I'm going to run and get doughnuts. I'll be right back. Oh, and there's a stack of magazines on the shelf if you want something to do. Kate said she'd be here at one o'clock," Peggy said. She went out the door and shut it behind her.

"What do you want to read Tara? There's Consumer Report, Time, Money, O the Oprah Magazine, Forbes, Entrepreneur, Fortune, and Inc," Rachel said.

"I'll take O the Oprah Magazine," I said.

"Okay, I wanted that one too, but you can have it," she said as she handed me the magazine. "I'll look through the stack and see if I can find last months. Then we can trade when we're done."

"Thanks Rachel."

I started thumbing through the magazine. A few minutes later Peggy was back with a box of doughnuts and orange juice.

"Here girls, I know this isn't the most nutritious meal but it'll do for now. I have a pile of papers on my desk I want to look through before Kate shows up. The bathroom's down the hall to your left if you need it. I'll be in my office it's down the hall to your right, the door next to the lobby. I called and gave my employees the day off, so we won't be disturbed. I'll see you in a while," Peggy said as she grabbed a doughnut and a bottle of juice and headed out the door.

"Okay," Rachel and I said.

Rachel and I sat quietly reading our magazines, eating doughnuts and drinking juice.

The morning went by quickly and before we knew it, Peggy was in the room bringing us each a hamburger.

"Here's lunch girls, burgers, fries and pop. Kate should be here in about an hour," she said.

"Where did you say the bathroom was Peggy?" Rachel asked. We peeked our heads out the door.

"It's down the hall and to your left," she pointed as she went down the hall to her office.

"I'm going too," I said.

Rachel and I went out the door to the bathroom, went and washed our hands and were back in the room eating lunch a few minutes later.

"Do you want to swap magazines?" I asked.

"In a few minutes, I'm almost done reading this article," Rachel said.

"Okay," I said as I looked through the O magazine one more time to see if there was any stories I missed, but there wasn't. I ate my burger and watched Rachel as she finished reading her magazine.

"Here Tara, you can look at it now," she said as she closed the cover and scooted the magazine down the table to me.

"Thanks," I said as I slid mine to her.

I opened the magazine and started reading.

A little while later the door opened, Kate came in, and shut the door behind her.

"Oh, my gosh, look at you girls," she said.

Rachel and I stood up as Kate reached out her arms and hugged us both at the same time.

"You're just as beautiful as ever. I'm so glad you're okay. How are you girls doing?"

"We could be better. You've probably heard about Danny and Drake by now," Rachel said.

"Heard what?" Kate asked as we sat down around the table.

"You didn't hear?" I asked.

"Hear what?" Kate was confused. "Tell me girls. What?"

"You didn't hear about Danny and Drake?" Rachel asked.

"No, what about them?"

"They passed away the night before last," Rachel said as she put her arm around me. She knew it crushed me every time we talked about it.

"What? No, I didn't hear. Oh no...I'm so sorry Tara. I've been so busy in the last couple of days I haven't turned on the TV and no one tells me anything around there. I'm sorry Tara." Kate put her arms around me and hugged me. "I know you really cared for Danny."

The tears welled up, and I started to cry.

"She's fragile right now," Rachel said.

"I'd be fragile too," Kate said. "Tara you have to think of Danny as going ahead of you on the journey of life. He isn't gone from your life for good. He has just passed on to another place. You'll see him again someday."

"I know Kate, but I already miss him," I cried.

"I know Tara, I know." Kate and Rachel held on to me while I cried.

"The funerals are tomorrow Kate. We're going to go," Rachel said. "Can you help us? We need dresses."

"Of course I can help you. You both know you are welcome to go through my closet anytime. I was hoping to start packing tomorrow. I want to get moved this weekend. Well... I guess I can still pack... it probably wouldn't be a good idea for me to go to the funeral anyways since I'm trying to keep a low profile with Mr. Parker. Tara, you girls can stay the night at my house. Trevor would love to see you two. You can see Billy too."

"Billy? Is he still in Windyn? I thought Mr. Parker was going to relocate him?" I questioned.

"He is planning to, but when the boys went into the hospital he put the plans on hold," Kate said. "I don't know what he's going to do now under the circumstances."

She looked at me and could tell I was upset.

"Tara, are you going to be okay?"

"I don't know Kate. I don't feel like I'll ever be okay again."

"I feel so bad for you. You know, I was watching the news a few days ago. All's the news ever talks about are the boys, they never say anything about you two girls. They did have a story about Nichole Beck. Peggy told me all about Nichole... and Amanda pretending to be her. I had no idea. Somehow, they're keeping information about you girls off the news. I don't know how they do it."

"The government agency is controlling the story. They're keeping it off the news because they don't want anyone to see our faces, since we're clones and we all look alike it would cause a lot of problems," Rachel said.

"Problems?" Kate asked.

"Yeah, can you imagine how people would react if they saw a news story about two girls named Tara and Rachel, who were missing and they put our

266

picture on the TV. Imagine what would happen if people saw the story on the national news everyone who knows a girl who looks like us would freak thinking it was the girl they knew. Now imagine people freaking out in small towns across the country. People would be talking about the girl who looks exactly like me or Tara, Selena, Nichole, Amanda or whoever. I'm sure the government agency saw the bigger picture. That's why we think they're controlling the news, and that's why they won't show a picture of us," Rachel said.

"Oh, That makes sense. You know now that I think of it they didn't have a picture of Nichole on the news either," Kate said.

"So Kate, I'm really glad to see you. Why did you want to meet with Peggy today?" I asked.

"Mr. Parker found some people who are going to help you girls and maybe our nieces too," Kate said.

Peggy came into the room and shut the door behind her.

"Did Kate tell you?" she asked.

"I was just about to, but since you're here, why don't you tell them," Kate said.

"Okay, Mr. Parker found a nurse who works at the island facility and he's on his way in here. His name is Frank, and he's going to help you girls," Peggy said.

The door opened and a man who looked to be in his late forties, came into the room, and shut the door.

"Frank, why don't you have a seat over there," Kate said as she pointed across the table from Rachel and me.

"Hi, Frank, I'm Peggy. My niece is a clone," Peggy said as she reached out and shook his hand.

"Nice to meet you Peggy. So, your niece is a clone specimen too?"

"Yes, her name is Selena, maybe you know her? She has curly red hair, big green eyes, and a beautiful smile and... oh what am I describing her to you for?" Peggy shook her head, smiled and laughed.

"Yeah, kind of pointless," Frank laughed.

"Tara and Rachel, this is Frank," Kate said.

"Hi Frank, it's nice to meet you," Rachel and I said.

"Hi girls, which one is which?"

"I'm Rachel." She put her hand in the air.

"I'm Tara." I did the same.

"Rachel and Tara, you're two of the missing clone specimens.

I've heard about the four who went missing and the one clone who drown. The four of you have caused quite a bit of commotion from what I understand. They actually packed up the clones specimens who were on the island, put them on a boat, and shipped them out to sea because of you," Frank said.

"Packed up the clone specimens and shipped them off the island... Really?" I gasped. I was thinking of lab mice.

"Yes it's standard protocol... of course they're back on the island now."

"Excuse me Frank, but could you please not refer to us as specimens? It makes me feel like a lab mouse," I asked.

"Sorry Tara, I can see how it could bother you. I'm so use to calling you girls that. Due to protocol, they don't allow staff workers to call clone specimens... 'girls, kids, children or babies.' They don't want the workers growing attached to any of you. I'm sorry."

"They don't want anyone to get attached to us...why?"

"Because we're told you clones are alive for studying... nothing more."

"So we are lab mice." Rachel shook her head.

"Look girls...I don't know what kind of testing they do on you. All's I know is you're asleep when you arrive and you're asleep when you leave. It's difficult for the medical staff to become attached to you under those circumstances, you understand don't you? He looked at us. "This is the first time I've ever seen any of you completely awake."

"It is?" Rachel and I questioned.

"Frank, you said they put them on a boat?" Rachel asked.

"Yes."

"Was it a big boat, like a cruise ship?" Rachel asked.

"Yes... it was, why do you want to know?"

"Tara and I were watching a cruise ship near the island when we stayed at the Parker's cabin. We wondered why they never turned on the lights. We thought there were probably elderly people on it and they all went to bed early... so... that's where they put all the girls?" Rachel asked.

"Yes, that's where they were. The agency wants to keep the operations top secret. After the clone drowned, they didn't want anyone coming out to the island and poking around in government affairs. So rather than shipping the girls home and then shipping them back to the island again they just loaded them on the boat. They slept the whole time."

How long did they keep the girls on the boat?" Kate asked.

"Oh, they were on the boat for about a month...maybe a little longer."

"Really, they kept those girls sleeping for a month? That's a long time," Peggy gasped.

"They've had them sleeping longer, it's nothing new."

"Really? I can't believe they keep us asleep like that. It makes me angry," Rachel yelled.

"Yes, I know it sounds bad, but with the type of medication they have you on, when you clones wake up, you don't remember anything about being on the island," Frank said.

"You say it like it's a good thing Frank," Kate said. "What do they do to those girls and why don't they want them to remember any of it?"

"I don't know." Frank shook his head.

"You work there and you don't know?" Peggy questioned.

"No, I don't know," he repeated. "I don't have access to any of the floors below ground level."

"So what do you do on the ground level, Frank?" Peggy asked.

"My job is to take the clone's vitals. You know, the regular stuff. I take their blood pressure, their pulse, their temperature, and I take them off the IV. You know... things like that. Then they move them to the lower level."

"Why do they put us on an IV?" I asked.

"Well, the sleeping med tends to cause dehydration. What happens is your parents are responsible for giving you a powder dose of sleeping medication, which they put in your food or drink the night before they ship you to the island. Two male nurses come to your house hook you to an IV and place you in a plastic sleeping chamber for the trip. They put the sleeping chamber in the back of a van, take you to the airport, and fly you to the island by private helicopter or jet. When you girls arrive on the island, it's time for me to do my job. I'm an intake nurse. I give you an orange pill. The orange pill takes your memories of home and replaces it with memories of the island. Then I give you a purple pill, which brings you from Delta sleep to R.E.M. sleep, or what we call the dream state. After about an hour I know the medication is working, I take you off the IV. I take your vitals and then your nurse takes you to your room on the lower level.

"What happens on the lower level, do they do the testing there?"

"No, not on the lower bedroom level anyway. My sister-in-law's a nurse, she works on one of the lower floors. She told me the lower floors are strictly female nurses, and she's responsible for the dressing, health, and cleanliness of the clones. They don't do any testing on her floor either. She said they are strictly sleeping quarters."

"So, does she know what kind of testing they do on the girls?" Kate asked.

"No, she has no idea. They do all the testing on the levels below the sleeping quarters. There are levels upon levels down there. When they're finished with testing the nurses are responsible for bringing the girls up the elevator to the top floor. A discharge nurse takes their vitals, gives them an orange pill, and a heavy dose of sleeping medication. Two male nurses come in and hook them to an IV, place them in a plastic sleeping chamber, and take them out of there."

"They give us another orange pill?" I asked.

"Yeah, the orange pill takes your memories of the island and replaces it with memories of home. You may have small memories from the island, but the combined effects of the orange and the purple pill, makes you think those memories are just dreams and nothing more."

"Frank, it sounds like they have the girls pretty doped up. Do they ever have problems with the medication?"

"Yes they have... quite a few times over the years, but they straighten it out on the lower level. The problems only happen with the first group of clones, the oldest ones. As the girls grow older, we have to adjust their medication to suit their growing bodies. Sometimes getting the medication adjusted is hard when the girls are going through a growth spurt. We have had occasional problems getting the medication adjusted, but once the medications adjusted for the first set of clones, we know how to adjust it for the rest of the girls."

"The first set... do you know how many girls are in the first set?"

"I think there are twelve," Frank said. "They try and keep employees from knowing too much. You all look alike so it's hard for me to tell how many times I've seen the same girl, so I don't know exactly. I know I see you older girls on the island more than the rest of the clones, because I'm the intake nurse for the older girls. Since you girls were the first, you've spent most of your childhood out there being tested."

"We have?" Rachel and I asked.

"Yes. They tried everything on you first."

"They did?"

"Yes, and Tara, I heard you almost died several times over the years. You see, clones don't have a long life span."

"I almost died?"

"Yes, but thanks to Professor Ziegler and all his research he was able to come up with the little green pill which keeps you and the other girls from dying prematurely."

"If Professor Ziegler has worked so hard to keep the girls from dying prematurely, why does he want to terminate them now?" Peggy asked.

"The professor doesn't want to terminate the clones, it's the government agency who wants to terminate them. The agency just sees them as a liability, a growing problem, nothing more," Frank said.

"Oh I see...they want to wash their dirty little hands of the whole thing, and walk away from this mess," Peggy nodded her head.

"So, the question is... how do we rescue the girls from the underground fortress without getting them killed?" Kate asked.

"That's a good question," Frank said, "You know it's my understanding, the government will stop at nothing until it has successfully terminated every one of the clones."

"I can bet they want you all dead before the President finds out anything about the clone project," Peggy said.

"I'm sure a lot of government people could lose their jobs and go to jail over this little scandal. I'm sure whichever government agency is over this project is trying to cover it up as fast as they can," Kate said.

"Frank do you know what government agency is over the project?" I asked.

"No, they don't give us any information. When I was hired, they ran me through background and security checks. They told me they assigned me to a top secret government project and they don't allow workers to discuss their work with anyone other than coworkers including friends and family. They gave me a cover story to tell anyone who asks about my job. I tell everyone I'm working in a hospital where the rich and famous go for seclusion while they have plastic surgery and hang out by the pool to heal. All employees are required to tell that story."

"Hey, I've heard that story before," Kate said.

"Yeah me too," Rachel and I said.

"There has to be something we can do to get those girls out of there," Kate said. "Do you know how many girls are on the island right now?"

"I have no idea. But I know they won't do anything to the girls until they have them all on the island together," Frank said.

"How do you know that?" Kate asked.

"The protocol," Frank said. "We were all trained on protocol and it dictates all clones must be present and accounted for before any termination process can be initiated. The board would have to meet before they could make changes to the protocol and that's highly unlikely."

"That's horrible," Rachel shrieked.

"We can't let them do that to any of us," I cried.

"Girls calm down," Peggy said. "I know it's horrible, but we're not going to let it happen. We're not going to let them find you."

"How are we going to keep them from finding us? We can't keep hiding the rest of our lives they always seem to catch up to us. We can't fight the government," Rachel cried.

"It's not the whole government, it's only one agency." Peggy shook her head. "We just need to find out which one."

"What good is it going to do? It's not going to stop them from wanting us dead is it?" I said.

"I don't know girls, but we have to start somewhere, and Peggy is right. It's only one agency. We just need to find out who's in charge of it," Kate said.

"One agency with a lot of thugs working for them." Rachel shook her head.

"What's going to happen when they track us down again?" I asked.

"Who says they're ever going to track you down?" Kate said.

"They always find who they're looking for. Either dead or alive," I said.

"We're going to figure out a way to keep you two alive along with the rest of the clones," Peggy said.

"You know I was thinking maybe we should just let them catch us and be done with it," I said.

"Tara you don't mean that. You're just upset over losing Danny that's all." Rachel put her arm around me and hugged me tight.

"You really don't want them to catch you Tara, because once they have you, Rachel and Amanda they will start the termination process and kill all of you including the littlest clones," Frank said.

"Oh, that sounds so awful," Peggy cringed. "We need to stop them and we need to do it now. I can't imagine little Avery being taken from her family and being put to death. Just because some highfalutin person who thinks he's important doesn't want to get fired from his high paying government job."

"Yeah, that's just wrong. If they think they're going to keep themselves from going to jail by destroying the evidence, they're wrong about that too. I'll make sure everyone knows what they're doing. They'll have to kill me to shut me up. And I'm not going down without a fight," Kate said. "Peggy... who's Avery?"

"Oh, Avery is the cutest little girl ever. She has curly red hair, big green eyes, and a smile that would melt your heart," Peggy smiled.

"You mean she's a clone?" Kate looked at her.

"Yes, she's a clone," Peggy nodded. "I seem to forget they're clones. Avery's just a cute little girl to me."

"Girls, how would you feel if we put a tracking device on you?" Frank asked.

"A tracking device?" Rachel and I looked at each other.

"I guess it would be all right," I nodded.

"Yeah, I guess so," Rachel nodded.

"Mr. Weber, who works for Mr. Parker, will be here soon. He has the equipment and the tracking devices which I will insert underneath your skin before we leave the office today," Frank said.

"Eew, you're going to insert something underneath our skin?" I groaned. "Are you sure you can do that?"

I looked at Rachel. She had the look of dentist pain in her eyes.

"He's a nurse." Kate looked at me.

"Oh yeah, he's a nurse. I forgot," I smiled.

"That's okay Tara. I forgot too," Rachel said.

"So, is Mr. Parker coming here?" I asked.

"No, just Mr. Weber and he should be here any time now," Peggy said.

"Good, because I'm not sure if I could ever face Mr. Parker again." I broke down and cried.

"What do you mean Tara." Kate put her arms around me and hugged me.

"I'm the reason his sons are gone," I bawled.

"Tara, you are not the reason the boys are gone. You didn't have anything to do with their deaths," Peggy said.

"Yeah, I did. If it wasn't for me they'd be home right now," I cried.

"You poor girl," Frank said. "It's not your fault at all Tara."

K J Scott

CHAPTER 11

A Bad Decision

The door opened and Mr. Weber stepped inside with a black briefcase.

"Am I interrupting something?" he asked.

"No... you must be Mr. Weber," Peggy said.

"I am," Mr. Weber said. "Is everything all right?"

"Well, not exactly... Tara's having a meltdown Mr. Weber," Peggy said.

"I'm sorry to hear that. Is there anything I can do to help?"

"Tara, are you going to be okay?" Kate asked.

"Uh huh," I sniffed as I tried to pull myself together.

"You girls have been on Mr. Parker's mind a lot. He has been worried they were going to catch up to you and hurt you. You gave him quite a scare. I'm glad to see you've made it this far. I'll be able to report back to him I saw you and you both look well." Mr. Weber shook Rachel's hand. "Now you must be Rachel since you don't look like you're having a meltdown," he smiled.

Mr. Weber came over to where I was sitting and sat in the chair next to me. "It's going to be all right Tara. I'm here to help you."

I nodded my head and tried to stop crying. Mr. Weber wiped away my tears and smiled at me.

"Okay," I nodded.

"I brought the equipment and the tracking devices so we can keep close tabs on you girls." Mr.

Weber opened his briefcase, reached in and pulled out two small plastic bags. He pulled out a pair of scissors, cut open one of the two bags, and handed it to Frank. He reached in his briefcase, pulled out a pair of rubber gloves, tweezers, a cotton ball and a small bottle of rubbing alcohol. He poured a little alcohol on the cotton ball, and wiped the tweezers.

"Here Frank," he said as he handed Frank the rubber gloves.

Frank put the gloves on and took the tweezers from Mr. Weber.

"Okay, who wants to go first?" Frank asked as he took the tweezers, pulled a tiny piece of metal out of the little bag, and looked at Rachel and me.

Rachel and I looked at each other. Rachel could see I was still a mess.

"I'll go first," she said.

"Okay, take off your right shoe and sock," Frank said.

Mr. Weber pulled out another cotton ball, soaked it in rubbing alcohol, waited for Rachel to take off her shoe and sock.

"Here, wipe your ankle right behind the inside bone," he said as he handed her the cotton ball.

"Here?" Rachel pointed.

"Yes," Mr. Weber said.

Rachel wiped her leg where Mr. Weber told her.

"Put your foot up here on the table," Frank said.

Rachel put her foot on the table so Frank could get a closer look.

"Do you need better lighting?" Peggy asked.

"That would be helpful," Frank said.

Peggy left the room and came back a minute later holding a desk lamp. She plugged it in and shined it on Rachel's foot.

"Now, this is going to sting a little it's just like getting a shot at the doctor's office. It's just a little piece of metal, like a needle, only it's flexible like wire." Frank showed it to Rachel and me. "Once I insert it into your skin and the stinging stops, you won't feel a thing after that. In fact, you'll forget it's even there. So are you ready Rachel?"

"I think so," Rachel said.

Frank took the tiny piece of metal and inserted it into Rachel's ankle.

"Ouch," Rachel said as she watched it go into her skin. "I guess that's not so bad," she said when Frank was done.

"Okay, it's your turn Tara. Are you ready to do this?" Mr. Weber asked.

"I guess I am," I said.

Mr. Weber opened the second little bag with the scissors and handed it to Frank. I took off my right shoe and sock. Mr. Weber handed me a wet cotton ball, and I wiped my ankle in the same spot Rachel wiped hers. Mr. Weber wiped the tweezers and handed them to Frank. Frank took the tiny piece of metal from the bag and waited for me to put my leg on the table. I watched while Frank inserted the metal into my ankle.

"Ow," I said.

"Okay, you're done," Frank said as he handed the tweezers to Mr. Weber. I took my leg off the table and put on my sock and shoe.

Mr. Weber took a cell phone out of his briefcase and looked at the screen. He tapped the screen with his finger and then typed something with his thumbs.

"Okay girls, I want you on opposite sides of the room please. Rachel, you can stand over there and Tara, stand over there," he pointed. "I need to set the app so I know who's who. All's I can see right now are two little blips."

Rachel and I moved to the opposite end of the room. We waited for Mr. Weber to tell us what to do next.

"Okay girls, I have you each locked in. Now I can tell who's who by the different colored blips. I'll be able to track your every move."

"Thank you, Mr. Weber. You really make me feel safe," Rachel said.

"Yeah, I'm feeling safer too," I said.

"Good, I'm glad to hear that," Mr. Weber smiled. "That's only the first step in keeping you girls safe."

"Next, we are going to move you to a safe house in Maine until we can get the two of you out of the country," Mr. Weber said.

"When are you going to move us?" I asked.

"We are planning on moving you tonight," Mr. Weber said.

"Tonight? But Mr. Weber. I can't go tonight. Danny and Drake's funeral is tomorrow and I want to go," I started to cry.

"Tara, I don't think it would be a good idea for you to go to Danny and Drake's funeral. The people who want you dead could be looking for you there. They know you were with the boys on the boat and in San Diego. Danny and Drake told Mr. Parker what happened before they died. I know you really want to go to the funeral, but I don't think you should go," Mr. Weber said.

"I have to go. I have to say good-bye," I said.

Mr. Weber looked at me and shook his head.

"Tara, you could put yourself and Rachel into danger. We don't know who could be watching," Mr. Weber said.

"Mr. Weber I know you think I'm just a kid, but kids have feelings too and I loved Danny. He was my first love. I need to be there to say good-bye to him," I sobbed.

"Okay, okay, I understand," he nodded.

"Are you sure Tara?" Kate asked.

"Yeah, I'm sure. Rachel you don't have to go if you don't want to, but I need to go," I said.

"Tara I'm going with you. Danny and Drake were my friends too I want to say good-bye to them," Rachel said.

"Okay, let me make a phone call to Mr. Parker," Mr. Weber said as he pulled his phone out of his pocket. "Excuse me."

Mr. Weber excused himself from the room, went out into the hall, and shut the door.

A short time later, he was back in the room.

"Okay, Mr. Parker isn't happy, but he understands. Now let's talk about the safe house in Maine. We'll leave tomorrow after the funeral. The funeral starts at two pm. They scheduled the service for an hour then they'll continue with a procession to the gravesites. I want you girls to be very careful when you are at the funeral. I wouldn't be surprised if the government agency didn't have their people watching to see if one of you girls turns up there. Mr. Parker heard the news story about Nichole. He knows they have the story wrong, but it still causes him and me concern about you going.

Who knows who's going to show up looking for Nichole?"

"Don't worry, leave it to me, I'll make sure no one will recognize these two," Kate smiled.

"Thanks Kate," I said as I wrapped my arms around her and gave her a hug.

"Okay, but I want you girls to leave the service as soon as it's over which should be right at three o'clock. Kate if you could pick them up, there's a small airstrip just east of Windyn. I want you to bring them there. I'll be waiting in a helicopter for you two girls," Mr. Weber said. "I will bring you here to Sacramento where you will board one of Mr. Parker's private jets to Maine. Once we have you at the safe house you'll be staying for a week while we get passports for you."

"You haven't said anything about our families, are we going to leave them behind?"

"I can't give you any information on your families right now, but I want you to know we are working on things. Trust me... it's for your own protection. With that being said, we want you girls to be able to protect yourselves if we can't be there to protect you," Mr. Weber said.

He looked in his briefcase and pulled out a plastic bag with two small pouches, which had big blue capsules in it, and handed them to Frank.

"You see these capsules. They are pure caffeine. Do you know what caffeine does girls?" Frank asked.

"Ah, it wakes you up?" I said unsure if the answer I gave was what he wanted.

"Yes, the million dollar answer. It wakes you up," Frank laughed, "Caffeine is in coffee, it's in soft drinks, it's in chocolate, and that's what it does. It wakes you up. Do either one of you girls know how caffeine wakes you up?"

"No not really. It just does." Rachel shrugged her shoulders.

"Caffeine works by changing the chemistry of the brain. It blocks the action of a natural brain chemical associated with sleep. Here is how it works," Frank explained. "The way sleep works is the chemical adenosine binds to adenosine receptors in the brain. The binding of adenosine causes drowsiness by slowing down nerve cell activity. In the brain, adenosine binding also causes blood vessels to dilate most likely to let more oxygen in during sleep. Adenosine is produced by your daily activity. Your muscles produce adenosine as one of the by-products of exercise. To a nerve cell, caffeine looks like adenosine. Caffeine, therefore, binds to the adenosine receptors. However, it doesn't slow down cell activity as adenosine would. The cells cannot sense adenosine anymore because caffeine is taking up all the receptors adenosine binds to. So, instead of slowing down because of the adenosine level, the cells speed up. You can see that caffeine also causes the brain's blood vessels to constrict, because it blocks adenosine's ability to open them up. With caffeine blocking the adenosine, you have increased neuron firing in the brain. The pituitary gland sees all the activity and thinks some sort of emergency must be occurring. So it releases hormones, which tell the adrenal glands to produce adrenaline (epinephrine). Adrenaline is, of course, the 'fight or flight' hormone and it has a number of effects on your body. Are you following me girls?"

Rachel and I looked at each other.

"Uh yeah, kind of," we said.

"Okay, maybe this is a little over your heads, but what happens is your pupils dilate. Your breathing tubes open up. Your heart beats faster. Blood vessels on the surface constrict to slow blood flow from cuts and also increases blood flow to muscles. Blood pressure rises. Blood flow to the stomach slows. The liver releases sugar into the bloodstream for extra energy, and muscles tighten up ready for action. This explains why, after consuming a big cup of coffee, your hands get cold, your muscles tense up, you feel excited, and you can feel your heart beat increasing. You may begin to feel the effects within fifteen minutes. Caffeine reaches its peak level in the blood within one hour and can stay in your system for four to six hours." Frank handed us each a small pouch with adhesive tape on one side of it. "Here girls, I want you to stick this to your skin underneath the arm of your shirt. That way it's easy for you to grab in case of an emergency."

"Emergency?" Rachel asked.

"Yes, if someone grabs you and tries to take you get to the caffeine capsules as quickly as you can. The dosage of medication they give you will not work as well if you have just taken a caffeine pill. You'll still be groggy from the sleeping medication but we're hoping you'll be able to think clearly enough to handle whatever situation they have you in."

"You're very smart Frank," Rachel said. "You know a lot about medications?"

"I have been administering medication to you girls for years. Just remember, if you ever get caught, take at least one of the caffeine pills as soon as you possibly can. There are no guarantees, but we are hoping it will give you a fighting chance."

"Girls we can't really help you much more than that," Mr. Weber said. "The quicker we get you to Maine the safer you'll be, we hope."

"Mr. Weber... what about my niece Selena and Kate's niece Isabella what if they're on the island?" Peggy asked. "And Avery... what about little Avery... what's going to happen to her if they take her to the island too?"

"From what I understand, there are several dozen people working on the island it's going to be a huge undertaking for us to find the girls and take them from the island. Mr. Parker has a lot of financial resources to get things done. But we have to have a plan that's not going to cause the destruction of many innocent lives, clones, and workers included," Mr. Weber said.

"Frank, do you know how many people work on the island?" Kate asked.

"Let's see. I know there are three shifts of nursing staff on the building level and three shifts on the lower level. There's the cooking staff, the cleaning staff, maintenance people, the doctors, and the scientists. I would say there are probably over six hundred people coming and going from the hospital on any given week."

"Over six hundred? Wow that's a lot of people," I said.

"There's over six hundred people coming and going every week? I would have never guessed it," Kate said. "I never see boats going there with passengers on it. Are the workers flown to the island like the girls?

"No. There's a tunnel from Water's Edge," Frank said.

"There is?" Kate asked.

"Yes, you have to have access onto the naval base in Water's Edge in order to use the tunnel," Frank said.

"How do all those people keep a huge secret like this for years and years?" Rachel asked.

"They are paid very well to keep their mouths shut," Frank said.

"They paid you well Frank?" I asked.

"Yes, they paid me very well, but I have learned money isn't everything. And it's sure not anything worth killing innocent kids over." Frank shook his head. "The island was a navy base during World War One and Two. At one time, the underground facilities were underground bunkers for enlisted personnel. They stayed there before shipping out to sea. They closed it shortly after the Second World War and it remained empty for years. Then some rich guy bought the island and moved there. He turned the bunkers into a grand showplace and had parties for all of his rich aristocratic friends. The man was supposed to get married out there I guess. I heard something happened and he ended up selling the island to the agency running the clone program."

"Yes, I remember the story. The guy used to throw parties for his favorite charity. He was young, and he had a beautiful girlfriend. I remember hearing about their wedding day. I heard an old boyfriend of the bride grabbed her, held a knife to her throat, and told everyone she belonged to him and if he couldn't have her, no one would. He took her somewhere on the island and she begged him to let her go. After hours of pleading, he agreed and let her go. She was running back to be with the man she loved and she fell down an open well. Everyone thought the old boyfriend had her. They arrested him and put him in jail. They questioned him for days and he said he let her go, but they didn't believe him. They found her about a week later down in the well after someone noticed a piece of her torn wedding dress on the ground. When they pulled her out of the well, she was alive but barely holding on. She died the next day. The man went crazy with grief and no one's seen or heard from him since. He stopped throwing parties and stopped coming to town. All these years I thought he still lived there," Mr. Weber said.

"That's a sad story," Peggy said.

"Tragic," Kate said.

Rachel and I looked at each other. We weren't going to tell them about our dreams.

"Peggy and Kate, we would like to discuss a few matters with the two of you alone. Do you have a place for Tara and Rachel to go for a few hours?" Mr. Weber asked.

"I can take them to my hotel right up the road from here," Peggy said.

"Okay, why don't you take the girls to the hotel and get them settled in. Frank and I can wait here. I need to call Mr. Parker and let him know the girls are ready to go," Mr. Weber said.

"Here girls, I have something for you," Kate said as she reached into her purse. She pulled out our wigs and set them on the table. "I thought you might need them," she smiled.

"Thanks Kate," Rachel said. "Can I wear the blonde one Tara?"

"Hey yeah, let's switch it up. Thanks Kate," I said, "You wouldn't happen to have a hair tie would you?"

"As a matter of fact I do." Kate pulled two hair ties out of her purse and two hairbands and handed them to us.

"Now that's a great idea," Peggy said.

"The girls used these wigs when they stayed at my house. They left them when they went on the boat." Kate pulled our makeup pencils out of her purse and set them on the table. "You left this stuff behind too."

"Thanks Kate," I said.

"Yeah thanks Kate." Rachel picked up a pencil off the table. "Does anyone have a mirror?"

"I do." Peggy searched through her purse, pulled out a small mirror, and handed it to Rachel.

Rachel and I put the wigs and makeup on while everyone watched.

"You two look nothing alike anymore, who taught you to put your makeup on like that?" Peggy asked.

"A lady working the makeup counter at a store in Oakland we stopped in a while back," Rachel said.

"Wow, that's amazing," Peggy laughed. "I'd like to meet that lady. Maybe she could teach me a few things."

"Oops, Tara you missed a ringlet." Kate pointed to the red lock of hair streaming out of the wig and down my shoulder.

"Oh," I said as I grabbed the lock of hair and tucked it into the wig. "This wig isn't as tight as the blonde wig. Rachel, how did you keep your hair from falling out of it?" I asked.

"I don't know, maybe my hair is a little longer than yours so I have more hair taking up the extra space. This wig is much tighter," she said.

290

"Okay, come on girls let's head over to the hotel and get checked in," Peggy said. "You girls can hang out and watch TV for a few hours while we talk to Frank and Mr. Weber."

"I'll drive us," Kate said.

"You'll drive?" Rachel and I asked at the same time.

"Sure, I'll be happy to."

Rachel and I looked at each other. I knew she was thinking the same thing I was. If Kate was a terrible driver in a small town, I wonder how terrible she will be in the big city.

We followed Kate to her car. I noticed a big scratch on the driver's side as I hopped in the backseat.

"Kate what happened? How did you get that scratch?"

"Oh, just pulling in to the store parking lot. I came a little too close to a light pole," she laughed.

We climbed into the car and fastened the seat belts.

"The hotel is just up the street here on your left," Peggy said.

Kate took off at a high speed, and then slammed on the brakes when she came to a four-way stop.

Rachel and I lunged forward and almost hit the front seat. Our seat belts saved us. I looked at Peggy and saw her seat belt held her back from going through the windshield.

Peggy didn't say a word. She looked over at Kate and shook her head. Kate drove on down the street.

"There's the hotel right there," Peggy pointed. Her voice was trembling as if she was nervous.

Kate pulled into the parking lot and took up her usual two spaces.

"Okay, we're here," Peggy sighed.

I climbed out of the backseat and said a little prayer of thanks for keeping me alive another day.

"Kate, you, Martha and Rita can sit in the lobby while I check in," Peggy said.

"Martha and Rita?" Kate looked at us and rolled her eyes.

"Martha and Rita Cook," Peggy laughed.

Rachel and I flashed our driver's licenses at Kate.

"Oh Martha and Rita Cook," Kate laughed.

Kate, Rachel, and I went in, sat on the couch in the lobby, and waited for Peggy.

"This looks like a very nice hotel, doesn't it Rita?" Rachel spoke with a British accent. Kate looked at her and laughed.

"Why yes, yes it is Martha," I said in my British accent.

An elderly couple sat across from us on a couch.

"Ah, where are you ladies from?" the woman asked in her British accent.

Rachel and I looked at each other and burst out laughing. Kate shook her head and rolled her eyes.

"I beg your pardon?" the British woman said as she looked at the two of us with a puzzled look on her face.

"Nothing, nothing, top of the morning to you," Rachel said in what sounded like an Irish accent. She stood up and walked away.

I sat looking at the woman for a minute not knowing what to do or say.

"What's a matter Missy? Cat get your tongue?" the elderly man said.

"No sir, not my tongue," I said in a Scottish accent, which wasn't very good. I stood up looked at Kate, who didn't say a word, and walked around the lobby looking to see where Rachel went. She was standing on the other side of a tall fern watching me look for her and trying not to laugh.

"There you are. You left me with that old couple. They probably thought we were from the same country they're from," I said.

"I know that's why I left. I wanted to tell them we were from London, but I couldn't lie to them or I'd turn all red, so I left," Rachel laughed.

"Martha, Rita let's head up to the room now," Peggy said.

We followed her and Kate to the elevator. Peggy pushed the button and waited for the door to open. We hopped on the elevator and Peggy pushed the button to the fourth floor.

"The British couple thought you girls were very cute," Kate smiled. "They were wondering if you were my little sister, Rachel."

"They were?" Rachel asked.

"Yeah, the makeup is working great. I don't think they thought the two of you were related at all."

"Good," Rachel and I said.

We went up, found our room, and went inside.

"This room is huge," I said.

"It's a suite. It's like a one-bedroom apartment. I always stay at this hotel," Peggy said.

"You girls make yourselves comfortable, watch TV, take a nap, or whatever you want to do. Kate and I are going to head to the office. We'll be back later with food. Okay?"

"Yeah, that sounds great Peggy," Rachel said.

"Okay girls, keep the door locked and don't go out of the room. We'll see you later."

"Bye girls, see you in a little while," Kate said.

"See you," Rachel and I said.

Rachel and I plopped ourselves down on the couch. Rachel turned the TV on and surfed the channels.

"Kate's driving skills haven't improved since we were with her last," Rachel laughed.

"I know she's just as scary as the last time I rode with her. You know Jess was driving like that when he was trying to outrun the other car, but Kate drives that way all the time," I laughed.

"Scary for sure."

"Rachel should we have told them about our dreams we've had about standing on the altar and someone grabbing us?"

"No, it's just too weird." Rachel shook her head. "I haven't dreamed the boat or the wedding altar dream in a while. Most of the time those weird dreams happened when I was at Amanda's house."

"Yeah, me too, it's just really odd we would both dream about the same things."

"I know huh." Rachel shook her head.

Rachel found a news channel and turned up the volume just as the reporter started reporting about Danny and Drake. Their pictures flashed on the screen.

"Rachel, I don't want to see that. Can you change the channel please?" I asked.

"Oh sorry Tara, I wasn't thinking," she said as she turned the channel to cartoons.

We watched cartoons and waited for Peggy and Kate to return from the meeting with Mr. Weber.

"Hey Rachel, I wonder why Mr. Weber didn't want us there while he met with Peggy and Kate?"

"I don't know. Maybe they want to keep us in the dark about the horrible stuff."

"Do you think it could get horrible?"

"I don't know. It could."

"I don't want anyone to get hurt. I think enough people have been hurt already."

"Yeah me too, but who knows what they're planning to do to make us safe."

"All this talk about people grabbing us, and hurting us, I just want to go somewhere no one knows us."

"Maybe we should leave and head to the woods."

"There you go again Rachel. All this talk about heading to the woods makes me sad now. It was making me have good dreams about Danny rescuing me, but now I know that's never going to happen." I shook my head. "You know what would make me feel really good?"

"What?"

"Seeing Billy and Trevor... it would make me feel really good."

"You know Billy probably doesn't know Amanda is still alive. He is going to be so happy when he hears she's alive and well."

"Oh yeah, I can't wait to see the look on his face when we tell him."

"Oh, I just thought of something, maybe we shouldn't tell him Tara."

"Why? He was feeling so bad when all this stuff happened to his family. If he knows Amanda is still alive he will be happy."

"I know, he will be happy, but what if something happened to her since we saw her last?"

"Oh, I never thought of that. You're right maybe we shouldn't tell him. I wouldn't want to get his hopes up only to crush them again."

"Do you think she's okay?"

"I have no idea Rachel. She didn't want to come with us. She could still be hiding on the boat for all I know."

"You think she would stay on Mr. Parker's boat all this time?"

"If I were sitting on the boat alone I would've jumped off the side and waited in the water until I knew it was safe. Then I would've climbed on the boat and stayed as long as I could. There was plenty of food for one person to last awhile."

"I wonder if the boat is still in San Diego or if Mr. Parker brought it back to Windyn?"

"Well, if he brought it back to Windyn and Amanda was on it I'm sure Mr. Weber or Frank would have told us. Don't you think?"

"Maybe," Rachel said.

We sat and watched cartoons the rest of the afternoon.

Peggy and Kate came into the hotel room with something that smelt good.

"Mmm... what smells so good?" I asked.

"Chinese food," Kate said as she placed the bag on the table. "Come and eat."

"I think I'm going to lie down for a while," Peggy said. "I'm not feeling all that great."

"Are you okay Peggy," Rachel asked.

"Yes, I'll be fine after I lie down for a while." Peggy went into the bedroom and shut the door.

"What's wrong with her?" I asked.

"Oh, Frank wanted to test the dose of sleeping medication and see if the caffeine would be enough to counteract the drug. He didn't want you girls having a false sense of security," Kate said.

"So, did it work the way he said it would?"

"Oh yeah, she's groggy, and it made her dizzy and nauseous, but she's wide awake too."

"Well, I guess that's better than being asleep," I said.

"Yeah, at least we'll have a fighting chance to run away if we get caught," Rachel said.

"That's the intention," Kate said as she opened the boxes of Chinese food, grabbed spoons out of the drawer, and put one in each container.

"Why did they test it on Peggy and not us?" I asked.

"You girls have been through enough Peggy didn't want to see you girls go through more experiments than you've already been through. She volunteered to be the Guinea pig. I did too, but they wouldn't let me since I have to drive home."

"That was really nice of her and you," Rachel said.

We ate our Chinese food and watched cartoons. I could hear the sound of Peggy throwing up in the bathroom.

"Oh, that doesn't sound good," Kate said.

"Yeah, nothing worse than hearing the sound of someone throwing up while you're trying to eat," Rachel laughed.

"Yeah, there's nothing worse than hearing the sound of someone throwing up while you're trying to eat and watch the coyote chase the road runner which you know he'll never catch," I laughed.

"Yeah, there's nothing worse than hearing the sound of someone throwing up while you're trying to eat and watch the coyote chase the road runner which you know he'll never catch. But you keep watching anyways because you're addicted to cartoons," Kate laughed.

Everyone laughed.

Peggy came out of the bedroom moving slowly, sat at the table and looked at us with a dazed look in her eyes.

"I feel much better now," She groaned. "Okay, I'm kidding. I don't feel that much better. I have a headache like you wouldn't believe. You poor girls, I don't know how you've done this for so long."

"We don't remember any of it. And I'm sure we didn't have to go through what you're going through Peggy," I said.

"Well, that's a good thing," Peggy said as she put her head down on the table.

"I'd like to know how they tested us while we were in a dream state," Rachel said.

"Yeah, me too," I said.

"I can't even imagine what kind of testing they would be doing on you girls." Kate shook her head.

"I want to know why they just couldn't ask us to go in for testing instead of doping us up and testing us while we're drugged out," I said.

"I wonder how accurate a test is when the subject being tested is sleeping." Kate shrugged her shoulders.

"I just wonder why they test us over and over again. Amanda said they tested us every two years. Now we find out we were on the island regularly," Rachel said.

"Did you hear what Frank said? It sounds like we practically live on the island. I don't remember any of it. It makes me angry my childhood has been spent in a lab as a lab mouse," I said.

"As far back as I can remember I've dreamed the same dream of laboratory mice. I wonder if it was my subconscious trying to tell me something," Rachel said.

"I think you're probably right Rachel. I've had those same dreams myself," I sighed. "I dream of thousands of little white mice underneath my bed, they used to wake me up in the middle of the night. I'd be scared and have a hard time getting back to sleep," I said.

"I wonder if they test us with mice," Rachel groaned.

"You poor girls, I feel so bad for you both," Kate said.

"I wouldn't wish that on anyone." Peggy picked her head up off the table. "I think I need to lie down." She stood up, went into the bedroom, and closed the door again.

Rachel, Kate, and I looked at each other and shook our heads.

"I hope we can keep you two safe. I don't want you to experience what Peggy is feeling."

"Frank can fix that I'm sure," Rachel said.

"Yeah, you're right. We just need to tell him what happened to Peggy and he will know what to do. He's a nurse. That's what they do. They fix people," I said.

"Let's hope he knows how to fix it," Kate smiled.

"Kate, so how is Trevor doing in school?"

"Oh, he's doing great. He really likes his teacher," Kate nodded. "I think he has a crush on a little girl at school named Olivia. That's all he talks about, Olivia this, Olivia that," she laughed.

"He's starting young," I laughed.

"Oh, he's always had an eye for the ladies. When you girls left, he wouldn't stop talking about the two of you either. I'm sure he had a mad crush on both of you," Kate smiled.

"Little boys are so funny," Rachel said.

"The older they get the funnier they get," Kate laughed.

"How's Billy doing?" I asked.

"Oh, he's hanging in there. He likes his Aunt Abby and Uncle Rob so that helps," she said.

"Did you tell him we found Amanda?" Rachel asked.

"No, I just found out from Peggy yesterday. I didn't have time to sit Billy down and tell him."

"That's probably better. Rachel and I think we shouldn't tell him a thing. We don't want to get his hopes up and then find out later something happened to Amanda. Then he'll have to relive the pain all over again," I said.

"You know you're right about that. We should wait until this whole mess is straightened out. If everything works out for the best and she's still alive he'll see her again. Let's hope for everyone's sake things work out for the best," Kate said.

"Yeah, let's hope it all works out for the best," I said.

"I'm with you on that one," Rachel nodded.

"Hey girls, why don't we find a movie to watch like we used to do when you were staying at my house? You girls are coming to my house tonight but I think we should stay here for at least a couple of hours to make sure Peggy is going to be all right," Kate smiled.

"Okay Kate, that would be nice. We can sit on the couch and curl up next to each other like we used to do at your house," I said.

"To bad Trevor isn't here," Rachel said.

"Well, we're not going to tell him when we see him. He won't be happy we watched a movie together, and he wasn't here with us," Kate laughed.

"Oh, we won't tell. We'll just have to watch a movie with him before we leave your house Kate," I said.

"Sounds like a plan," Kate smiled. "Do you see a movie guide around here?"

"I have it," Rachel said as she handed the guide to Kate.

Kate turned a few pages then looked at the clock on the wall.

"Okay, there are a couple of good movies starting in ten minutes. Which one do you want to watch? We have the Pirates of the Caribbean Dead Man's Chest and Maleficent."

"Let's watch Maleficent," Rachel, and I said at the same time.

"I was hoping you would pick that. Turn to channel one-o-seven," Kate said as she put the movie guide on the coffee table.

We sat on the couch and watched the whole movie together. By the time the movie ended it was close to eight o'clock.

"That was fun Kate. You know you have always been like family to Rachel and me. Just sitting here watching a movie with you made me feel like I was at home again," I said. I reached my arms around her and gave her a hug.

"Ah, well you girls are like family to me too." Kate hugged me back and then added Rachel for a group hug. "I love you both."

"I love you too Kate," I said.

"I love you Kate," Rachel said.

"You girls are making me all teary eyed," Kate smiled.

Everyone laughed.

"Well, I'm going to check on Peggy and then we're going to get on the road. It's a four-hour drive home, so it's going to be close to midnight before we get there," Kate said as she went into the bedroom.

She came out a few minutes later.

"How's she doing?" I asked.

"She'll be right out," Kate said.

Peggy came out of the room looking a little groggy.

"Are you okay Peggy?" I asked.

"Oh, I think so. I'm half-awake and half-asleep. The little purple pill Frank gave me was supposed to be the dream maker med they give you girls. It puts you in a dream state. I'm feeling a little loopy from it. The caffeine pill he gave me is keeping me awake so now my body wants to go to sleep and my mind wants to stay awake. I have a feeling I'm going to be up all night." Peggy shook her head. "Well, at least I'm not sick to my stomach anymore. The headache's going away a little. Come and give me a hug girls. I don't know when I'll see you again. You girls be careful. Keep an eye out for strangers. Remember... *Stranger Danger!*" Peggy said.

"Stranger Danger!" Rachel and I nodded our heads and smiled.

Rachel and I gave Peggy a big group hug.

"Peggy, thanks for everything. I hope we get to see you again soon," I said.

"Yeah, me too," Rachel said.

"Kate, take good care of these two. I don't expect to see you in the office until Monday morning," Peggy said.

"Okay, I will," Kate said. "Come on girls grab your bag and let's get out of here. We have a long drive ahead of us."

"Bye Peggy," we said as we went out the door.

"Bye," Peggy said.

We hopped in the elevator and pressed the button for the lobby.

"Oh, I can't wait to see Trevor and Billy," I said.

"Me too," Rachel said.

"You can see them for a few minutes tonight if we wake them up. Billy's at my house babysitting Trevor."

We went out to Kate's car, and I climbed in the front seat, Rachel climbed in back.

"Okay girls, are you ready?"

"I think so," I said. Then I remembered Kate was a terrible driver.

"Ah, Rachel do you want to sit up front?" I asked.

"Ah... no. I'm good," Rachel laughed.

"Don't worry girls you can switch at the halfway point," Kate said.

She had no idea why I wanted to sit in back, but Rachel did.

Kate flew out of the parking lot, came to the same four-way stop, and slammed on the brakes.

"Thank goodness for seat belts," Kate laughed.

I couldn't wait until we were out of the city. I wanted to go where there weren't as many cars, curbs, poles, and other things Kate might run her car into.

"There's a stop sign Kate," I said.

Kate slammed on her brakes.

"Oh, thanks Tara I didn't even see it. I almost went through it," she laughed.

"I'll let you know if I see any more," I said.

When we came to the place Kate referred to as the halfway point I was happy to give the front seat to Rachel.

I lay down in the backseat exhausted from the ride. It took me a little while to let go of the fear of Kate's driving skills, but once I did, I fell right to sleep.

CHAPTER 12

I Should Have Listened.

I woke up when we pulled into the driveway and parked. I climbed out of the backseat and looked at Rachel. She looked as white as a sheet.

"Are you okay Rachel?" I whispered.

"She almost hit a deer," Rachel whispered. "I thought we were going to hit the ditch. Didn't you feel us swerve?"

"No I was sleeping."

"Wow, if that didn't wake you up, you must have really been tired. I almost peed my pants." Rachel shook her head.

"I can't believe we almost hit a poor little deer," Kate said as we followed her into the house. Billy and Trevor didn't look up from the TV program they were watching.

"You boys should be in bed. It's almost midnight and you have school tomorrow. I can't believe you're still up!" Kate scolded.

Billy and Trevor looked up and saw Rachel and me.

"Tara? Rachel? Oh wow, I can't believe the two of you are here!" Billy came over and gave us each a big hug.

"Hi," Trevor smiled. "My turn, my turn." He had his arms out waiting for Rachel and me to hug him.

I knelt down and gave him a big hug.

"You have your fake hair on again?" Trevor touched my wig with his fingers. "I like your real hair better."

Rachel bent down and gave Trevor a hug.

"You remember me?" Rachel asked.

"Of course I do. I'm not a baby," Trevor laughed.

"What's my name?"

"Tara," Trevor smiled.

"Nope, we switched wigs just to mess with you," Rachel laughed.

"You're Rachel?" Billy said

"Yep, Rachel that's my name," she laughed.

"Oh well, you had me confused too. So, how are you two doing?" Billy asked.

"We're still in hiding Billy," I said.

"Yeah, that's too bad." Billy shook his head. "I don't think I could do it. I don't know how you do."

"Sometimes we don't know how we do it either. We've been very lucky making our way through this with the kindness of strangers," I said.

"Yep, that's how we do it... Tara and I would be nowhere without the kindness of strangers," Rachel said.

"I know what you mean. I really didn't know my Aunt Abby and my Uncle Rob until they came here to help me out. They were like strangers to me. I've been very lucky they could come here and take care of me like they have," Billy said.

"Billy, how are you doing? Have you stayed out of the hospital lately?"

"Yeah, I'm fine. I haven't had a seizure since I've been home with my Aunt Abby and Uncle Rob."

"I still think those neighbor guys hit you on the head with something." Kate shook her head.

"I know Kate, you told me, but I don't know why they would do something like that. I've known them since I was little. Rick and Brian saved me from drowning when I was little," Billy said.

"I know, I know, but I find them very odd."

"Tara, I'm so sorry to hear about Danny. I just heard about it this morning." Billy shook his head. "He was a really good guy."

"Yeah he was," I said.

"Well it's late, so I'm going to head to bed. Billy, tell Abby I'll be over in the morning to drop Trevor off before school," Kate said. "Come on Trevor, time for bed."

"Okay Kate, I'll see you later," Billy said.

"Night Kate," I said.

"Night," Rachel said.

"Ah, do I have to go to bed too?" Trevor whined.

"Of course you do. You have to go to school in the morning," Kate said.

"But Mom, the girls just came to visit me I want to stay up."

"No, it's time for bed," Kate said in a stern voice. "Oh, girls you know where the blowup mattress is."

"Yeah, Kate we'll get it. Thanks," I said.

"Night girls," Trevor said as he put his arms up for a hug. I bent down and gave him one and so did Rachel.

"Night, I'll read you a book tomorrow," Rachel said.

"Okay." Trevor smiled and waved as he went down the hall.

Rachel and I smiled and waved back.

"He just keeps getting cuter and cuter," I said.

"Yeah, but he's getting to be a little terror," Billy laughed. "He went outside, brought a bucket of sand in the house, and dumped it in the middle of the carpet. I made him clean it up and put him in time-out for an hour." He shook his head. "I think he's just missing his mom. She's been gone a lot looking for a new job and she hasn't had time for him the last few weeks."

"How are you doing Billy? Are you missing your mom and dad too?"

"My aunt Abby took me to see them a few weeks ago. It's hard to see them sitting behind bars like that. They both say they never laid a finger on Amanda. I believe them, but no one else does," Billy said.

"I believe them too," I said.

"Me too," Rachel said.

Rachel and I looked at each other. It was hard keeping this secret from Billy, but we didn't know for sure where Amanda was or if she was still alive.

"Well, I'm going to head home now, it's late. I'm going to the funeral tomorrow, I'm sure I'll see you two. I won't tell anyone who you are." Billy hugged us both and went out the door.

"Bye, Billy," I said

"See you tomorrow," Rachel said.

Rachel and I took the blowup mattress out of the hall closet hooked it to the blower, grabbed the blankets and sat on the couch while the mattress filled.

"Rachel, I really feel bad we can't tell Billy we saw Amanda. His mom and dad are sitting in jail rotting away for no reason. They didn't hurt Amanda at all," I whispered.

"I know, I feel the same way. I wanted to tell him too. I feel sorry for his parents. It must be hard being in jail for something you know you didn't do," Rachel whispered.

"Yeah, it was good seeing him and Trevor. You know, I like staying here. I don't know what I like about this house, but it feels more like home to me than anyplace else I've been."

"I feel the same way Tara. I think it's the most comfortable place I've been since home."

I watched as Rachel took the blower off the mattress and put the plug in it. She took her wig off, lay down, and covered up with a blanket. I took my wig off, grabbed a blanket and lay down next to her.

"Night Rachel."

"Night Tara."

The morning came early. I heard Kate turn on the shower. I rolled over fell back to sleep until Trevor poked me in the cheek with his finger.

"Which one are you?" he whispered.

"The mean one," I said hoping he would get the point and let me sleep.

"Which one is the mean one?" he asked.

"It's me, Tara," I grumbled and rolled over hoping he would leave me alone.

"Can you tie my shoe? I can't seem to get it to stay tied like this one," he said as he stuck his tied shoe in my face.

"Sure." I sat up, tied his shoe, lay down, and closed my eyes.

"So, why are you the mean one?" he asked.

"I'm not the mean one. I said that to throw you off," I grumbled.

"So, is Rachel the real mean one?"

"No, Rachel isn't mean at all," I groaned.

"Then who's the mean one?" he asked.

"Trevor, there is no mean one. Can you let me go back to sleep now please?" I shouted.

"Oh, so you *are* the mean one."

"Yeah, I'm the mean one, leave me alone please."

"Mom... Tara was yelling at me." he ran down the hallway.

I shook my head and went back to sleep.

When I woke up the house was quiet. I looked over at Rachel and she was still sleeping. I lay there and thought about Danny. I remembered the time he came over and took me for a walk on the beach. Today was his funeral, and I wasn't ready for it. I knew I needed to go and say good-bye to him, but my heart wasn't ready to let him go. I stood up and I looked out the window at the beach. I went to the window and opened it. I looked out at the water and saw the buoy where Danny rescued me months ago. I could smell saltwater in the air and hear ocean waves as they hit the beach. I knew life was never going to be the same without Danny.

I looked out at the island. I remembered being out there thinking I was going to die. It made me sad and happy at the same time. It made me sad because if it hadn't been for the island I would have never met Danny. If I had never met Danny, he would be alive today. It made me happy because meeting Danny was the best thing that's happened to me in my life so far.

I went back and crawled under the covers. I lay on the mattress and looked at the ceiling. I thought about Danny. I pictured his smile in my mind. I could hear his laughter ringing through my head and it made me smile. I knew he was gone, but he was still alive in my mind, and in my heart.

"Danny," I whispered to him. "I love you." I felt a single tear roll from my eye, it crossed my temple, rolled into my hair, and straight into my ear.

I pictured him in my mind saying "I love you too Tara," laughing with me and kissing me gently on the lips. I pictured us holding hands and walking together across the beach. I pictured him putting his arms around me and holding me. I could hear him saying, "It's going to be all right Tara. It's going to be all right." In my mind, I was looking into his big green eyes. I whispered, "No... it's not." I felt another tear make its way out of my eye it followed the path the one before it took. I felt the warmth of the teardrop in my ear. "No... it's not," I cried.

Rachel rolled over and looked at me.

"Are you thinking about Danny again?"

"Uh-huh," I sniffled.

"Do you need a hug?"

"Uh-huh."

We sat up and Rachel held me tight.

"Does this help?"

"Uh-huh, I needed this," I sniffed.

"I have them for you any time you want."

We sat on the mattress for the longest time just holding each other tight.

"Rachel, now that Danny is gone, what am I going to do without him?"

"I don't know Tara, I don't know."

"I know what I'm going to do." I nodded my head.

"What's that Tara?"

"I'm going to keep him in my heart and I'm going to love him forever." I nodded and squeezed Rachel tightly.

"You'll see him again one day. I'm sure of it," Rachel whispered.

"Me too Rachel, me too."

I started feeling better again, and I looked at Rachel.

"Rachel you know the right words to say to make me feel better."

"Yes I do," she smiled.

"I'm just going to lie here for a while longer," I said as I lay back down on the mattress.

"Okay, I'm going to hop in the shower," Rachel said.

I fell asleep in minutes.

I woke up a little while later to the smell of bacon.

"Rachel, are you cooking breakfast?"

"It's done I put your plate in the oven to keep it warm," she yelled from the bathroom.

"Thanks."

I went into the kitchen, opened the oven door, grabbed a pot holder, and took the plate out of the oven.

There was bacon, eggs, and toast on the hot plate.

I took a hot pad and placed it on the table, set the plate down, and grabbed a fork from the drawer. I noticed a note when I took a seat at the table, it was from Kate it read... *"I'm glad you girls are here, you're my family and you've been missed. I'm running errands I'll be back shortly."* She signed it Kate, with a little smiley face.

"Hey, Tara I left you some hot water," Rachel said as she sat down at the table.

"Thanks Rachel, and thanks for making me breakfast."

"You're welcome," she smiled. "Hey, did you see the note from Kate?"

"Yeah, I just read it. She is our family Rachel."

"I know. I want to stay here. I've always feel comfortable here in this house. It's like home."

"It feels like home to me too. I kind of want to stay here but I kind of don't," I said.

"I know you kind of don't because of Danny huh?"

"Yeah, it's hard being around here. I have memories of Danny here."

"They're all good memories aren't they?"

"Yeah," I nodded my head as I took a bite of a piece of bacon.

"Danny's going to be in your heart forever huh?"

"Yep, I'll never let him go," I smiled.

I finished my breakfast, rinsed the plate, and put it in the dishwasher.

Rachel and I went into the living room and sat on the couch.

"Hey Tara, do you think Kate would mind if we went through her closet and tried on her dresses?"

"No, she told us we could try them on any time."

"Do you want to?"

"Of course I do."

We went into Kate's bedroom and opened her closet doors.

"Where do you want to start?" I asked.

"Well, I remember we only made it to here." Rachel pointed at a red dress hanging in the closet. "I didn't try on this one. We need to try on the black ones again because we need to wear black to the funeral."

"Yeah, the last time we wore black we were going to Dillon's funeral," I sighed.

"We don't have to try the dresses on right now if you don't feel like it Tara."

"No... I want to, it will take my mind off things."

"Okay, which one of these red dresses do you want to try on first?" Rachel grabbed two red dresses from the closet and held them up to her, one had sequins, and the other was lace.

"Oh, I think I want to try the lace one on first." I ran my hand across the neckline of the dress. "This is beautiful."

I tried the dress on and looked in the mirror.

"How do I look Rachel?"

"Stunningly beautiful if I do say so myself. Can you zip me up Tara?"

"I sure can." I zipped her up, and she turned around to face me. "Wow you look great in those sequins."

"Do I?" Rachel looked in the mirror.

We tried on dresses and made our way through Kate's closet.

"Oh, look...this is beautiful, I want to try on this white ball gown," I said.

"Oh yeah, it's beautiful it almost looks like a wedding dress if you had a veil to go with it."

I put the dress on and stood in front of the mirror.

"It does look like it could be a wedding dress Rachel." I twirled around. "This is beautiful isn't it?"

"Yeah, and you look beautiful in it. I want to try it on next," Rachel smiled.

"Okay... Rachel I could have married Danny someday," I said as I stopped twirling and looked at myself in the mirror. A tear rolled down my cheek.

"I know Tara, sometimes life doesn't turn out the way we think it should," she said.

Rachel hugged me tight.

"I'm glad I still have you," I cried.

"Me too," Rachel cried.

I took off the dress and handed it to Rachel. She put it on and twirled around in it.

"Oh Rachel, you look beautiful."

"Thank you my dear." She smiled as she looked in the mirror.

We moved on to the black dresses, found the ones we wanted to wear to the funeral and put the rest of the dresses back in the closet.

By the time we finished Billy was walking through the door with Trevor.

"Hey girls you still here?" Billy yelled.

"Yeah, we'll be right out," Rachel yelled.

We grabbed the black dresses and took them out into the living room with us.

"Hi boys, how come you're out of school so early today?" I asked.

"We had early dismissal because of the funeral. Danny's and Drake's schoolteachers are going," Billy said.

"Wow, that says a lot," I said.

"It's a small town and the Parker family is well known around here," Billy said.

"I'm glad they let us out early. Olivia wasn't there. I think she's sick today," Trevor said.

"Is Olivia your girlfriend Trevor?" Rachel asked.

"Yeah, and she's really pretty, and she is smart and she smells like chocolate all the time, because her mom owns the bakery by the pizza place."

"Oh that's nice Trevor," I smiled.

"You said a mouthful," Rachel laughed. "So it's eleven-thirty, and the funeral doesn't start until two. We have an hour-and-a-half to hang out with you before we need to get ready. What do you want to do Trevor? Do you want me to read you a book?"

"Maybe later, I know what I want to do. Why don't we make a fort?"

"Oh, that sounds like fun Trevor," Billy said.

"So, do you boys usually do this when you're hanging out together?" I laughed.

"We do sometimes. Do you want to play with us?" Trevor asked.

"I guess we can," Rachel laughed.

We took the cushions off the couch, set them on the floor, took the chairs, put them around the cushions, and put blankets over the chairs. We built a nice fort in the middle of the living room and climbed inside.

"I haven't sat in a fort in a long time," I said.

"Why not?" Trevor asked.

"I don't know, maybe because I'm too big," I said.

"You're not too big. You fit in here just fine." Trevor pointed to the blanket ceiling above our heads. "See your heads not touching the ceiling. So... you're not too big."

"Okay, I'm not too big," I laughed.

"I'm bigger than both of you and I fit," Billy smiled.

"You have grown taller since we saw you last, Billy."

"I know, my aunt Abby says either my pants are shrinking in the wash or my legs are getting longer," he laughed.

We sat in the fort awhile then put stuff back where it belonged.

"How about a book Trevor," I asked.

"Yeah." Trevor grabbed a book off the shelf and everyone sat on the couch while I read it to him.

"I'm back," Kate said as she came through the front door with her hands full of boxes. "Billy can you help me and bring the rest of the boxes out of the car for me please?" she asked as she went into the kitchen.

"Sure Kate," Billy said as he headed out the door.

"Girls it's almost one. I'm going to fix sandwiches for lunch. I think you should start getting ready to go," she yelled from the kitchen.

"Okay Kate," Rachel said as she headed to the bedroom with her dress.

I continued reading to Trevor. I didn't want to get off the couch, I was scared about going to the funeral.

I knew this afternoon was going to be the toughest afternoon of my life. I was going to have to pretend I was just a person at someone's funeral, not someone who just lost her first love. It was going to be a truly hard undertaking, and I wasn't sure if I could pull it off the way I felt.

I knew I had to start getting ready now, or I wasn't going to make it through the rest of the day.

"Okay Trevor, I have to start getting ready. Mommy's going to have to finish reading the rest of the story to you later. Is that okay?" I asked.

"Yeah it's okay," Trevor said as he took the book and put it back on the shelf. "I'm going to go play with my cars," he said as he headed out of the living room.

"I'm going to go get ready too," Billy said. "I guess I'll see you later Tara, but I won't get to talk to you."

"I know," I said. "Give me a hug Billy. I don't know when I'll see you again," I started to cry.

"Oh, Tara," Billy cried. "You're making me cry."

"Sorry Billy. I can't help it," I said as I hugged him.

"Rachel I'm leaving," Billy called.

Rachel came out of the bedroom in the black dress she picked and gave Billy a hug.

"Bye Billy, I don't know when I'll see you again," she said.

"See you later Billy," Trevor yelled from his bedroom.

"See ya," Billy yelled back.

"Here Billy." Kate came out of the kitchen and handed Billy some money. "Here's your babysitting money, thanks. I'll see you tomorrow."

"Thanks Kate," Billy said as he headed out the door.

"I'm going to take a shower now," I said as I headed down the hall.

"Okay, lunch will be ready when you get out," Kate yelled from the kitchen.

I showered then I stood in the bathroom staring in the mirror, trying to talk myself into going to the funeral without becoming an out-of-control mess.

"You have to do this Tara. You have to say good-bye without crying," I whispered.

"Tara are you okay?" Rachel knocked on the bathroom door.

"No, I'm not okay," I whispered.

"Can I come in?" Rachel whispered.

"Yeah, I guess so."

Rachel opened the door and gave me a hug.

"I needed this," I said as I put my head on Rachel's shoulder.

"Yeah, me too. I'm going to help you make it through the day Tara." Rachel brushed the wet hair out of my face.

"I don't know if I can see Danny lying there. I don't know if I can do it."

"Tara you don't have to see him if you don't want to. We can sit in the back like we did at Dillon's funeral."

"But I need to say good-bye to him."

"I don't think you can say good-bye to him. He's going to be with you forever in your heart."

"I know. He's probably watching over me right now. He'll follow me everywhere. He'll be my guardian angel and keep me safe," I nodded.

"Yeah he will," Rachel smiled. "You just keep thinking about him watching over you and you'll be fine."

"Yeah, I'll be fine," I said, as tears welled up in my eyes and rolled down my cheek.

"Oh Tara." Rachel hugged me again.

"This is the hardest thing I've done in my life Rachel."

"I know... letting someone go is probably one of the hardest things we ever have to do. I've said good-bye to my brother Robert more than once. He's been close to death so many times. I don't even know how he's doing now or if he's still alive," Rachel started to cry.

"Oh Rachel I'm sorry," I hugged her.

"I wish I knew how he was doing or if he's still alive," she sobbed.

"We'll talk to Mr. Weber maybe he can find him for you."

"Yeah, okay," Rachel sniffled and nodded her head.

"Are you girls okay in there?" Kate asked through the door.

"No," Rachel and I said.

"Can I come in?"

"Sure," I said.

Kate came into the bathroom and shut the door.

"Girls, I'm so sorry." Kate hugged us. "I know it's hard right now, but you're going to get through this. They say... *'That which doesn't kill us, makes* us *stronger*,' and I believe it with all my heart. You're going to get through this, girls."

"What's going on in there?" Trevor knocked on the door.

"Come in Trevor," Kate said.

Trevor opened the door and looked at us.

"I need to go, it's my turn," he said.

"Okay," Kate said.

The three of us stood hugging in the bathroom.

"Uh, can I have some privacy?" Trevor looked at us.

"Oh, of course Sweetie," Kate said.

We left Trevor in the bathroom and went into the living room.

"I'm going to get dressed," I said. I grabbed the dress from the chair.

"You can use my room," Kate said.

"Thanks Kate," I said as I went down the hall to Kate's room and closed the door.

I put the dress and the short black wig on and looked in the mirror.

"You can do this Tara," I whispered to myself.

I went out into the living room and sat on the couch.

"Do you know what time it is Kate?"

"It's one-thirty, doesn't the service start at two o'clock?"

"Yeah, it does," I said.

"Rachel go knock on the bathroom door and tell Trevor to hurry up in there. I don't want you two to be late," Kate said.

Rachel stood in front of the bathroom door about to knock and Trevor opened the door and looked at her.

"You can go in there but it doesn't smell very good," he laughed.

"There's a can of spray under the sink," Kate laughed.

"Ick." Rachel went in and shut the door.

"Tara, you have the short hair now? Why'd you trade?" Trevor asked.

"Just wanted to change it up a little," I said.

"You have a big red curl sticking out of your wig right there." Trevor pointed to a ringlet sticking out of the wig and flowing down my back.

"Oh, thank you Trevor, I'm not used to this wig. It's a little looser than the blonde one. I guess I'll need to wind my hair up a little tighter so it will stay in better next time." I shook my head, as I took my finger and pushed the curl under the wig. "How's that?"

"Better I guess, but I like your regular hair the best," Trevor smiled.

"Thanks Trevor."

"I'll be ready in a minute," Rachel yelled through the bathroom door.

"Kate, can you help me with my makeup? I don't think I can get it on right today."

"Sure, where are your pencils?"

"I'll get them." I took them out of the backpack and handed them to her.

"It's doing it again," Trevor laughed.

"What's doing it again?" Kate asked.

"Tara's bouncy curl fell out of her hair," he pointed.

I reached up, grabbed it, I wadded it up tight, and poked it under my wig.

"I don't know how Rachel kept her hair up so well in this wig. It's looser than the blonde one. Is that better?" I asked.

"Yep," Trevor nodded his head.

"You had the same problem yesterday. Maybe you should switch back to the blonde wig," Kate said.

"No, this one is fine. Rachel wants to be blonde for a while and I don't feel like messing with it," I said.

"You're just a little out of it today, that's all. Don't worry you'll be fine. It's just going to take some time," Kate nodded.

Rachel came out, grabbed her pencils, and headed back to the bathroom.

She came out a few minutes later and stood in front of Kate and me.

"How do I look?" she smiled.

"You look fantastic as always," Kate said as she put the final touch on my eyes. "And so do you Tara," she smiled.

"Thanks Kate," we said.

"Okay, let's get going. We don't want to be late," Kate said.

I sat up front with Kate while Rachel and Trevor climbed in the backseat.

Kate started the car and headed towards the funeral home. She drove like a madwoman down the street. It didn't take us long before we were in front of the building. There was a crowd of people already gathered outside, slowly moving towards the door, and making their way inside.

I looked at the building and sighed.

I took a couple of deep breaths before I climbed out of the car.

"Are you okay Tara?" Kate asked.

"No, I'm not. I really don't think I can go in there. I thought I could," I said as I opened the car door and stepped onto the sidewalk. "I don't think I can go in there it's too real."

"Tara, get back in the car and I'll take you home. You don't need to go in there. If you can't do it then just don't."

"But I have to say good-bye to Danny. I have to let him go."

"Tara you don't have to go in there."

I could feel my heart beating fast as I stood on the sidewalk looking at the building. My head was pounding, and I started to cry.

Rachel climbed out of the backseat and put her arm around me.

"You don't have to go in there Tara. Danny would understand," she whispered.

I looked at all the people who came to pay last respects to Danny and Drake. They walked right by me unaware of my heartache from the loss of Danny. I knew they were grieving too, but not like I was.

Kate turned off the car, came around, and gave me a hug.

"You don't have to do this if you don't feel up to it Sweetie."

"No, I need to," I cried.

"Okay, Okay. I'll come back in an hour and pick you up," She whispered. She kissed me on the forehead and said, "You girls better get in there. It looks like they're getting ready to start the service. They'll be closing the doors soon. I'm going to go. I'll pick you up, right here at three o'clock." She climbed back in the car and drove off down the road.

"Are you ready to go inside?" Rachel whispered.

"Not really," I cried.

Rachel and I stood on the sidewalk hugging each other for a few minutes. I looked up just as the funeral home door closed. We were standing on the sidewalk by ourselves.

"Are you ready to go in?" Rachel asked again as she grabbed ahold of my hand and gave it a little squeeze.

"I guess," I nodded my head.

"Look Tara, you have a big red curl coming out of your hair." Rachel pointed to the ringlet flowing down my back.

"Oh, not again," I said as I reached around to find it.

The next thing I knew someone grabbed me by the arm and pulled me away from Rachel. I looked up and there was a big man who I had never seen before staring me in the face.

"Aah," I screamed at the top of my lungs.

"Let go of her!" Rachel screamed.

He pulled me down the sidewalk while I dragged my feet and screamed at the top of my lungs. No one was around to help.

I tried to break loose, but he had ahold of my arm so tight I thought he could break it.

"You're coming with me," he yelled as he pulled my wig off and threw it on the ground.

Rachel was kicking and hitting him trying to make him let go of me. Nothing seemed to stop him.

"Stop dragging your feet!" He yelled. Then he picked me up and carried me.

I kicked and threw my arms around trying to break loose. Rachel was pounding on him with her fists.

"You girls need to settle down," he yelled. "There's no one here that's going to save you."

Rachel was punching him in the face and pulling his hair. I bit him on the hand and he yelled. He pushed Rachel on the ground, put me over his shoulder, and carried me down the street.

"Aaaah," I screamed as I was hitting him in the back as hard as I could.

Rachel stood up and ran after us.

He put me in the backseat of his car, shut the door, and climbed in the front seat.

I pulled on the handle, but the door wouldn't open. I tried to open the other door but it wouldn't open either. I beat on the window hoping it would shatter, but it didn't. I tried to climb over the seat but the man pushed me into the backseat again.

He put the car in drive and took off speeding down the street. I grabbed him by his hair and pulled as hard as I could.

"Let me out of here," I screamed.

He pulled out a gun and pointed it at me.

I sat back in the seat.

"Go ahead! Do it! Do it! Go ahead and shoot me! I don't really care anymore!" I yelled.

"If you keep this up, believe me I won't hesitate. I'll shoot you." He looked over the seat at me. "What's your name?"

"Don't you know who I am?"

"What's your name?" He pointed the gun at me.

"Go ahead and shoot me." I shook my head.

I looked out the back window and I could see Rachel running after the car until we turned the corner and she was out of sight. As we drove down the road, I was thankful Rachel was safe.

The man drove down the road awhile, found a dirt road in the middle of nowhere, pulled off, and parked.

I knew he was going to kill me and leave my body out there where no one would ever find it. I sat there saying one last prayer. Praying I would feel no pain and thanking dear heavenly father for the life he had given me.

Then the man picked up his cell phone and dialed someone.

"Yes, I have one of them," He said. "No, she won't tell me her name." He looked at me in the rearview mirror. He said, "Okay, I'll bring her."

He pushed the pedal to the floor and backed down the dirt road at high-speed until he reached the main road. He looked at me in the rearview mirror one more time as he took off down the main road.

I had no idea where he was taking me. I paid attention enough to notice we drove by the Parker Family cabin where Rachel and I stayed a while ago. I knew we were heading down the road towards the little town south of Delphin.

"Are you going to kill me?" I asked as we drove down the road.

"Yes," he laughed a deep and evil laugh.

He took me to an airstrip where I saw a cargo plane sitting with the rear door open like it was waiting for me. He jumped out of the car and opened my door.

"Get out," he said as he pointed his gun at me.

I jumped from the car and ran as fast as I could go. He was chasing me, but I was running faster than he was. I felt a tug as he grabbed me by the hair then he yanked me to the ground.

"Aaah," I screamed.

He put his hand over my mouth and I bit him.

"Oow," he yelled.

He let go of me for a moment and I scrambled to my feet. I stomped on his foot as hard as I could and took off running.

He grabbed me by the hair again and pulled me back. Then he slapped me across the face.

"Oow," I screamed.

"Knock it off girl or I'll kill you now. I don't care what they say," he yelled. "I'll kill you now."

I started to cry.

"Shut up!" He yelled as he grabbed me around the waist, picked me up, and carried me towards the car.

"Let go of me!" I screamed as I squirmed and tried to loosen his grip.

He held onto me tightly and wouldn't let go of me. I jabbed him in the ribs with my elbow.

"Knock it off or I'm going to knock you out," he yelled.

He took me over to the car and opened the trunk. He pulled out a rope and tied my hands together. Then he pulled the rope tight, pushed me to the ground, and wrapped it around my feet. He grabbed a rag and stuffed it in my mouth. He picked me up, stuck me in the trunk of the car, and closed it. I was in total darkness. I tried to scream but couldn't the rag was in my mouth. I cried. I was scared.

I heard him get in the car and start the engine. We were driving down the road again and he drove for a long time. I wondered if he decided to take me to some remote place and kill me instead of meeting up with whoever he had spoken to on the phone.

I felt the car come to a stop. He shut the motor off and we sat there awhile. We sat there for so long I thought he abandoned the car and left me in the trunk to die a slow and agonizing death.

Then I heard voices outside. The trunk opened and a man in a suit stood next to the man who threw me in there.

"Well, that's one of them. Is it Tara?" he asked.

"I don't know, she wouldn't tell me her name."

"Get her out of there."

The big man reached in, picked me up, and took me out of the trunk.

I looked around and noticed we were at the same place we were earlier. The plane was still sitting in the same spot with the rear door open.

"Put her on the plane," the man in the suit said.

The big man carried me to the plane. He took me up the ramp into the plane and he put me in a seat. Then he left.

I looked out the window and watched the big man as he walked over to the man in the suit and started talking to him. Then he closed the trunk, hopped in the car, and drove away.

I watched as the man in the suit pulled out his cell phone and talked to someone. Then I saw a car pull up, three people climbed out of it. One was dressed in a nurse's uniform, one was wearing dark glasses and looked like an undercover police officer, and one was wearing what looked to me like a captain's hat. They were walking towards the plane. I started to cry. I didn't know what to do.

They boarded the plane.

"Let's get this greyhound off the ground," the man in the suit said to the pilot.

The nurse came to where I was sitting and looked at me. "You poor little specimen," she laughed as she took the gag out of my mouth and untied my hands and feet.

"Can I get some water please," I coughed.

"Poor little thing." She shook her head and walked away.

I grabbed the capsules Frank had me tape to my arm and stuffed all four of them in my mouth. I figured they were going to kill me anyways, so it didn't really matter.

The nurse came back a few minutes later, handed me a bottle of water, and I drank the whole thing.

"So you're the ginger causing Victor so much trouble." She smiled and pulled a syringe out of her bag. "You're not going to cause anyone else any trouble," she said as she gave me a shot in the arm.

"Ouch!" I screamed and pushed her away from me.

"Oh, you're an evil little specimen. I'm sure you can't help it though. Everyone knows gingers don't have souls. That's why you make such good specimens," she laughed, grabbed the rope, and tied my wrist back together.

I'm not a ginger? I thought... what's a ginger anyways? I thought I was a clone. I didn't know what she meant by that statement.

I could feel my eyelids getting heavy. I felt groggy in a matter of minutes. I fought to stay awake hoping the caffeine would kick in soon. I wasn't going to let the power of the drug overtake me. I closed my eyes and pretended to sleep.

We were heading off to parts unknown. I was nervous and scared this time. I was embarking on a new adventure leading to the end of the road for me.

This is the end of book 4, continue to book 5 "The Gathering."

Made in the USA
Las Vegas, NV
04 April 2024

88219751R00187